Praise for the novels of
SUSAN JOHNSON

"Her romances have strong, intelligent heroines, hard, iron-willed men, plenty of sexual tension and sensuality.... Anyone who can pull all that together in a book is one of the best."
—*Romantic Times*

"Smart . . . sexy . . . sensuous . . . Susan Johnson's books are legendary!"
—Robin Schone

"Johnson delivers another fast, titillating read that overflows with sex scenes and rapid-fire dialogue."
—*Publishers Weekly*

"A spellbinding read and a lot of fun . . . Johnson takes sensuality to the edge, writing smoldering stories with characters the reader won't want to leave."
—*The Oakland Press*

"Sensually charged writing . . . Johnson knows exactly what her devoted readers desire, and she delivers it with her usual flair."
—*Booklist*

"Susan Johnson writes an extremely gripping story . . . . With her knowledge of the period and her exquisite sensual scenes, she is an exceptional writer."
—*Affaire de Coeur*

continued . . .

"An enjoyable literary experience . . . [A] well-developed and at times quite suspenseful plot . . . I simply couldn't put it down. . . . The next time you're in the mood to read a piece of erotic literature, I recommend picking up a copy of *Tempting*. The plot and suspense angles of the novel are Susan Johnson at her finest and the romance is both solid and endearing."

—*The Romance Reader*

"Fans of contemporary erotic romances will enjoy Susan Johnson's latest tryst as the blondes heat up the sheets of her latest novel."

—*BookBrowser*

"No one . . . can write such rousing love stories while bringing in so much accurate historical detail. Of course, no one can write such rousing love stories, period."

—*Rendezvous*

"Susan Johnson's descriptive talents are legendary and well-deserved."

—*Heartland Critiques*

"Fascinating . . . The author's style is a pleasure to read."

—*Los Angeles Herald-Examiner*

HOT

SUSAN JOHNSON

BERKLEY BOOKS, NEW YORK

B

A Berkley Book
Published by The Berkley Publishing Group
A division of Penguin Group (USA) Inc.
375 Hudson Street
New York, New York 10014

This book is an original publication of The Berkley Publishing Group.

Copyright © 2003 by Susan Johnson.
Cover design by George Long.
Text design by Kristin del Rosario.

PRINTING HISTORY
Berkley trade paperback edition / July 2003

Library of Congress Cataloging-in-Publication Data

Johnson, Susan, 1939–
    Hot pink / Susan Johnson.—Berkley trade pbk. ed.
       p.   cm.
    ISBN 0-425-19010-2
    I. Title.

PS3560.O386458H68 2003
813'.54—dc21

2003041774

PRINTED IN THE UNITED STATES OF AMERICA

10 9 8 7 6 5 4 3 2 1

ONE

I LIKE MY MEN TALL, DARK AND HANDSOME.
I don't mean six-foot-one in hiking boots.
I mean barefoot *and six-foot-four.*

And when I say dark, I don't mean brownish hair and a light tan.

I mean Goran Visnjic on ER—black-as-sin hair and swarthy skin.

And handsome? Well, that's all a matter of mood . . .

And Chloe was definitely in the mood after working day and night for three weeks on a humongous web site that she'd *finally* finished for a new kids' cereal.

So what the hell was she doing sitting across from this really smarmy-looking guy with a button-down collar and hair the shade of snail shells who had his elbows braced on the table to look taller? Was he even within shouting distance of her tried-and-true criteria for desirable men? No. Did he meet even *one* of her criteria? The answer to that was obvious. More to the point, hadn't she sworn that she would never, *ever* again fall for that line: You have to meet this friend of mine?

Particularly when the speaker was Tess, who everyone knew had absolutely no taste in men. Okay, to be fair, not *Chloe*'s taste in men. Or possibly that of any female with normal vision.

But what made a bad decision even worse was that her be-nice-to-Tess obligation had inconveniently fallen on the day she'd *finished* her project.

This was *not* her idea of celebrating.

"Huh? Sure." Chloe quickly smiled, not sure she'd heard what the annoying little man had said, but he was holding up her glass and pointing to the bar so she was probably on track. "Thanks," she added with another smile, because her mother had insisted she not only learn but *use* good manners, and all those years of training kicked in independent of reason or alcohol consumption. Politeness aside, though, there was no way she was going to spend the rest of the night listening to this man's unending complaints about his work environment.

One more drink and she was outta here.

So when he returned with her drink—an umbrella drink that Chino's was famous for—she was really, really polite and smiley and sort of listened while he told her about his new turntable that cost three million dollars or something. But as soon as she'd sipped the last drop of mango-juiced alcohol, she uttered the lie that always saved her from any disagreeable obligation. "Thanks so much, but I have a project that has to be finished, so tomorrow's a workday for me." Easing down from a bar stool that overlooked the night sky of downtown Minneapolis, she teetered briefly on her really adorable green-lizard strappy Jimmy Choos, smiled her last artificial smile and waved. "Say hi to Tess."

"Tess didn't tell me you had pink hair."

Her fake it's-been-nice smile froze on her face at his peevish tone. Her pink hair went with a damn nice face if she said so herself, along with her three-times-a-week-in-the-gym toned body—well, okay, *ideally* three times a week. And her pink hair sat atop a reasonably fine brain, certified by a couple degrees from reputable schools. "Pink hair's a problem?"

"I usually don't go out with up-towner types . . ."

Or anyone at all, she wanted to say, but damn those childhood lessons on civility were hard to break. "Well, then, everything worked out great," she replied in her best fuck-you tone. Swiveling around on stiletto heels that clearly were made for such dramatic gestures, she walked away, half pissed, totally relieved and seriously on her way home because she suddenly felt wasted after three weeks of little sleep.

FIVE MINUTES LATER she was still waiting for the elevator outside the bar.

These were, without doubt, the slowest elevators in town, and if the best bar in town wasn't on the top floor of this building, she'd not be reduced to a state of frustration too many times a week for a serious working girl. Swearing softly, she jabbed the down button again.

While she waited, any number of pithy retorts for Mr. Dweeb had come to mind. Isn't that always the way? But— bottom line—did she really give a damn if he didn't like pink hair? Fuck no. Did she care about anything at all he liked? Same answer. Did she care if he lived or died? Well, it was only ostensibly a drink date or meeting or whatever that miserable encounter could be designated . . . life or death was probably extending the thought process into the surreal. Although, let's face it, Dweeb Man had to be damned near the last person in the world who could afford to be picky about a date. Unless a subset of women existed who were turned on by whiny men or lengthy descriptions of stereo equipment.

Finally . . . finally—the elevator. *Thank God.*

Seeing it was empty, she offered up a double thank-you to God, Buddha and her own personal goddess, who had curly red hair and was trés understanding of her foibles. She thanked all three because she was superstitious. She counted stairs way too much for her own good as well, but when you had a grandma like hers, it was inevitable. Genetic, even.

The doors began closing and she leaned back against the rosewood wall, relieved. She'd escaped; she was on her way home.

"Hey!! Hold the doors!!"

She almost didn't look up; she almost pretended she hadn't heard. But her mother had much to answer for, she resentfully thought, already lunging to catch the doors. Between her leaping and glancing up and fear of having her fingers crushed, it took her synapses an extra millisecond before the explosive *wow* registered in her brain.

The man sprinting toward her had black ruffled hair, increasingly ruffled by his headlong pace. His lean, broad-shouldered frame was well over six feet, even estimating it at a distance. And he was racing toward her on what could only be hand-sewn black custom-made shoes because she knew shoes like nobody knew shoes.

"Thanks," he gasped, charging into the elevator. He immediately began punching the door-close icon.

Thank *you* she felt like saying, absorbing the full impact of his stark beauty. Definitely a ten, maybe even a twenty, certainly a damned fine representative of his gender.

The elevator doors finally started to slide shut. Blowing out an explosive breath, he turned to Chloe. "Thanks again."

"Were the fiends of hell after you?" Okay, so she never talked to strangers in elevators; she never even looked at them if she could help it. But Jesus, anyone would make an exception for this very close approximation to Visnjic on *ER*.

"Yeah, absolutely." He suddenly grinned. "Nice hair."

Obviously he was not only a TV star but a man of impeccable taste. "Thanks."

She would have said more, but the elevator abruptly came to a stop on the observation-deck level and a crowd of sightseers jammed in, separating them. The IMC Tower was a favorite date-night destination for too-young-to-drink teens. They all seemed to be from one incestuous social group, so the decibel levels were ear-shattering.

Thankfully, they emptied the elevator in a lemminglike rush at the ground floor.

Her *ER* fantasy smiled faintly and moved toward the door. "Thanks again. For saving me from the fiends of hell and all . . ."

"No problem. Anytime," she said like some klutz, when in her fantasy world she would have said something incredibly clever and witty.

She watched him walk out and turn left.

Unfortunately, she was going the same way, and for an awkward moment she debated standing in the empty lobby until he was out of sight. Deciding that was juvenile for someone who owned her own company—albeit a very small one—or for anyone who perceived themselves as a modern, independent, take-charge kind of woman, she followed him—although she hung back, hoping he wouldn't notice.

Just because she read the books on assertiveness and empowerment didn't mean she practiced the art every *tiny* second of the day. Okay?

Additionally, she was experiencing that twinge of fear that reflexively comes from being alone in the vastness of an empty hallway . . . at night . . . in the city. With serial killers and rapists too much in the news, this was definitely a creepy venue. And regardless of the man's incredible good looks, he might just be a very *handsome* serial killer.

"Are you following me?"

Jolted from her musing, she glanced up to see him standing at the side doors, looking bemused—*and* drop-dead gorgeous.

Could serial killers be über-charming?

How much had she drunk that she was obsessing about serial killers?

"Or are you parked in the same loading zone?"

"My permit's legal." If she was Catholic, she'd have to go to confession.

"I didn't say it wasn't. I just thought a woman with pink hair might be driving that silver Audi TT next to my car."

"Tell me you're not a serial killer." Christ, she *must* have had too much to drink.

"I was tempted tonight, but no."

"The fiends of hell, right?"

He grimaced. "I probably would have lost the fight anyway."

"So we both had an evening from hell. Mine didn't like pink hair."

"Stupid man."

"How did you know it was a man?"

"Pursed lips like that. I know that look."

"Woman trouble?"

He grinned. "Not anymore."

TWO

HE HELD THE DOOR OPEN FOR HER. "IT'S dark out there. I'll save you from the serial killers."

"Thanks." Maybe she'd been fantasizing about Visnjic too long, she thought, walking through the opened door out into the alley, because her mind was as blank of witty rejoinders as a tongue-tied adolescent. And what thoughts were racing through her mind were highly inappropriate—like, are you married? engaged? have a steady girlfriend? sleep with women you've just met? Although the first three questions didn't really matter if he answered yes to the last—which really meant that she'd had way too many of those mango drinks at Chino's and should probably call a cab to take her home.

On the other hand, it might not be the liquor talking so much as her three long weeks of hard work and barely any sleep and *no sex* for what seemed like *forever,* her slightly—all right, more than slightly—aroused senses reminded her as she stopped at her car.

Quickly running through "Peter Piper picked a peck of pickled peppers" twice under her breath, she decided it wasn't the umbrella drinks after all.

"Keys?" he said in that hesitant have-you-gone-to-sleep-on-me tone.

Damn—when she was already fantasizing about croissants and lattes in the morning—apparently only *one* of them was aroused. She began digging in her little teeny, tiny embroidered evening bag that held no more than three extremely small items if squeezed in very tightly, and managed to ferret out her key without breaking a nail. Discarding all her gauche comments having to do with him and sex, she uttered, "Thank you," *again*, instead of something charming or clever, smiled and unlocked her car.

"Seeya." With a wave, he walked toward his black, racy, expensive-looking car.

Sliding into her driver's seat, she turned the key in her ignition and heard a metallic clicking sound that wasn't at all reassuring. Fuck. Then even the clicking stopped. Double fuck. A rush of tears to her eyes. Jesus, she *must* be tired.

Get a cab, go home, deal with the car in the morning. But she'd have to hike three blocks in stiletto heels to find a cab in front of the hotels on Seventh Street. Minneapolis wasn't a cab town. It was the kind of town where you phoned for a cab and it showed up in half an hour—and at this time of night that scenario was even more iffy.

Maybe she'd just rest her eyes for a minute. . . .

The knock on the window startled her.

Visnjic.

He was making a rolling motion with his hand, and after a brief pause for her fried brain to make the connection, she realized—one, it wasn't a scene from *ER;* two, it was better because this was real and she was playing a starring role; and three, *her* Visnjic was smiling.

The automatic window wouldn't work with that clicky thing going on, so she shoved the door open. "This definitely isn't my night," she said with a sigh. "First what's his name and now this." She waved at her ignition switch. "It's making funny noises."

"Yeah, I heard. It's either your starter or alternator. Would you like a ride home?"

Then again, maybe it was her night after all, because she was feeling like it must be her starter all right—although her starter didn't have anything to do with car parts. Dweeb Man and her car troubles vanished into the ether. "If you don't mind," she said, swinging her long legs and Jimmy Choo'd feet out of the car.

He noticed her legs.

She noticed he noticed and bit back a highly improper comment; the mango drinks had much to answer for tonight because Peter Piper aside, her inhibitions were definitely juiced. "I should introduce myself," she said instead of telling him what she was thinking about her legs and his legs, and getting out of her car, she put out her hand. "Chloe Chisholm."

He was tall, taller up close or maybe she was just more aware of his size when he looked at her like that. Like she might be his favorite dessert.

"Rocco Vinelli." He smiled and shook her hand.

The last time she felt a tingle like that a vibrator was involved. "I have a friend from the Range with relatives named Vinelli," she said, telling herself to get a grip. So he was good-looking. It didn't mean he'd be good in bed. Oops, wrong thought—not at all helpful.

"Where on the Range?" He started moving toward his car.

She had to rerun his question in her mind as she followed him because she was still on the "good in bed" speculation and sort of undressing him in her mind when she shouldn't be doing any such thing. When she should be reminding herself that sexy good looks and a hugely buff body like his were superficial and much less important than, say, integrity or intelligence. Why was he looking at her like that? Oops, the question. "Tess is from Gilbert," she quickly said.

He smiled. "She must be a relative. One of a couple hundred."

"Then we're practically friends."

"Sounds good to me."

How good, she wanted to say—I mean you in bed? She didn't, of course; she censured her errant libido, which was really aiding and abetting way too much tonight. "Nice car," she said instead. Men always liked their cars. That was safe, conversational, like talking about the weather.

"Thanks. I like the sound system."

He was standing very close as he opened her car door— his cologne filled her nostrils; she could practically touch the dark sweep of his brows.

"The seats are low." He held out his hand.

She took it and sucked in a breath—as in constraint. She was literally trembling. A decided first in her life.

Jesus, he thought, his own constraint not fully functioning; he had an instant hard-on. "Careful," he said. "It's a long way down." Or in, a perverse little voice murmured inside his head as she sat.

He had a serious conversation with himself as he walked around the back of the car and opened his door—something to do with picking up strange women in elevators. But his next thought had to do with condoms, which was serious, he supposed, but not exactly the voice of reason he was trying to sustain.

"Are you married or engaged?" she blurted out the instant he slid into his seat. Flushing with embarrassment, she began to stammer some implausible excuse that didn't even make sense to her.

"No, I'm not," he said, interrupting her erratic, jumpy explanation, his voice calm as though the question wasn't way out there. The party from which he'd just escaped flashed into his mind. "No," he said again, more firmly this time. "Neither one."

Yesss! she thought. "I shouldn't have asked," she said instead, lying through her teeth.

"Not a problem." He jabbed the CD button and shot her a quick smile. "Really. Where do you live?"

"On Grand, just east of Marshall. I've been working for three solid weeks, not sleeping much, so I'm slightly loopy."

"Doing what?" He didn't need U2 telling him to make love tonight. He hit NEXT and was relieved to hear the Red Hot Chili Peppers rocking up a storm.

"Graphic and web design. I have my own small firm. What about you?" He had the longest lashes she'd ever seen on a man; his hands on the wheel were strong and tanned; when he pressed on the accelerator, you could see his thigh muscles flex under the pale linen of his slacks—just . . . like . . . that. Oh. My. God.

"I'm in marketing for Diversified Foods." He backed out of the no-parking zone into the street.

"Small world. I just did the web site for their new Graham Crunchies." She was pleased to hear the bland civility in her voice. Now if she could only rein in her more troublesome inclination to run her hand over his leg and feel his muscled thigh and everything else hard and male and—STOP THIS INSTANT, she silently screamed, gripping her purse as though it was her lifeline to sanity.

"You're dealing with Bill Martell, then." His voice was low, taut, his dark gaze holding hers.

She nodded, having run out of civility, unsure she could keep her voice steady.

Lust was palpable in the darkened interior, almost suffocating.

Neither was entirely sure of what they were saying . . . or cared.

"This is very weird," Chloe whispered.

Rocco blew out a breath, his hands clenched hard on the wheel. "Definitely."

"I'm figuring it's because I haven't had sex for so long." She couldn't say it was him, that he was like a King Kong–sized magnet for her libido. And don't even think about the phallic symbolism in the Empire State Building, she warned herself.

Going without sex wasn't Rocco's problem. Nor was her statement very helpful when he was trying to talk himself out of sleeping with a woman he'd met in an elevator ten minutes ago. "You're probably overtired."

She slanted a glance at him, one brow raised. Was he blowing her off? Did she care if he was blowing her off? Was she losing her mind that she was questioning if she cared if he was blowing her off?

He grinned. "I'm trying to be polite."

A flooding relief inundated her psyche, and she came face to face with the unsavory realization that she was perhaps more vain than she would have liked to acknowledge. "That's fine. There's always my vibrator." One casual comment deserved another.

"I could help you if you like." Not a scintilla of casualness was evident in his tone this time.

She met his dark gaze for a potent moment. "Are you asking?"

He focused on the complexities in his life for an equivocal moment. "Yeah," he said, his libido taking charge. "I'm asking."

He was really astonishingly handsome. Or charismatic. Or both. Or maybe she was just highly charged—hormonally—and the Empire State Building was turning her on. "I'd like that."

"Good." He pressed his foot down on the accelerator and the car leaped forward.

How could so simple a word make her tremble with desire? Bracing her hands on the seat, she drew in a deep breath.

He touched her arm. "Are you okay?"

"Yes—no—probably not." She grinned. "This is way out of my league."

He dipped his head. "Maybe we're both walking the edge tonight." He smiled. "But say no anytime. You can change your mind."

Her brows raised. "I don't need your permission."

"No doubt."

She shot him a censorious look. "What does that mean?"

"It means it looks as though you can take care of your-self."

"Well, I can."

"No argument there."

Her mouth twitched in a faint smile. "Are we fighting?"

"I never fight."

"Never?"

"What's the point?"

"What if I tell you to do something?"

"Something?" He grinned.

"You know."

"I'd do it."

"Liar."

"I'd probably do it."

"Sounds good."

"I'm glad."

"You're going to say whatever it takes, aren't you?"

He laughed. "Wouldn't you?"

"No."

He shrugged. "We're different then."

"Not that I'm complaining about the differences."

He smiled. "Amen to that."

"You certainly are amenable. What am I going to have to do to get a rise out of you?" she inquired playfully.

"No problem there." His glance flicked downward.

Her gaze followed his, she felt her body open in welcome at the glorious sight, and she was right back where she'd been a few moments ago—trembling and ravenous.

He could tell. He punched the accelerator, ravenous too. And focused.

She could have taken issue with his speed, but she was feeling such a wild impatience she watched the streets zipping by with a sense of relief. The smell of the river struck her nostrils as they crossed the Hennepin Avenue Bridge, and bracing herself as he downshifted for the turn off the bridge onto Marshall, she seriously considered the concept of pheromones for the first time in her life. She'd never felt like this before. Not once.

It wasn't as though Rocco had never picked up a girl in a bar and slept with her before, he thought, feeling the car's rear end drift a little on the squealing turn. What was different was the jolt in the stomach or—okay—lower, when he'd first seen Chloe in the elevator. He didn't get jolts like that. Never.

"Turn right at the corner." She pointed and at the next cross street, she said, "That's my place. That brick building."

He turned left, pulled up to the curb and cut the engine. The sudden silence was electric.

Taking his keys from the ignition, he looked at her. "You're sure now?"

"Aren't you?"

He smiled. "Oh yeah."

"Then come see my place." Feeling the way she was feeling, there was no way she was going to change her mind.

He swung out of the car, came around to help her out and then stood on the grassy boulevard and looked at the two-story brick building. "The old corner grocery, I'll bet. Nice," he said.

The neighborhood had originally been home to Eastern European immigrants, so there was a church practically on every block. Polish Catholic, Roman Catholic, Eastern Orthodox, the occasional Lutheran church or Jewish temple, every ethnic group was represented. But in the last decade, the NordEast neighborhood had become home to an increasing number of artists' studios, architects' offices, small galleries and edgy cafes. Chloe's graphic-design business had fit in perfectly.

"I bought it a few years ago. An artist friend of mine was moving to Nepal—to find himself. And he had a trust fund so he could find himself just about anywhere in the world. It was affordable. He didn't care about making a profit."

"Nice kind of friend to have."

She frowned. "He wasn't *that* kind of friend."

"Sorry. None of my business."

"He was married."

So? he wanted to say. "Ah . . ." he said instead.

"Women aren't like men. They can be *just* friends with the opposite sex."

"I didn't say anything."

"It was your tone."

"Sorry."

A tenuous moment of indecision assailed her. "I don't ever do this—invite someone I don't know over," she said slowly. "But then, I don't expect you to believe me." She shrugged away her brief moment of unease. "Why should you?"

"I believe you." Maybe he did and maybe he didn't, but he'd never wanted to sleep with a woman he'd met in an elevator before—so what the hell . . . she could be telling the truth.

"Not that it matters." She didn't have to explain anything to him.

"True. It looks like you have your office downstairs," he said, nodding in the direction of the large plateglass windows on the ground floor.

He was changing the subject, being polite enough to get laid. "You had a fight with some woman tonight, didn't you?"

"Not really. A difference of opinion."

"Are you using this"—she waved her hand in the general direction of her bedroom—"to get back at her?"

"Not even remotely. Are you trying to get back at the man who didn't like your hair?"

"No, and it's not pink."

"I know. Only under certain lights."

She grinned. "I won't ask you how you know that."

"My sister has hair your color. Well, almost that color."

"You have a sister?"

"Yep. She's an accountant. She works on her own."

"She doesn't like to take orders."

"Same as you."

"I can see we're going to get along real fine."

"That's what I was hoping," he said with a grin. "Are we done now?"

"With the interrogation?"

"Yeah . . . did I pass?"

"So far."

He nodded at her building. "Why not ask the rest of your questions inside?"

"You're impatient," she murmured, pulling him toward the side door.

"And you're not?"

"I'm already in overdrive." She laughed. "I don't mean to frighten you."

"No way. I'm counting my blessings."

She punched in the numbers on her code lock, opened the door and flicked on the lights. The stairway to the second floor was carpeted in a riotous floral carpet in tones of pink and green.

"You do like pink."

"I like color."

An understatement, he realized as they reached the top of the stairs and entered a small foyer resplendent with emerald green moire wall covering, gilded mirrors and a large stuffed bear.

"Jesus," he said under his breath, the bear looming, arms raised, claws out and teeth bared, over his six-foot-four-inch frame.

"Meet Yogi Bear."

"Where the hell did you get that?" The bear was eight feet tall, shoulder-height.

"It came with the building. My friend Cecil's grandfather shot it in Alaska, I think, poor dear. But Yogi's found a good home. We talk."

He pulled her to a stop. "How serious are you about this?"

"Sleeping with you?"

"No, talking to this bear."

She smiled. "If I talked to this bear, wouldn't you sleep with me?" She glanced down at his blatant erection.

He slipped his finger under her chin and lifted it. "Hey."

"What do you want me to say?"

"Something normal."

"I haven't had sex for a long time. I shouldn't have invited you up here, since I don't know you other than you're some relative of Tess's. But I'd really like to see that"—she brushed his hand away from her chin and pointed at his erection—"up close and personal. So, I guess it's your move."

"Don't be shy."

"I never am."

"Is there another bear in your bedroom?"

"Come in and see—or don't. It's your call."

They were only inches apart, the sudden tension thick enough to cut with a knife.

Abruptly bending, he scooped her up into his arms and began walking across the foyer. "Where's your bedroom?"

"Through that door, turn left, down the hall. It overlooks the park across the street."

"Good. I'm interested in a view."

"I thought you might be."

He looked down at her, his gaze heated. "I'm going to eat you alive."

"It depends who gets to the buffet first. You forget, I've been starved."

He laughed. "A race to the buffet line."

"It better not be a race."

"You give orders in bed?"

"Sometimes." She could practically see the gears clicking in his head, but he didn't break stride, and when he finally looked at her again, he winked.

"Should be interesting."

"Yeah," she murmured, his effortless strength in carrying what was not a size-four woman revving up her already revved-up libido. "It looks that way." And then in an altogether different tone, she quickly said, "That door there, and I'm warning you, I like color."

He braced himself after the brilliant stair carpet and foyer—this man who lived in a home furnished in earth tones. Even then, when she reached over, opened the door and flicked on the lights, he was momentarily stunned at the blinding colors and textures. The large room fronted the building, the view of the park no doubt visible through the run of French doors, now curtained in swagged, flowered chintz. The huge bed was decoupaged in literally thousands of roses—bouquets, garden scenes, single blossoms, the seven-foot headboard sinuous and faintly art nouveau. Large overstuffed chairs were upholstered in fringed and tasseled silks, their colors bright as an Arabian bazaar. And pictures and paintings were everywhere—on the walls, on tables, leaning against shelves. But the light was even more fantastic than the furnishings, soft, golden, glowing through patterned silk shades dripping with shimmering glass beads.

"Wow," he whispered.

"Does it pass?" But she was pleased. It was a good wow.

"You'll have to show me your work."

"Later." Reaching up, she pulled his head down and kissed him—a light, brushing kiss.

It shouldn't have triggered such an intense reaction. He'd been kissed like that by his aunts or grandmother. It was something about her; there had been something about this girl named Chloe even before he knew her name.

Something that had brought him here to this Aladdin's cave of a room.

Something—fuck if he knew . . . but something.

Chloe was in a more practical mood, attributing her unusual attraction to more mundane reasons: Rocco's drop-dead looks; her outrageous sexual neediness, hunger, craving—whatever this current insanity was; and of course—his drop-dead good looks. Okay, at times, she could be as shallow as the next guy. But it wasn't only his handsome face. Rocco knew when to shut up and when to talk and most of all, when to pick up on her cues.

Like now.

He'd set her on her feet as though he could read her mind.

Then turning her gently, he'd begun unzipping her dress.

THREE

HER DRESS WAS ONE OF THOSE SUMMER
dresses for clubbing, the ones that looked more like
slips than dresses, the ones you couldn't wear with a
bra—green flowered organza, little straps, short, ruffled
hem and it lay at her feet in about three seconds flat.

She kicked it aside and spun around—so easy on four-
inch heels. "My turn," she said with a smile.

He smiled back. "Be my guest." His gaze flickered down.
"Nice pearls." Her thong was a tiny triangle of seed pearls
just covering what it was supposed to cover.

"I like pearls."

His gaze was appreciative. "So do I."

He wore a black linen sport coat, a cream-colored shirt,
natural linen pants and those nice shoes she'd noticed from
a dozen yards away. The ones he was currently kicking off
as he shed his jacket. "Just helping," he murmured, tossing
his jacket on a chair. Then he lifted his arms away from his

body and looked at her from under his dark brows and luscious long lashes with the hottest, sexiest look she'd ever seen, and that was counting the scene years ago from *Thelma and Louise* where she'd first seen Brad Pitt—where he was paying for his ride with something better than money.

"You're really considerate," she murmured, reaching for a button on his shirt, not sure she was going to last for the entire undressing with the hard steady throbbing between her legs.

"We try."

"We?"

His gaze flicked down and then up again and met hers— causing her to discard her unbuttoning of his shirt and start unzipping his pants.

He was doing that mind-reading thing again, because he quickly stripped off his shirt, said, "Let me. I'm faster," brushed her hands away and had his pants, boxers and socks off in a blur.

"Now then." He smiled. "Standing or lying down. You're the one giving the orders."

"Wow," she whispered, her gaze lifting from his erection.

"You in only your pearls and those fuck-me heels— double wow," he said, husky and low. "I'm waitin' for your orders, Ma'am. . . ."

She didn't think it would really matter where she was when that enormous cock slid inside her. It was sure to be pure heaven.

His ramming speed mentality was hard-pressed to wait for an answer. He'd come here tonight for this—for her— and trailing his palms over her hips, he slid her thong down. As it dropped to the floor, he grasped her around the waist, lifted her away from the pearls lying on the carpet, set her down again and drew her close. Stroking her back in a lazy descent, his hands came to rest at the base of her spine and he kissed her lightly—waiting for her cue.

But she was way past kisses, had been since he'd said, "Do you want a ride home?" and moving her hips against his outrageously large erection pressing into her stomach, she whispered, "I can't wait—and that's an order."

He laughed, her words warm on his mouth, her urgency matching his, her style of fiat like getting the newest PlayStation when you were a kid. Perfect wish fulfilment. And she was a damned convenient height in those spiky shoes—almost perfectly aligned. "At your service, boss," he murmured, and steadying her with one hand, he bent his legs, deftly positioned the head of his penis with his other hand and took a small breath of restraint. She was flagrantly ready—slick, slippery, panting. He sent up a small prayer of thanks to the elevator gods and pushed into her welcoming body with a smooth upward thrust of his hips.

She shivered, trembled as his rigid length slowly filled her, crammed her, stretched her—her senses flame-hot, needy, feverish with longing.

She was sleek and tight, yielding bit by bit to his invasion. He shut his eyes against the wild, fevered lust exploding in his brain, and cautioned himself to prudence.

"More . . . more," she panted.

"I don't want to hurt you."

"No—no—it's fine," she gasped, "perfect . . ."

"Here, then . . . how's this?" And he eased in a discreet distance more.

"Oh, God, oh, God . . ." The phrase "die of pleasure" was lit up in ten-foot neon in her brain and she panted and sighed and held on for dear life.

After a deliberate, measured forward progress, when he

was almost fully submerged and she was teetering on her tiptoes impaled on his erection, he whispered, "Can you take a little more?"

Eyes shut, she nodded, believing and disbelieving, already stretched taut but wanting the staggering pleasure more. She sunk her nails into his shoulders, bracing herself.

In the grip of his own unequivocal need, he didn't notice; he was picking her up with his hands under her bottom and lifting her up, wrapping her legs around his waist so he could thrust in deeper, hard, hard—like that . . .

She whimpered.

But she was liquid, pliant, hot, hot around his firmly lodged erection. He stayed where he was, gently rocking from side to side.

She sighed then in a low exhalation of satisfaction and kissed his neck and felt him lift her in a slow, leisurely up-and-down motion that brought her pulsing clitoris in exquisite contact with his hardness, blissfully grazed her G-spot, brought her by rapid, pulsating degrees to a sexual frenzy, drenched them both in the glossy heat of her arousal.

She was featherlight in his arms, his adrenaline pumping so fiercely he could have lifted a Mack truck, his mind focused laser-sharp on his furiously approaching climax. Quickly moving to her mirrored armoire, he braced her against the solid piece of furniture; needing more leverage and flexing his powerful thighs, he drove in deeper, wanting what the woman riding his cock with increasing wildness wanted. Now.

She suddenly went still in his arms, as though in some esoteric sexual harmony, and knowing what that meant, he stopped mid-withdrawal and plunged to meet her climax.

His intellect, too long dormant, suddenly came to life, reminding him of what he'd forgotten in this full-speed-ahead racing fuck.

A condom.

For a flashing millisecond, reason quarreled with libido—should he, shouldn't he? Could he stop even if he wished? Did it matter at this late stage? Or more to the point, how much did it matter? Then, a pulse-beat later, the decision was taken out of his hands—she screamed a high, keening cry, her tight cunt seized his cock in a death grip, her orgasm began rippling up his hypersensitive, damned-near-ready-to-detonate penis. Ohmygod—and, breath held, his orgasm exploded in a furious, high-voltage dam-breaking deluge.

At the same instant the soft golden silk-shaded ambiance of the room was shattered by clamorous waves of Chloe's high-pitched screams.

Not that anyone cared.

Not that anyone heard.

When he came up gasping for air, he instantly knew he'd been incredibly stupid. Resting his sweat-drenched forehead against the armoire mirror, coolheaded reason, now restored, began enumerating all the possible calamities that could befall him.

But Chloe licked a warm path up his throat a second later and hitched herself up a fraction higher and said, "Ummmm . . ." in the sexiest of whispers that made his penis instantly surge higher. His imprudent, fearless penis was apparently calling all the shots tonight, because it was rock-hard again and engulfed in the velvety sweetness of the tightest cunt he'd ever had the good fortune to bottom out in. Moving faintly as though testing his good fortune, he felt her yield infinitesimally, the lambent, honeyed friction melting through his body; the extraordinary unalloyed bliss torching his brain, and decided, what the hell. He'd see how long he could last.

Raising his head, he smiled at her. "I think we should try that bed of yours next."

Her lashes lifted slowly. "Anything you say. . . ."

"In my current mood, you might want to rescind that statement," he whispered, noticing the color of her eyes for the first time, thinking purple was as unusual as everything else about her.

"In *my* current mood, you're going to have trouble keeping up," she murmured, moving her hips in a slow, gliding undulation that added inches to his erection.

He laughed. "Is there a prize for the winner?"

"I'll think of something," she purred, feeling his laugh in the shimmering heat of her body, "on the way to the bed."

It was his cue, and shifting her weight slightly in his arms, he turned from the mirror.

"Look," she breathed.

His gaze swiveled around and he caught sight of them in the mirror, their bodies in profile, hers cradled in his arms, only the base of his penis and his testicles visible at the point where they were joined. He moved slightly, withdrew fractionally so they could see what he was doing to her, what she was doing to him, what they were doing to each other.

She sighed and shifted downward so his penis slid back in.

He moaned deep in his throat and kept her there, his rampant erection pressed hard against her cervix.

"You're strong," she breathed, her eyes closing as she felt herself melting inside, quickening, shuddering with desire. "So very, very, gorgeously—strong."

"And you're soft." He pulled her closer, his hands hard on her bottom. "Really soft," he whispered, swelling larger and larger, the sensation of pleasure so intense it momentarily blotted out reality.

A pulse beat later when his brain began functioning again, he murmured, "Watch."

"What if I don't want to." Teasing and playful.

"You have to or I won't fuck you. Look, it's all slippery and wet from you."

She clutched at his shoulders and whimpered as he slowly withdrew.

"Are you watching?"

"Yes, yes . . . please, I want it back."

"Like this?" He moved forward the merest distance.

"No, more . . . more."

"Are you watching?"

"Yes, yes . . . oh, God, oh, God, oh, God," she panted as he slowly drove forward.

"More?" he whispered, her sweet-as-candy cunt doing disastrous things to his self-control—not that it was even a priority any longer.

"Please, please . . ." Obsessive, avaricious need pulsated in her whispered plea.

And he obliged her, driving into her in a fierce rhythm of thrust and withdrawal as he held her two steps and brief minutes away from where he'd just come in her—unaware of anything but his own raging lust, no longer prudent or cautious, pounding—pounding—pounding into her.

She welcomed him, opened herself to him, every cell and nerve and tissue pulsating with need; receptive, hungry, craving what he could give her, surging pleasure washing over her and through her like molten gold.

He was the one who panted this time. "I can't wait."

"I know," she breathed, already floundering in the turbulent prelude to climax.

And they came a second later in an orgasm that rocked them to the core.

He looked around afterward, not sure for a second where he was, understanding a second later with a lively sense of gratitude—where he was and who he was with and where his cock was buried.

It was inside the luscious Chloe with the fuck-me shoes and the tiny pearl thong and the most seductive, obliging, indulgent, *sensational* body.

"My legs hurt." She almost didn't complain because she liked the feel of him inside her, because he'd just given her the most mind-blowing orgasms of her life and if her thighs were being torn apart, perhaps that was a small price to pay for such splendor.

"You should have said something," he murmured, quickly moving toward the bed. But on reaching it, he hesitated. The magenta silk coverlet looked pristine while its owner had his semen dripping down her thighs.

"Pull back the covers."

Either she could read minds or this had happened before. But he did as he was told because this definitely was not a night for undue speculation.

As he lowered her to the bed, she smiled the luxurious, gloating smile of a supremely satisfied woman. "You deserve a reward," she purred.

"I think you already gave it to me," he said with a grin, placing her on startlingly chartreuse sheets.

"You're not leaving—I hope."

"Not a chance," he murmured, coming upright, gazing on her lush nudity. "My Pavlov reflexes are on high alert. I'm the rat, you're the sugar pellet and I'm gonna keep pushing that feel-good button until I drop."

She laughed. "Definitely a romantic image."

"Speaking of romantic images," he said with a flicker of

his brows. "You're dripping all over. Point me to the bathroom and some towels."

"That way and there's towels over there too." She indicated the bathroom with a stab of her finger and the towels with a wave of her hand toward a bedside table.

He'd bet if he opened that cabinet beside the bed there would be condoms alongside the towels. Chloe definitely liked sex. Not that he was complaining.

He washed up quickly in the bathroom and then brought her both a wet and a dry towel, dropped them on her stomach, unbuckled her shoes, tossed them on the floor and lay down beside her. Turning on his side, he wiped her once wet and then dried her while she lay eyes-closed and smiling.

"Maybe you'd like to stay on as my houseboy. You're damned good."

"I've slept in the last three weeks. I'm one up on you."

"I'm going to have to stay awake for you," she whispered, opening her eyes as he ran his hand over her stomach to check if he'd dried all the dampness.

"I'll have to find something to keep you awake."

"That's working pretty well," she said, reaching out to run a finger down his erection.

He sucked in his breath. "He likes you."

"The feeling's mutual, believe me." She ran her finger slowly around the flange bordering the large showy head of his penis, then measured the rigid length with a downward stroke. "Word of God—*that* is fantastic—ummm . . . look at him grow."

He slipped a finger in her newly washed and dried cleft, found the nub of her clitoris and circled it gently, felt it lengthen under his touch, pulse, swell. She moved faintly against the pressure of his finger and moaned, a quiet, almost inaudible sound.

Within seconds, his finger was drenched, the thought of sliding inside her hot, wet cunt was too much to resist, and he eased himself between her thighs in a ripple of muscle and sinew and entered her with exquisite slowness.

"Jesus," she whispered, arching up to meet him. "Jesus, God . . ."

He buried himself hilt deep, she sobbed—an erratic little rapturous sound—and he found the lines from "Let's Get It On" filling his mind.

Capturing her hips, his fingers splayed wide, holding her firmly in place, he drove in deeper while she panted and whimpered and ground herself against his engorged hard length, coming before he'd even settled into a rhythm. She was definitely primed, ravenous, insatiable, but it didn't matter because he knew how she felt.

He was going to fuck her until he couldn't move.

That's how it felt.

And that's what they did until the sun came up and the birds in the trees across the street in the park reminded them it was morning.

Rising from the bed, he threw back the swagged chintz drapes and, bracing his palms on the door frame, hung there exhausted. Ravenous still. Restive and surly.

He didn't want to leave

Not a useful feeling.

Because he had to go.

She must have felt something or seen something in his face when he turned around.

"Morning and reality—right?"

"No shit."

"Well, thanks." She stretched lazily. "It was worth a long wait. Definitely worth it."

He glanced at the clock buried in bric-a-brac on the desk. "I gotta go."

"I figured."

"I really enjoyed—everything . . . you—the night"—he smiled—"you. Thanks." He began gathering up his clothes.

She rolled over in bed, pulled the quilt up to her chin and let the torpor of three nearly sleepless weeks overtake her. There weren't going to be croissants and lattes, she could tell. But everything else had been a dream come true. C'est la vie to the rest of it, she drowsily concluded.

Rocco let himself out, sullen and moody.

He didn't want to go, but he had a breakfast appointment.

And it wasn't as though she'd notice anyway.

Apparently she'd wanted a stud last night and the night was over.

This was a first for him.

Although, had she wanted more, he couldn't have given it to her anyway.

His life was unbelievably complicated right now.

Fucking-A it was.

FOUR

 WHEN HE WALKED INTO HIS HOUSE, HE IMME-
diately picked up his phone messages. He knew he'd
have a slew. Amy—predictable message—angry,
hurt, crying; then Amy-Amy-Amy-Amy-Amy-ditto, ditto,
ditto. She'd finally stopped calling at two in the morning.
A message from his brother saying he had a call from
Amy—call him back. A message from his sister saying she
had a call from Amy—do not call her back; it was midnight.

He glanced at the clock. Almost eight. Apparently Amy
was still sleeping. Thank God. He had time to take a
shower and dress.

He was meeting Amy and her father, his sister and his
brother at ten.

And then, if he could deal with what was sure to be a
peevish, overindulged princess, the rest of them could discuss the particulars of the business they were about to

launch. He, along with his brother and sister, were developing a line of natural shampoos, soaps and a few simple cosmetics. Amy's father was financing half the venture. And therein lay the proverbial fly in the ointment.

His family and the Thiebauds lived in the same neighborhood when he was growing up. Amy's older brother had been his best friend all through school, and they still got together whenever Steve was in town from Los Angeles, where he produced a segment for Fox Sports. Amy had always been the little sister who got in the way until she'd graduated college and they'd begun dating occasionally. Occasionally being the operative word.

Although she had an altogether different interpretation of their relationship.

They were meant for each other, she insisted.

They'd been soul mates since grade school, hadn't they?

Everyone said they made the perfect couple.

A fortune teller had once told her she'd marry someone named Rocco.

Apparently, she lived in some fantasy world he didn't inhabit.

But she'd always been her daddy's darling, and when Rocco had talked to Jim Thiebaud about investing in their business, Amy had immediately insinuated herself into the venture. She'd model for their ads—be the marketing image like Elizabeth Hurley had been for Estée Lauder. She was blonde and beautiful and certainly suitable; she'd cajoled her daddy into endorsing the concept.

Jim Thiebaud's construction company had build most of the suburbs south of the city, and he was always open to new investments. Rocco hadn't realized Amy would put her own creative (read: perilous) spin on her father's cooperation and segue their business partnership into a marriage proposal for herself.

In fact, that's what he'd been running from last night.

She'd invited him to a family party, then whispered to him over dessert—"Why don't we take this opportunity when everyone is drinking champagne anyway to announce our engagement?" He'd tried to be pleasant. He'd tried to be tactful. He'd tried to explain to her that while they'd dated occasionally, there had never been any understanding between them. She'd turned pouty and sulky and switched to drinking martinis—dangerous fuel to a demanding, self-centered daddy's girl.

He'd made his excuses to Jim and Marcy Thiebaud and left.

And now he had this breakfast meeting, and Amy was sure to be there.

God help him.

HE DIDN'T ANSWER the phone, although Amy started calling at nine.

He hated arguing over the phone.

Or maybe he was a coward.

Either way, he had no intention of listening to her bitch at him after his sleepless night—the thought of which brought a smile to his face. Perhaps the only one he'd have today, he speculated.

Café Latte was packed.

But his sister, Mary Beth, had made sure to come early and save a table; she had that plan-ahead-for-every-eventuality accountant's mind. She was currently waving a menu at him.

"Where's everyone?" he asked, sitting down, picking up her latte and drinking most of it.

"Probably looking for a parking place. It's Saturday. You

have five minutes tops before they all descend on us. Why the hell was Amy calling me at midnight?"

He grimaced, picked up her latte again and finished it off. "She wanted to announce our engagement last night at Fiorollo's with all her family in attendance."

Mary Beth smiled. "That must have been a surprise."

"Yeah, no shit. My heart stopped for a second."

"And she's calling me for help in corralling you into marriage?"

He shrugged. "Who the hell knows? Why don't they have waitresses? I need about six espressos, and look at that fucking line."

"You haven't talked to her since last night, then."

"I was gone last night."

"A smile like that must mean you were gone somewhere interesting."

"Definitely interesting," he said, not able to suppress his grin. "I met a woman in the elevator when I was running from my surprise engagement party. She has pink hair—sort of . . . a little like yours. A graphic artist."

Since her brother rarely—actually *never*—discussed his dates (which were numerous), Mary Beth was instantly alert to the nuances. But before she could ask another question, as predicted, the rest of their party appeared: their brother Anthony, Jim Thiebaud and a glowering Amy.

In the following few minutes, greetings were exchanged, and Mary Beth and Rocco—who was quick to volunteer—got into line to pick up lattes and croissants et cetera for the table.

When they returned, Mary Beth kindly took the seat beside Amy because she was an older sister and still protecting her baby brother. Jim and Anthony had been discussing formulas and prices for supplies; Anthony had sheets of paper piled up between them. Amy was lounging in her chair, looking sullen in a melon linen Prada jacket

HOT PINK 37

and pants, her heavy blonde hair pulled back in a ponytail
to show off her coral and pearl earrings.

She didn't say a word throughout the meeting, spooning
whipped cream from the top of her hazelnut latte into her
pouty mouth, tearing her chocolate croissant into shreds,
eating maybe two bites, swinging her melon-colored
leather mule from the tip of her toe in as close an approximation to boredom as her acting abilities would allow.
Until her father finally said, "Jesus, Amy, sit up and cut
out that infernal fidgeting."

"Yes, Daddy." She stopped swinging her mule for thirty
seconds and started again.

Jim Thiebaud went back to the numbers he and the Vinellis were crunching and didn't notice.

They'd already leased an old factory building; they were
beginning to buy supplies and equipment, hire employees
and draw up an advertising budget. If their business plan
remained on schedule, they would be up and running in
six months. Mary Beth was overseeing the accounts and
employees, Anthony the supplies and manufacturing, and
Rocco was in charge of marketing. He'd already been to
New York and Los Angeles with samples and brochures,
was scheduled to go to San Francisco, Chicago and Dallas
soon and then Miami, Boston and Atlanta. It was getting
to the point where he'd soon have to give notice at Diversified. Once he had some initial sales and had set up some
of the larger accounts, he'd have to hire some sales reps.

In the animated discussion that ensued, the level of enthusiasm was almost palpable. Anthony, a chemist, had
come up with some great formulas—totally organic, wonderfully scented, and affordable. The Vinelli siblings had
always gotten along well. They were looking forward to
working together.

And Jim Thiebaud was always pumped when he could

get in on the ground floor of a profitable business. There were handshakes and smiles all around when the discussion ended. Minus Amy, of course, who was intent on not smiling even once.

"I'd say we're lookin' good. Right on schedule," Jim said, coming to his feet. "Same time next Saturday?"

Since the Vinellis were still all employed in other jobs, Saturdays were their best option. And Jim didn't mind when he talked business.

Everyone nodded and agreed.

"Come on, Amy." Jim tapped his daughter's shoulder. "Your mother's waiting to golf."

"Don't forget the Art Tour, Rocco," Amy murmured as she came to her feet. "You said you'd take me."

Shit. She'd been sitting there the whole time just waiting to pounce. And the sorry fact was he *had* said he'd take her, in a moment of weakness two months before. "Ah . . ."

"You promised!"

Jesus God, she'd stamped her foot. He couldn't fucking believe it, but there was Jim, looking expectant. "I'll pick you up at two."

"It starts at noon," she said, pettishly.

He glanced at his watch. Almost eleven. And he hadn't slept last night; it would be helpful to rest an hour or two. "I have an appointment with a buyer at noon."

"On Saturday?"

"It was the only time I could see him," he lied.

"Well, I suppose if it's for the business."

She said it like she was saying *our* business, meaning his and hers—fucking terrifying thought. "I'll pick you up at two." He couldn't get out of it with Jim smiling at his daughter like she'd just invented the wheel.

"Don't be late."

And the thought popped into his mind of another

woman who gave orders too, but much more tantalizing orders, and he smiled without realizing it. His voice changed, the edge was gone. "I won't be late. Promise."

"She certainly is a grade-A little bitch," Mary Beth murmured as the Thiebauds walked away.

"As long as she's not *my* grade-A little bitch, I don't give a damn. I can be polite to her once in a while."

"But not go out with her anymore?"

"I haven't taken her out for—jeez—a year or more."

"What about those movies and the museum opening and the Christmas party at the Thiebauds'?"

"And the fund-raiser at the zoo?" Anthony added.

"Those were not dates. I made sure they weren't dates."

"And she's still dreaming of marrying you?"

Rocco shrugged. "Go figure. She's got too much spare time on her hands."

"And she's designated you her Prince Charming." Mary Beth threw her hands up. "It's inevitable. Tall, dark and handsome—pretty blonde princess . . ."

"No way. I'd kill myself first."

"Don't kill yourself until we have this business up and running and we've either paid Jim back or he's made enough in profits to break even," Anthony said, his frown in the way of warning.

"I know, I know. But Amy's a handful."

"Why did you date her in the first place?"

Rocco rolled his eyes. "I must have been out of my mind. She was always underfoot, coming to the house on some pretext, bringing me some message from Steve or her family, hanging around, pressing me. I found her in my bed one night when I came home, and finally gave in. But, bottom line and most important—that was a long time ago."

Anthony grinned. "We should find her another Prince

Charming." Anthony was happily married with two children. He could afford to grin.

"Do that with my blessings." Rocco glanced at his watch again. "I gotta go. I didn't sleep last night and if I have to actually listen to Amy this afternoon, I'm going to need at least an hour of shut-eye. Ciao."

"He told me about the woman he met last night," Mary Beth murmured, as their brother strode away.

Anthony's brows rose. "No joke?"

Mary Beth shook her head. "She has pink hair and he met her in an elevator."

"Sounds like Rocco. Let's hope that's all he did in the elevator."

FIVE

CHLOE SLEPT THROUGH TEN OF TESS'S phone calls, three of Rosie's, one of her mother's without so much as a break in her breathing. But finally, at two in the afternoon, the ringing of the phone marginally invaded her sluggish brain and she rolled over just as the sound died away. Squinting at the clock, she forced her brain to recognize the numbers, understood it was daylight and shut her eyes again.

But Tess wasn't known as the Gossip Girl for nothing, and ten minutes later when the phone rang again, Chloe groaned and reached out to grab the receiver.

"It's about time!" her best friend Tess Carlson exclaimed. She tended not to speak in a monotone. It had something to do with her undergraduate degree in drama. "And don't tell me *Fred* kept you awake all night!"

"Damn you," Chloe said, her voice still heavy with sleep. "You knew he was a dud. You owe me big time."

"Yeah, yeah, like you owe me for the time I went out with Grant so you didn't have to. So who *did* keep you awake? I've been trying to call you since nine."

"I've been working my ass off for three weeks. Did you ever think I might be sleeping because I was tired from working?"

"If I didn't know you since third grade I might. You always get up at the crack of dawn—tired or not. So what was his name? Tell me everything . . . including the size of you-know-what."

Chloe chuckled. They'd been exchanging pertinent information on penis sizes since they'd first begun having sex. "The size was good—better than good. I met him in the elevator at Chino's and he gave me a ride home 'cause my car wouldn't start—which reminds me I have to get it towed to the car dealership for repairs. Anyway, my elevator pickup is hotter than hot, or *was*. He's gone and I don't think I'll ever see him again."

"Why not?"

"Because he said thanks this morning and just thanks and left, that's why."

"The bastard!"

"Well, it was a very, very fine night, so he's not a complete bastard. He can do it all night and every which way and I've never felt so good. So I'm feeling a degree of indulgence I wouldn't ordinarily feel if it had been a wham, bam, thank-you-ma'am fuck."

"Was he good-looking?"

"A movie star, rock star, polo star all rolled into one."

"Wow."

"Exactly."

"What's his name?"

"Oh . . . that's the cool part. I think he's some relative of yours. His name is Rocco Vinelli."

"Never heard of him."

"I'm not surprised. He said he had a couple hundred relatives in Gilbert. And when was the last time you went to Gilbert?"

"When my grandma died in 'ninety.' "

"There you go. That was a long time ago."

"So are you heartbroken?"

"About the sex . . . yeah. But let's face it, the chances of meeting the man of your dreams in the elevator at Chino's are pretty slim."

"You're sounding very mature today. Does that mean I don't have to bring over chocolate truffles and a double cheeseburger?"

"Ummm . . . that does sound good. I can't remember when I ate last."

"I'm not touching that line; I'm being mature."

Chloe laughed. "Come on over and I'll tell you about it—him . . . it. My God, the man was hung."

"Should I bring a cheeseburger?"

"Bring two, and hash browns if it's not too late."

"Hello . . . it's two o'clock. And we have that Art Tour to go on. If you dress while I'm on my way over, we can still see some of it before they close at six."

"I forgot . . . sorry." Chloe shook herself awake. "Okay, I'll be ready."

CHLOE LET OUT a little shriek when she walked out of the shower and into her bedroom.

Tess was lounging on her bed, the bag from Mac's in her lap.

"Jesus, Tess, didn't you see *Psycho?* Shout when you come in next time. Give me some warning."

"Sorry. So I'm impatient. It's not often we run across a

man of what sounds like very grand proportions. Tell me everything."

Chloe grinned. "Food first." Grabbing a towel, she rubbed her hair semidry as flopped down on her bed. Between bites of cheeseburger, she told Tess all she could in good conscience disclose. Tess had a habit of being outspoken, and since Rocco was a relative of sorts, she didn't want him to be embarrassed at the next family reunion with one of Tess's unedited blow-by-blow accounts.

"So you're not going to see him again?"

"I suppose it's possible I might run into him; there's only a million and a half people in the Twin Cities."

Tess grimaced. "Cute. You could call him."

Chloe shook her head. "He had a funny look on his face this morning." She shook her head again. "I don't think so."

"You're not ordinarily so composed." Chloe was impulsive as hell, as Tess well knew, having followed her through a succession of outrageous escapades over the years, starting with the time they threw water balloons from the middle school windows and accidently hit the principal.

Chloe wrinkled her nose. "I don't know . . . maybe he's too good to believe—like maybe I dreamed everything last night. Or maybe I don't want to be his four thousandth lay who's still pining for him."

"Are you talking pride? Like he can come to you?"

Chloe shrugged. "Maybe. I don't really know. Look, I'm still too tired to actually think straight. Give me a few days and I'll set this whole night into some kind of reasonable perspective."

Tess glanced at the clock and shifted in her chair. "We should go soon, although I don't want to get to Dave's until the tour's almost over—just in case."

"You can talk him into spending the night with you."

Chloe smiled. "I know what this is all about." And she did, because she'd been listening to Tess's pretty much unending longing for Dave Lepinski for weeks now. But then, Tess was more subtle than she when it came to men. While Chloe preferred the direct approach, Tess subscribed to some polite code of female behavior that resisted options like calling up a guy when you wanted to or making the first move. Not that Tess was a prude. She just couldn't say "I want you" first.

Tess held up crossed fingers and grinned. "Maybe I'll get lucky. So hurry and get dressed. We don't have to wait for Rosie. She can't come. She had to go to her mother's birthday party."

"She called yesterday," Chloe replied, bundling up her wrappers and climbing from the bed. "I forgot until now, but, yeah . . . I heard. How is darling Markie Mark?"

"She cried her eyes out last night. He didn't show— again."

"What a prick. I thought they were going to the Guthrie?"

"I went with her."

"She shouldn't even talk to him again. He's such a horse's ass."

Tess rolled her eyes. "She's in luvvv . . ."

"With a horse's ass," Chloe said, heatedly. "Does he have one redeeming feature? Even one?" She turned back from her armoire. "He hit on me the other night. I wasn't going to mention it, but—" She shrugged. "I said to him, why the hell would I want to go out with you? You already have a girlfriend—actually, I believe you're *engaged!* It didn't fucking faze him a bit. Maybe some other time, the jerk said!" Chloe pulled out a lavender T-shirt.

"Don't wear that. It shows your nipples."

"Everything shows my nipples. I don't wear a bra."

"Wear something dark, then."

"Are you the fashion police today? Since when did you care. I've never worn a bra."

"Since we're going to Dave's studio, and I want him to look at *my* nipples."

Chloe laughed. "And well he might in that very tight T-shirt. How about I wear black?"

"Black's good."

In deference to her best friend, who had had a crush on Dave Lepinski for over two months and he'd barely noticed her, Chloe wore a black linen man's shirt that hardly showed her body, a pair of khaki slacks and sandals. "Do I pass?" she asked with a grin, holding her arms out and twirling around.

"Perfect. Thanks, Chloe. I want him so bad." Tess made a moue that emphasized her really lush, full lips—lips Chloe had envied since she'd first understood what boys noticed in women . . . besides big tits.

"And you're asking me if I'll ever see Rocco? Hey, babe, take some of your own advice and call him up. You know Dave's shy as hell. Why else does he paint those Escher-like paintings that take a year to finish? He's the world's biggest introvert." He was also the type of man she wouldn't give a second look at, but there was no accounting for Tess's myopic taste.

"I suppose I should."

"Damn right, you should."

"I thought I'd buy one of his paintings and ask him to help me hang it."

Tess was a bank manager so she could probably afford a painting that took a year to finish. "And then greet him at the door naked and see if he notices. I'm not sure he would."

"I'm not as brash as you."

"True." Which thought brought to mind a man she

knew who was as brash and audacious as she; her vagina did a little flutter in remembrance. Damn, he was good. But then she returned to the real world where Tess was waiting to go and see Dave and she smiled at her best friend. "Let's go and give shy Dave a hard time."

SIX

 BY THE TIME THEY REACHED DAVE'S STU-
dio, it was almost five and the crowds were thinning.
They'd looked at a dozen studios on the way; Tess
had been gauging the time, waiting for the tour's end so
she could more easily talk to him.

Chloe wanted to say, "He doesn't talk anyway, crowd or
no crowd," but was being supportive and kept silent. She'd
not calculated the influence of five hours of wine-drinking
on Dave. All the studios were offering wine and hors
d'oeuvres, and he'd taken the opportunity to overcome his
shyness by imbibing, perhaps a little too much.

The artist Lepinski, dressed as usual in jeans and a denim
shirt, his long pale hair disheveled, was between the lounging and the passed-out stage. Ensconced in a large upholstered chaise at the back of the studio, he was looking up
at a tall, dark-haired man with a beautiful, polished blonde
hanging on his arm.

Even from the back, Chloe's breath caught in her throat.

She immediately told herself to get a grip. How many tall, dark-haired men were there in the Twin Cities? she firmly asked herself. How many indeed? And she wouldn't have gone another step closer if Tess hadn't literally dragged her by the arm, hissing, "Help me think of something to say to him."

Which turned out to be her problem as well.

At close range—much too close range as it turned out—that little vaginal flutter immediately set in. She came face to face, not only with Dave . . . but with her bed partner of the previous night. Along with his beautiful, model-perfect, designer-clothed girlfriend, who was clinging to his arm as though he were the last crew member on the *Titanic* who could lead her to safety.

Chloe couldn't think of a thing to say.

Tess was equally bereft of conversation.

Thank God Dave was drunk; he literally lurched into the breach, coming up from his chaise and falling into Tess, muttering, "Wanna shleep wish you, wanna real bad."

"They must be friends," Rocco said smoothly, watching a smiling Tess lead the stumbling artist away.

"Apparently," Chloe replied, having gotten the necessary cogs in her brain wheeling into action. "I'll see if she needs some help." She began to turn away.

"We've met, haven't we?" Rocco's voice was bland and urbane.

Chloe turned back, stunned. Did she answer yes or no? Could she even meet his gaze with equanimity? Who was that bitch blonde looking like she'd just smelled something bad?

"I think we met at Diversified Foods," Rocco said, polite and genial, as though they'd just bumped into each other at a church picnic and were actual churchgoers too. "Aren't you doing the Graham Crunchies web site?"

"Yes." It just went to show what a master's degree could do for your vocabulary.

"For Bill Martell, wasn't it? I saw you there."

Okaaay, she wished to say. Now what? Are you going to mention where you spent last night to the woman creasing the hell out of your linen jacket?

"You must know this artist." Rocco nodded at a nearby painting. "He does nice work. I like the black-and-white one best."

He lifted his arm slightly as though to show her and almost touched her. She backed up a step so she wouldn't embarrass herself by throwing herself into his arms—okay . . . arm—the other one was held captive. "My friend, Tess, knows him. And yes, that black-and-white interior is well done," she said, finally managing to get out two sentences in a row.

"Aren't you going to introduce me, darling?" The beautiful blonde's expression had changed from one of distaste to petulance.

"It was Chloe—right?"

The shit. She wanted to say, "You didn't have any trouble remembering my name when we were having sex all night," but said, instead, "Yes, Chloe Chisholm. I don't recall your name." Two could play that memory-loss game.

"Amy Thiebaud, Chloe Chisholm," Rocco said, with apparent calm, when he was hard-pressed not to send Amy on her way and take Chloe into the back room and fuck her on the floor or against the wall or anywhere at all. That should make her remember his name.

That Thiebaud? Chloe wondered. The sleek blonde looked rich enough to be the daughter of the man who'd begun and sustained the suburban sprawl south of the Cities. Thiebaud Homes had ads on TV every thirty seconds.

Amy nodded faintly in Chloe's direction, as though she were acknowledging the hired help.

Chloe said, "Nice to meet you," because her mother had always insisted on courtesy with admonitions like, "Do unto others as you would have them do unto you, kindness is within our power," and old habits become involuntary. But beyond the reflexes of politesse she was wondering what would happen if she stepped on the toes of those cream-colored pumps matching the cream-colored silk sheath and smooth blonde tresses that were in stark contrast to her windblown curls and casual outfit.

"If you really like that painting, darling, let me buy it for you," Amy murmured, turning her shoulder to Chloe, looking up at Rocco and smiling. "It would look wonderful in your living room. Or maybe even in your bedroom," she added in a sultry undertone. "Over the fireplace . . ." She swung back to Chloe, a sudden briskness in her voice. "Could you get the artist for us? I want to buy this for my boyfriend."

Chloe's mouth firmed, temper sparked in her eyes. "Sorry, I can't help you. If you'll excuse me."

"Wait." Rocco had no idea what he was going to say or do, but he didn't want her to leave. "Help me pick out a painting," he said quickly. "You know art. I'll buy something."

If looks could kill, Chloe thought, she'd be dead on the spot from those mascara'd and heavily eye-shadowed baby blues. Definitely incentive to respond. "Sure. Let's take a look around." She almost felt like quoting something from Karl Marx under Amy's withering patrician disdain. "Each of these paintings takes a year or so to finish," she added, moving toward the next painting on the right. "I hope you have piles of money."

It was acid sarcasm, but he didn't care. All he could think about was touching her—correction, fucking her. Reason had left on vacation.

Stopping before the next painting, Rocco's presence no more than a foot away doing predictable things to her addicted sensual receptors, Chloe quickly launched into art speak before she gave in to impulse and embarrassed herself. "The reds in this painting are especially vibrant, evoking a heated, energetic mood and tempo. As does the asymmetrical composition and vanishing perspective. The horizon line keeps disappearing and reappearing. See. Here and here and—"

"I'll buy it. She's not my girlfriend."

Her gaze snapped up. "Liar."

"She isn't."

"Then what are you doing with her?" She was speaking in an undertone, albeit a sharp, acerbic one.

"It's an obligation."

The softness of his voice brought back lush memories of the night past, and if she wasn't wondering how many times he'd cheated on his girlfriend, she might have surrendered to the seductive timbre. "Isn't this where you say, she doesn't understand me; I need more space? What the hell do you think you're doing?"

"Trying to see you again."

"Here she comes. Ask me out."

He didn't. She knew he wouldn't. Amy came up and slid her arm through Rocco's like she owned him lock, stock and barrel. Like she was the winner.

"Are you going to buy this painting?" All Chloe wanted to do was leave.

"You decide. I don't care." Rocco's voice was a low growl, discontent in every syllable.

"Take the black-and-white one then. It's Dave's best. You can put it over your fireplace in your bedroom," Chloe said with cloying sweetness.

"It will match your bedspread, darling." Amy did a little wave in the general direction of the painting. "It's perfect."

Certainly the very best reason to buy a work of art, Chloe thought.

"Can we go now?" Amy's perfectly formed lips curved downward into a little-girl pout, much practiced and generally effective. "I'm tired of standing here." *With her* was left unsaid, although the intimation hovered in the air like a Macy's Thanksgiving Day Parade balloon—conspicuous and unmistakable. "You said we could go back and buy that painted dress I want. Come on, pleeeease."

"In a minute," Rocco gruffly replied, ignoring her tug on his arm. "I'm buying that painting."

"The girl at the desk over there can help you." Chloe was finished with this charade—irritated with the prevarication and artifice—mostly with the possessive blonde if she wanted to be brutally honest with herself. "And if your girlfriend wants to buy something else, there's not much time." Go, go, go.

"There, see, Rocco. Cleo knows." Amy looked directly at Chloe and smiled smugly—their relationship properly accredited, everyone's territorial rights clearly defined. "You've been *ever* so helpful. Hasn't she been helpful, darling?" Leaning into Rocco's body, she lifted her gaze. "You know Daddy will love that painting too. He has one just like it in his study."

"Great." As if he needed the reminder that he was screwed. Or at least for the next six months he was screwed.

"I don't think we need you anymore." Amy did a little flick of her wrist toward Chloe.

"You two have a great life." Chloe walked away. She didn't need some little bitch being bitchy to her. She particularly didn't need a little bitch—actually Amy Thiebaud was probably five foot ten if she was an inch, which meant she was a big bitch, but anyway—she didn't need any crap from the girlfriend of the man who had spent last night with her. Damn him. It pissed her off that he was so typically male. Screw any female who stands still long enough, regardless of girlfriends or wives or fiancées. Hell, he wasn't any better than fucking dog-ass Markie Mark.

Which didn't exactly put her in the category of sensible women.

Because Rocco had looked really, really good.

Her vagina had thought so too.

It was a crying shame.

All the hot guys were already taken.

PUSHING ASIDE THE curtain that separated Dave's work area from his gallery space, Chloe came to a sudden stop and held her breath, hoping no one would notice she was there. Particularly the couple making love on the couch in the corner.

Jeez, she didn't know Dave had a tattoo on his— She looked away, began quietly easing out of the room. Standing in the back of the gallery a moment later, she stayed out of sight while Rocco wrote a check and finally left with his girlfriend. She didn't have the same blasé capacity that allowed him to converse with two women he was screwing without so much as breaking a sweat.

Thank God they were gone.

She'd walk home herself, because it didn't look as though Tess was going to have to buy that painting after all.

It also looked as though she'd be spending Saturday night alone.

Rosie was busy with family, Tess was . . . well—busy.

And she was fantasizing about a man she couldn't have because Miss Beautiful Blonde Moneybags had him clutched to her couturier-attired body and it didn't look real likely she was going to let go without a fight.

Besides, there was nothing to fight for.

Rocco wasn't hers.

He had never been hers; it had been a one-night stand.

Case closed.

Her only decision now was pepperoni or sausage, Pepsi or Coke?

SEVEN

 WHICH CONCLUSION ABOUT ONE-NIGHT
stands seemed sensible and reasonable and easily
managed until Chloe reached the halfway point in
the bottle of wine she was drinking with her pizza in lieu
of Pepsi. The first time her errant psyche said, "Why don't
you call him?" she resolutely ignored the suggestion. But
after another glass of wine, that niggling little voice in-
creased in volume, even adding the helpful phrase, "I'll look
up his number in the phone book."

She managed to tamp down the impulse to respond, but
less firmly this time, considerably less firmly, because she
actually dragged out the phone book, looked up Rocco's
number and circled it in red marker.

As she sipped on her wine, that red marked target kept
jumping into her line of vision, and even with the most
severe self-control, she was unable to keep her gaze from
that shimmering red image.

It was really quite amazing how powerful the sexual impulse was, she mused, wondering if she should get out her vibrator as a substitute. Which word, substitute, continued to bombard her increasingly inebriated brain, as though in stark reminder of the differences between Rocco's splendid equipment and the inherent wimpiness of her battery-powered appliance.

Coming to her feet in a burst of frustration, she slammed shut the phone book and threw it in the corner behind the couch where it would be very difficult to retrieve. Unfortunately, she had total recall of numbers, an advantage, of course, on numerous occasions, but not precisely now when she was seriously trying to CURTAIL HER LUST.

Ohmygod . . . when had benign longing turned to lust? She glanced at the clock and softly groaned.

How was she going to get through the night?

CALL! CALL! CALL! that persistent little voice inside her head screamed.

First lust and now screams . . . this was getting totally out of control.

She set her wineglass down and turned on the National Geographic channel, as a reminder of the consequences of poor judgment; an animal was always being killed in some brutal, gory way for entering dangerous territory. And surely this was one of those occasions when what she wanted was outside the pale—not necessarily in the relatively lax moral climate of contemporary society, but say in a more philosophical context.

As in good versus bad.

As in the Golden Rule.

As in *The Rules* book that she'd never actually read; but she suspected the authors would not condone calling up another woman's boyfriend to invite him over for a night of unbridled sex.

*   *   *

IN ANOTHER PART of town—a posher part, where the local police let strangers know it was best if they kept their cars moving until they reached the freeway, Amy was sitting immovable as the Rock of Gibraltar in the passenger seat of Rocco's car parked at the curb outside her house. "But I don't *want* to go home yet."

She had been rocklike in her obstinacy for at least twenty minutes, arguing with him, refusing to leave, giving him one hell of a headache. Almost making him wish he hadn't been born into a family of middle-class income. Then he could have asked his father and mother for the start-up money and Jim Thiebaud, or more importantly, Amy, would be out of the picture. But his dad was a high school football coach, much revered for his record of wins, but not a millionaire. And his mother's nurse's salary wasn't going to open any factory. He and his siblings had mortgaged everything they had to the hilt for their share of the investment, but—bottom line—they needed Jim Thiebaud.

So he decided to barter his current headache for a future one.

"Look. Why don't I take you out for dinner next week? I really do have to go now."

"Go where?"

That was the tenth time she'd asked, and the tenth time he'd lied. "Anthony and I have to take his kids to some Little League baseball game. He coaches and I help him out." He knew how Amy hated little kids—hence the fiction.

It was almost seven. He'd been with her for five very long hours. He didn't know time could go so slowly. And seriously, his headache was fierce.

"When next week?"

She could have negotiated for the Chinese. Never give an inch without getting something in return. "Thursday. We'll go to Zinc's." He knew she liked the small Parisian bistro.

"Right after work."

"Okay." She still hadn't moved, but he was praying hard.

"Who was that girl at the gallery?"

He suppressed his shock. "No one," he said.

"I didn't like her hair."

"I didn't notice."

"And did you see that horrid shirt? She looked—well . . . common, I thought."

"I didn't notice," he said again.

"You talked to her for quite a while." Amy's blue-eyed gaze was sharp.

"Bill Martell said she did good work. Bill doesn't say that often."

"What kind of work could she possibly do?"

"Web design, I guess. . . . I really don't know much about it other than Bill's comments."

She'd seen the way he looked at the woman in the gallery. But if he wasn't going to talk about it, she knew better than to press the issue. What she needed to press, however, was his obligation to her family, the closeness of their family bond. It was her trump card. Her ace in the hole.

And he had a sense of honor—so rare nowadays. But eminently useful.

"Do you remember the time you saved me from drowning?" She turned slightly more in her seat, so she could look into his eyes. "That summer at the cabin when Steve was holding me underwater?"

"You wouldn't have drowned. Steve would have let you up."

"I don't know if he would have in time. You were my

knight in shining armor," she whispered, reaching over to touch his cheek. "You were fifteen."

"Geez, Amy, Steve was just playing around."

"That was so sweet," she went on as though he'd not spoken. "I think I've loved you ever since—no—I've loved you from the first grade. Mummy always reminds me that I told her I loved you after you brought me that valentine."

His mother had sent him over with valentines for the whole Thiebaud family. He was twelve and embarrassed as hell. And look where it had landed him. "Amy, please, don't talk about loving me. Your family means a lot to me, but I'm not in love with anyone. Okay? We went out a few times, that's all. I wouldn't want you to get the wrong idea."

"I understand. But, darling, you can't keep me from loving you, no matter what you say." She half lowered her lashes in feigned shyness. "I just do." She smiled her most seductive smile, the one she'd perfected at seventeen after hours in front of the mirror. The one that normally got her what she wanted. "So there. And Mummy and Daddy just adore you too."

Jesus, he hated when she smiled at him like that, like she was sharpening her knife to eat him. "Look, we've been friends a long time. And I like your family. But we're in business together now, and I'd like to keep that relationship simple. No complications."

"Of course, darling. We're all so pleased to be part of your new venture. I won't complicate anything. I'll just continue to love you like I always have and be hopeful— no—don't say anything . . . I can be hopeful if I wish. Every little girl dreams of a Cinderella story of her own." She smiled. "It's a girl's prerogative. Just like it's a man's pre-rogative to try and escape that matrimonial noose," she added, playfully. "I understand the rules."

"There are no rules, Amy. And no story. Okay?"

"Whatever you say, darling."

She was impervious to his explanations; he might have been talking to a wall. There was no way he was going to continue this conversation. He'd been as polite as he could be for five hours. Everyone had their limits. Pushing his car door open, he said, "I'll get your packages from the trunk," and exited the car before he said something he'd regret. After gathering the numerous items Amy had purchased, he walked around to the passenger door, opened it and put his hand out to help her up.

Even Amy, who wasn't known for her perspicacity in terms of other's feelings, realized Rocco was looking grim. She knew that look from her daddy; his mouth would purse like that when she'd really overspent. Prudently deciding she could continue her subtle manipulation some other day, she emerged from the car with an amiable smile. "I adored the Art Tour. Thanks for taking me," she said as though he'd had a choice. "You must show me your new painting when they deliver it."

The phrase "when hell freezes over" came to mind, but he mumbled some vague reply, backing away, grateful to be holding several shopping bags as buffer when she looked like she was trying to figure out how to give him a hug. Moving toward her house, he walked Amy to her door, where he handed the bags to the housekeeper. Smiling tightly, he forced himself to mouth the vile statement exchanging one torture for another. "I'll see you Thursday."

" 'Til Thursday, darling." She blew him a kiss.

He nodded, incapable of even the most banal politesse after five hours of Amy's unsubtle machinations. Turning away, he walked down the brick path to his car feeling like someone who had made it through a mine field, rigid and tense but still alive.

Also feeling sorely—make that wildly—tempted to drive to NordEast Minneapolis.

But it was Saturday night. Chloe probably had a date.

And she'd barely lifted her head when he'd left that morning—correction, *hadn't* lifted her head. In fact, she'd been sleeping.

Fuck.

His head was pounding—compliments of Amy.

He'd go home, have a beer, watch some baseball and go to sleep.

To make up for last night.

He smiled.

Definitely a night for the record books.

EIGHT

CHLOE HAD PICKED UP THE PHONE AND
changed her mind at least a dozen times before she'd
actually dialed the number. But before the call had
even gone through, she chickened out and dropped the receiver into its cradle.

After pacing the room for ten minutes, she decided to
go for a run and rid herself of some of her sexual frustration.
After slipping on her sneakers, however, she took note of
the time and had second thoughts. It was after nine. Even
with longer daylight hours, it probably wasn't a good idea
to go running alone at this time. And let's face it, if running
truly released sexual frustration, there would be a whole lot
more runners.

She poured herself a glass of wine instead.

And then another—which may have been the impetus
for finally giving in to temptation. It was almost ten when
she dialed the number, actually let it ring *and* ring *and,*

dammit, ring before she quickly hung up when the message machine kicked in.

Damn, damn, damn—she almost cried, when she'd never cried for sex in her life.

Rocco was probably out with the beautiful blonde, having mouthwatering sex, and what did *she* have—cold pizza, the grease congealing on the cardboard box, the corners of the slices sort of curling up, looking gross, and one empty wine bottle that had been a leftover in the first place—like her tonight, she wretchedly thought.

If one wished to contrast the haves and the have-nots of the world in terms of sex on this particular Saturday night, she was a pathetic example of a have-not. While Rocco and the blonde beauty were probably making love on pale Porthault sheets—hand-hemmed, monogrammed and carefully ironed by some underling—smiling at each other like an ad for Doublemint gum . . . double the pleasure when two movie-star types hit the sheets . . . she was sitting home alone.

Reaching for the wine bottle on that miserable note, she belatedly recalled it was empty.

She was frantically searching her disordered cupboards for another bottle of wine when the phone rang and rang and rang because she was teetering on the kitchen counter about to reach the shelf over the fridge where she sometimes kept a good bottle of wine.

"Wait, wait, wait!" she screamed, trying to get down without breaking an ankle. Having reached the floor, she raced for the phone and picked it up just as the ringing stopped.

Now would be the time to have caller ID upstairs like she did in her office. She quickly checked her voicemail, but the caller hadn't left a message.

But all was not completely lost, her semi-inebriated brain reminded her. She had caught a glimpse of a very good bottle of wine above the fridge. But this time, she wouldn't teeter dangerously on the countertop, she decided. She'd find her small stepladder. Not a simple task as it turned out; she finally found it, oddly enough, under the bed. Which meant she could now get at the expensive bottle of Haut-Brion claret, which further meant all was not lost on this miserable, sex-deprived Saturday night.

She set the ladder carefully, making sure the legs were solidly planted. After drinking most of a bottle of wine, she intended to be caution itself. While holding onto the fridge she ascended the ladder. Having reached the fourth and top step, she was almost able to reach the high shelf. As she was stretching out her hand to take hold of the cupboard door handle, a familiar voice, close and sexy as hell, said, "You better change your door code. Four ones is too easy."

Chloe swung around, wobbled, arms flailing like a terrible cartoon character, she found herself thinking, when she would have preferred to look cool and beautifully composed when Rocco saw her. Her wobbling turned into free fall and she screamed.

Stepping forward like a man confident in his physical abilities, Rocco caught her, scooping her up in his arms with an effortless grace, kissing away her scream, kissing away her surprise, kissing away her feeling sorry for herself. And when his mouth lifted from the increasingly happy warmth of her mouth, he whispered, "Why don't you answer your phone?"

"That was you?"

"Yup. I was returning your call." He shifted her in his arms, but he didn't set her down. He tightened his grip.

"How did you know I called?" But she didn't really care about the hows and the whys when he was here, holding her ever so close.

"I saw your name on my caller ID."

"But you didn't answer."

"I was out for more beer. I was drinking away my frustration."

Her eyes flared wide. "Me too, me too, me too."

He could tell she'd been drinking away something, but he didn't care, no more than he cared that she'd waited so long to call. "A cop gave me a ticket for speeding or I would have been here sooner."

"A speeding ticket because of me?" It was much harder to censure those unfashionably gauche remarks when one had drunk a good portion of a bottle of wine.

"For you," he said in a sexy whisper that went with the sexy look in his eyes, that went with his obvious erection nudging her hip. "I had a helluva day and you were just what I wanted to make me feel better."

"I know—ditto here," she said, softly, when she should have asked him about the woman he was with that afternoon, when she should have told him about her resentment and frustration. "I almost called you a thousand times."

"I'm glad you finally did."

Which goes to show *The Rules* is just plain wrong for empowered women on a mission from God.

He opened his mouth, feeling as though he should explain how Amy fit into his life; he even said, "I want to explain about Amy," when Chloe began pulling his T-shirt over his head, whispering, "Please, please, pretty please . . . *hurry*," in the kind of tone no man with a pulse beat could ignore. He debated the necessity of setting the record straight for about six seconds more before giving up and doing what he'd come there to do.

He carried her toward her bedroom, moving down her now-familiar hallway at record speed, shoving the bedroom door open with his foot, the color shock scarcely registering on his retinas after a few beers and his hardcore focus on consummation. Dropping her on the bed, he stripped his clothes off while she unbuttoned the black shirt she wore, sans chinos and underwear.

He'd taken note of the fact in the kitchen, her bottom soft and warm when he'd caught her, and while he hardly needed any added temptation with his libido at the rocket-launching stage, he'd fully appreciated the lush sensation.

She was lying stretched out on the rumpled bed, pleading with him to hurry.

Life didn't get any better, he decided, pausing a moment to take in the view before dropping between her legs and taking advantage of her widely spread thighs.

"Finally," she said, as he plunged inside her, as though he were on contract to her and late.

"Amen to that," he breathed, feeling as though someone had let him back in paradise after a day in hell.

They made love that first time as though in homecoming, as though they'd been apart for months, as though he'd been adrift at sea and returned a survivor, a level of hysteria shimmering just beneath the surface, the physical sensations intense, acute, raw, seething. He didn't let her move, or at least not very far, holding her captive with his hands and erection, with the promise of pleasure he offered her in full and abundant measure until their first bout of starvation was sated, until they'd come enough times. Until they could consciously think beyond the need to feel the tactile closeness of each other—everywhere—and know it wasn't a dream.

An hour later, Rocco lay on his back, his breathing labored, Chloe beside him gasping for air. "I'm obligated to

Amy," he panted, "or I would have called first."

Chloe gave him a stare. "I don't want to talk about it." "Ignorance is bliss" was coined for this moment.

He hesitated for a second. "Okay." He was off the hook; she'd let him off the hook.

With a smile, he ran his finger down her arm, resting next to his. "Did I tell you I missed you today?"

She took his finger, slid it over her nipple, smiled back. "Not more than twenty times."

"I really did." He gently compressed the soft tissue and watched it spring to life.

"Ummm . . . I know." She arched faintly against his touch. "I drank a couple extra glasses of wine because I missed you."

"We could have drunk together." He transferred his attention to her other nipple, making a matching pair of taut, aroused crests.

"Exactly. Or do other things even more fun."

"Yeah. Like you need a shower."

"I do?"

"Let me reword that. I *need* to give you a shower."

"Ah . . . that's different." She stretched lazily and grinned at him. "Anytime . . ."

He was thinking "anytime" could be translated into now. When he'd brought his breathing back to normal, he carried her into the bathroom that he'd only seen in passing last time and sat her down on a little poufy chair he wouldn't dare sit on for fear of breaking. He didn't recall the tiger painted on the wall, the one staring out at him from a dense green thicket, no more than he remembered the size of her shower.

It was very small. He wasn't sure he could stand up in it.

Her tub wasn't much better—one of those old claw-foot

tubs made for a generation of smaller people.

But he was resourceful; he could improvise. He turned on the shower, sat down in one corner and beckoned her in.

"I can see you're not made for these cramped spaces," she said, grinning as she joined him, taking the hand he offered her, settling on his lap.

He couldn't stretch his legs out, but she fit just fine where he wanted her to fit.

She squirmed a little and sighed like she did when he was filling her and making her feel as though pleasure was not only pulsing through every cell in her body but enfolding her in a cocoon of glowing bliss.

He soaped her plump breasts, shifting to one side while he was soaping so the spray hit his shoulders and not her, running his slippery hands over and around the lush heavy curves, lifting the shiny weight in his hands, saying, "Look," so she had to look down and see the soft flesh mounded high in his palms, her nipples jewel hard, waiting for his touch.

She felt his erection grow inside her, stiffen, surge upward, and gasped a little and clutched at his wet, warm shoulders and bent forward slightly to kiss his smiling mouth. When she leaned in, the delicious friction of his penis sliding up her clitoris felt like a tiny bolt of lightning.

"Nice," he whispered. "Hot, wet sex . . ."

"Nice indeed," she whispered back. She rubbed her soapy breasts against his chest and moved her bottom gently and kissed him harder, wanting to mark him somehow, brand him, make him hers. If she'd been sober, she wouldn't have allowed herself to go that far. But she wasn't sober; she was feeling like an addict and he was her fix and if he left her she'd die.

"I need you, I need this"—she ground her bottom against him hard—"God, I need you . . ."

It was a momentary lapse. Even in her drunkenness she knew she'd gone too far. She felt him stiffen under her hands and mentally flogged herself for her stupidity.

But his muscles relaxed a moment later and he took her face between his hands and he kissed her even harder than she'd kissed him. And when his mouth lifted from hers, he said, low and soft, "The feeling's mutual."

"You don't have to say that—but thanks . . . you're sweet." She'd heard enough sex talk to know that guys felt they had to say nice things back.

He shifted back fractionally, so the spray fell on them both, but he'd not moved his hands from her face, and his dark eyes were very close and heated. "I'm not sweet—never—and for what it's worth, I meant it."

She liked the warm water running down her face and head and back, she liked him, here, now, like this—inside her and around her and holding her gently between his hands. "For what it's worth, I meant it even more."

He laughed and kissed her hard, hard, and held her, his hands on her hips, and raised and lowered her as though she were weightless, and brought her to orgasm with ease like he could because she was truly addicted.

And when they'd both come enough to ease their addictions, he washed her gently and sprayed her off and toweled her dry before showering himself.

She watched him from her poufy chair, wondering how much of the affection she felt was due to the wine, infatuated like a fourteen-year-old, without reason or rationale. He was too beautiful, she decided, and too good in bed, and if she had an iota of sense, she wouldn't lose sight of those irrevocable facts. And the sooner she reconciled herself to the carpe diem credo, the better off she'd be.

She had composed her wildly adoring sensibilities into a semblance of order before he dried himself off. And when he said, "I'm hungry. Let's order some food," she was able to reply like a reasonable person.

"Get some whipped cream too."

Well, semireasonable.

What? She might as well enjoy him while he was here.

THE GROCERY DELIVERY arrived first. She recognized the staccato doorbell ring of the delivery boy. Throwing on his jeans, Rocco tossed her his T-shirt. "Meet you in the kitchen."

His shirt smelled of cologne and masculinity and as she dropped it over her head, she felt such a rush of pleasure she shut her eyes for a moment. It was crazy and stupid, juvenile as hell, but he sure would be easy to love if he probably didn't have ten thousand other women standing in line ahead of her. Or if she'd known him more than twenty-four hours and could justify her outre feelings of affection.

Or better yet, if she had the slightest clue what love was.

Running a brush through her hair, she warned herself that falling in love literally overnight only happened in songs and movies, and instant attraction had more to do with lust than love. Staring at herself in the mirror, she reminded herself that men ran like hell from women who told them they loved them after the first date—not that their sex marathon was even remotely a date . . . but certainly a really great way of getting to know each other. She then ran through affirmations from numerous self-help books that she occasionally half-read—or at least looked at the chapter headings—the ones that affirmed female independence, inner confidence, real power and passing up good for great—which in her case, she'd definitely done this weekend. She smiled.

I AM WOMAN.

Maybe she'd tell him she loved him just to see the shock on his face.

On the other hand, maybe she wouldn't because she wasn't quite ready to relinquish his incredible dick and sexual skills. Call her selfish. Call her spoiled. Call her addicted.

Coming into the kitchen a few minutes later, she paused in the doorway to admire the view. Wearing only jeans, he was taking the groceries out of the sacks, looking sexy and very large in the narrow confines of her corridor kitchen. "It's not fair how men can walk around half naked and the world is unconcerned. Now if I'd gone to the door in a pair of jeans—"

"The delivery boy would have been mighty happy," he said. "You'd better let me answer the door for the Chinese food, too." He winked. "You look great in my T-shirt, but I'm not in the mood to share."

"What? I'm covered." His T-shirt fell halfway to her knees.

"Not enough, babe. Your nipples are giving me a hard-on and if I lift that shirt just a few inches every man who looks at you is thinking . . ."

"That's because men are hardwired for sex."

"My point exactly."

"It's still not fair."

"How about I make the whipped cream and put the groceries away? Does that ease the fairness issue? You can tell me what to do."

"Really?"

"Sure."

"Come here."

He hesitated a fraction of a second, she noticed, but he set down the bag of powdered sugar and walked toward her.

"Now what?"

She had to look up a considerable distance, barefoot as she was, no four-inch heels to mitigate the vast disparity in their heights. "I need a kiss."

His smile was instant, the measured look in his eyes fading. "Anyplace special?"

"Lecher."

His smile broadened. "Just trying to be accommodating."

"A plain kiss if you please. The accommodating stuff will have to wait until after I eat, and I'm talking about food before you say anything impudent."

"Yes, Ma'am," he said in a husky low murmur. "At your service, Ma'am." And he took her shoulders in the cup of his hands, dipped his head and kissed her with a gentleness that was irresistibly sexy and romantic.

Oh God, she thought. Oh, God, oh, God, oh God . . . feeling as though every girlish dream was being fulfilled. Not realizing until that moment that she even harbored girlish dreams. Suddenly in unfamiliar territory, she pushed him away. Sex she understood; feeling good she understood; lusting after a man she understood. But not this Disneyland feeling of wanting a castle and prince for her own. "Thanks," she said lightly, sliding her hand up his chest, taking a step back. "You do nice work."

He smiled. "Wait until you taste my whipped cream." His voice was playful too. He didn't want to acknowledge what he'd felt any more than she. "Sit down and watch me work."

Not that watching him work was necessarily soothing to her sense of unease. He was barely dressed, handsome as sin and willing to please her in any way she wished. Why wasn't that good? Why was she worried about feeling the way she did? With arch pragmatism, she decided to stop beating herself up, and like the classic line from *Gone with the Wind,* she'd worry about this tomorrow.

"I'm glad you came over," she said, taking her own advice and speaking the truth.

"I couldn't stay away."

"So we'll ride the wave."

He knew what she meant; it was as though they were in sync, on the same page, aware of the sorcery, giving themselves up to it. "Try and stop me."

"Could I?" Her gaze held his, but she was smiling as though she already knew the answer.

He grinned. "Not a chance. Now where's your vanilla?"

WHEN THE CHINESE food was delivered, he set the whipped cream in the fridge. "For later," he said in a delicious murmur they both felt strum through their senses. And then he carried the large box of takeout cartons into the living room, set it on the coffee table, said, "I hope you don't mind watching TV while you eat. It's a habit from living alone," and began opening the twenty different items they'd ordered from the menu.

"I love TV," she said, sitting down on the couch beside him.

He glanced up. "What programs?"

She named her favorites; the list was long and he kept nodding and saying, yeah and smiling at her.

"Do you watch baseball?" he asked.

"I help coach a Little League team."

He stopped opening the cartons and looked at her as though she'd suddenly sprouted a halo. "No shit. Me too—

with my brother. Why haven't I ever seen you?"

"It's way south."

"We're north."

She grinned. "There you go."

"Did you play?"

"In high school. I wasn't good enough for college."

He didn't say he'd played a year in the minor leagues after college ball. "I wasn't good enough for the big time either, but I love the game."

"What position did you play?"

"First base." He grinned at her startled look. "Karma, right?"

"This is getting weirder and weirder."

"But good weird." Leaning over, he kissed her. "Welcome to nirvana."

He liked to eat like she did, one thing at a time, no mixing. And they watched the end of a baseball game while they ate, trying to anticipate the pitches and plays, finding themselves in agreement so often, she teased maybe they'd been separated at birth.

"I hope like hell not. Considering my plans for you," he murmured, his gaze definitely smoldering.

She batted her eyelashes at him. "You have plans?"

"Several. I hope you're not too tired."

"My adrenaline is pumping so hard, I could stay up for a week. You turn me on like no one has ever turned me on."

It bothered him for a fraction of a second—her oblique reference to other men, but he tamped down his aberrant jealousy and touched the tip of her nipple pressing through his T-shirt. "I've had a hard-on since I first saw you. This is going to work out just fine."

"When?" she said, tossing her chopsticks on the table, setting down her nearly empty container of shrimp fried rice, leaning back against the couch cushions with a smile.

"Now's good." He jammed his chopsticks into the carton he was holding and set it in the box. Pushing her down on the couch, he lifted her shirt those few inches required and reached for the zipper on his jeans. They came the first time to the roar of the crowd on TV.

"Home run," he whispered, trying to catch his breath.

Her eyes were shut tight. "Out of the park . . ."

TESS CALLED VERY early Sunday morning, but she was whispering in the phone, so obviously Dave was over or she was at his place. "He's fabulous," she whispered, about ten times in a row.

"Great, good, way to go. Call me later," Chloe whispered back.

"Who's there?"

"Tell you later. Bye."

Tess called again Sunday evening, her voice all dreamy and giddy and no longer a whisper. "He's really fabulous and he's going to give me one of his paintings 'cause everything went really, really, wonderfully and he's really, really, well, you know—capable of—well just about anything."

"Can you call me later?" Chloe was still whispering.

"Jesus, who the hell is there?"

"Tell you later. Bye."

BUT OF COURSE, the real world eventually intruded, as it has a habit of doing, even in the fantastic world of round-the-clock sex. Early Monday morning, Rocco said, "I have to go to work."

"I know." He was holding her close, his body warm against hers, a kind of blissful lethargy inundating her senses.

"We have to talk."

God, she hated those words. You might as well say, "Line up for the firing squad." "I don't want to talk. Come over when you can. The rest doesn't matter."

"That's the problem. I can't come over—at least for a while."

She wanted to scream; she wanted to swear; she wanted to hit her fist into a wall if she wasn't so averse to pain. "Why not?" she said instead, in what she hoped was a reasonably calm voice. And she twisted around so she could see his face when he lied to her.

"It's complicated." He went on to explain to her in the abbreviated shorthand way men have of defining a situation without recourse to feelings or emotions, using mostly nouns and simple verbs. And she came to understand that he and his family were going into some business that Amy's father was funding and Amy was part of the package.

"Are you engaged to her?"

He shook his head.

In her mind that wasn't the firm no she would have preferred. And she suddenly thought of something even more terrible. "Jesus, are you married to her?"

"Fuck no!"

The intensity of his response was comforting. Although she told herself in a semireasonable frame of mind that surely she didn't contemplate Rocco falling in love with her in three days and them living happily ever after. She wasn't quite that wacky yet. This was not a Hollywood movie. "Okay," she said, pushing up into a seated position. "Okay."

"What the hell does that mean?"

"What do you think it means? It means okay, you have to go to work and get on with you life. I have to get on with my life. Life is fucking okay all around."

His expression went moody and he sat up too. "It's not as though I have a choice." He thought of the mortgages he and his siblings had taken out; he thought of this dream of theirs that was almost looking possible. And he didn't feel obligated to explain every little detail to a woman he'd met on Friday. He had no intention of jeopardizing his and his siblings future for a piece of ass—no matter how fantastic. He wasn't sixteen and driven by his cock. Although with Chloe that wasn't completely true. But he could restrain himself if he had to.

And he had to. For now.

"Thanks for everything." He tried to smile, but didn't quite manage. "I had a great weekend."

"You're welcome. I did too." She could be mature and adult. She knew sex was sex and nothing more. Even when it had been outrageously fabulous sex. She understood. "Good luck with your"—she wiggled her hand in a gesture of vagueness—"business stuff."

"Thanks." He rose from the bed, picked up his clothes and went into the bathroom to dress. As though she hadn't seen his nude body from virtually every angle this weekend.

But that's what Monday mornings were about.

Good-byes.

NINE

CHLOE CAUGHT TESS BEFORE SHE LEFT FOR work and whined something terrible—enough that Tess said, "Come into the office at eleven. I'll take an early lunch and you can tell me everything."

"Meet me at Aquavit instead. I'm a rumpled mess."

Chloe was seated in a corner at Aquavit waiting when Tess walked in. An espresso half drunk before her and she was slumped in the banquette like her best friend had died.

"So what happened? Tell me everything," Tess said, pointing at Chloe's espresso as the waiter came up with their menus.

"Rocco's gone."

"You told me that on Saturday and he came back."

Chloe shook her head. "He's really gone this time. You saw that blonde he was with at Dave's. Her father is financing some business he and his family are starting and she comes with the deal."

"Comes . . . as in what?"

Chloe made a moue. "That wasn't very clear. But he can't see me because of her—so you figure it out."

"It must be serious." Tess's brows arched. "But not serious enough to keep him out of your bed all weekend."

"There you go. Clear as mud. And don't get me wrong, I have no illusions about a weekend in bed with some guy leading anywhere. But he's fabulous and I'd like to keep the sex if nothing else. Is that too selfish?"

"No more selfish than any guy." Tess screwed up her mouth and then exhaled softly. "It does sound really weird. In my experience if you offer a guy carte blanche in terms of sex, most of them won't categorically refuse."

Chloe scowled. "You'd think."

"He must have some—"

"Fear of the bitch?"

"I was going to say—principles?"

Chloe snorted. "I don't think so. It's something else, but I can't figure it out and I'm frustrated as hell." She lifted her espresso to her mouth and drained it. "But enough of my useless whining. Tell me about Dave. Was he all you'd hoped? Was he charming and beautiful and all that?"

"Well, he's not precisely beautiful, as you know, but yes, he was very, very, very nice," Tess said, her voice softening, her smile appearing like a ray of sunshine in the shadowed room. "And we're going to one of his friend's fabulous studio on Lake Minnetonka on Thursday night for some party. He said he'd buy himself a car if we were going to date. Isn't that cute? Sort of proper and chivalrous. He said he never needed a car before. His father owns a bank up north so there's money I guess. And he sold everything in the gallery Saturday, so he's not poor either. Not that it matters," she added quickly. "I liked him even before—when I thought he was a struggling artist."

"It sounds so nice. I'm happy for you." Chloe was almost envious, but not completely, not with Dave. But she was happy for Tess. Their tastes in men had never been the same.

"Sometime you should think of going out with less-than-A-list-handsome men. They're easier on your emotions." Tess smiled. "But then you like all the flash and excitement and heat more than I do."

"I lived with Sebastian for two years. I don't always need excitement."

"You just liked his apartment with the view of the lake and his sailboat."

"I didn't know it at the time. We had fun."

"He was madly in love with you."

"I guess I didn't know that either—not completely." Although he was always telling her he loved her truly, madly and forever, so she probably had a pretty good idea. "Not that he knew what he was talking about anyway, as you well know." Chloe had broken up with Sebastian as gently as she could, hoping he wouldn't be too badly hurt. He'd married his personal assistant two months later and they were expecting their second child soon. It really made one view male protestations of true love with a certain cynicism. "And Sebastian might be in part—although not entirely," she added, realistically, "why I'm in the mood for less protestations of love and more sex. Can I put the blame on Sebastian?" she asked with a grin.

"No." But Tess was smiling. "And don't be too down about this guy Rocco. I'll bet he'll come crawling back."

Chloe grinned. "Now there's a picture. He's very good on his knees."

Tess hissed, "Shush," and looked around to see that none of her colleagues were in the restaurant. She was much more conservative than Chloe.

By the time Chloe had eaten lunch and listened to Tess's blow by blow of her weekend, she was feeling better. No way she would have wanted to spend a day in bed with Dave or have him buy a car so they could date. But that's what made the world go round. Diversity. And what the hey—her life was busy; she had ten projects in the works. She had so much work to do she should seriously consider giving up sex for a month anyway.

IN AN EFFORT to get back on track, she went to her office after lunch, sorted through her projects in terms of priorities and started on the most pressing one. When she was working, she often felt as though she was in the zone—her brain racing at top speed, her creative juices flowing big time, the screen lighting up before her in a brilliant collage, dancing with ideas, almost talking to her . . . sometimes *actually* talking to her.

During those moments, when everything was converging into a creative whole or she was experiencing a eureka moment or digging herself out of the black hole of a mediocre design, she sometimes didn't even hear the phone ring. And it wasn't unusual for her to work twenty consecutive hours without stopping.

Although on that Monday after her sexually gratifying but rather strenuous weekend, she only worked until midnight. And her creative fervor had been helpful in taking her mind off Rocco.

When she returned upstairs, however, evidence of his presence was everywhere, and her longing returned with a vengeance. The Sunday paper was still spread over the coffee table in the living room where they'd lounged on the couch and half read the paper and kissed and made love and kissed some more. She found his coffee cup on the floor near the bed where he'd dropped it when she'd attacked him once. The hassock on the sun porch remained in the middle of the floor where they'd left it after some of their amorous play, the bowl of whipped cream—empty in the corner. And wet towels were strewn about in the bathroom from a number of tub and shower diversions. Quickly shoving the towels into the hamper, she hauled it into her small laundry room and shut the door.

Pushing the hassock back where it belonged, she carried the bowl into the kitchen, picked up the coffee cup from the bedroom floor, put them both in the dishwasher. The Sunday papers went in the garbage. Everything out of sight, out of mind. Oops. There was his money clip laying on the counter by the back door. He'd paid for their takeouts and forgotten it. Now what? Should she call him? Would he prefer losing his money clip to having her call? Did she even *want* to talk to him right now? Sliding the clip in a drawer, she decided she wasn't up to deciding.

And that's how she dealt with the entire issue of Rocco. She didn't.

Every time he popped into her mind, she did that *ommm* yoga thing and cleared her brain.

So much for confronting one's problems.

THE NEXT MORNING the phone woke Chloe and for a flashing moment she wished and hoped. But even before picking up the receiver, in her heart of hearts she knew better.

"This is a warning call," Tess said, hurriedly. "Rosie's in tears and she's going to call you. I have to go to work, but I told her you'd be available today."

Chloe looked at the clock. Five forty-five. Who the hell had died?

It wasn't precisely a death, but as near to one as Rosie could handle. Or in her case, in the immediacy of her crisis, not handle. She was sobbing so hard when she called a second later that Chloe had to say, like they do in movies or in therapy sessions, "Take a deep breath, Rosie, count to three, and then tell me what happened."

"The bastard," Rosie said in a hiccupy little half-sob.

Must be Markie Mark, Chloe thought. The description fits.

"I went to surprise him with breakfast this morning before he woke up to go to work and found him—"

Loud, heaving sobs resumed and Chloe figured out the end of the sentence. "In bed with another woman," she filled in.

"The fucking bastard!"

That was better. The sobs had been replaced by outrage. "Do you want to come over?" Chloe asked. "I'll go get us some lattes from the coffee shop on Marshall. I'm home today, anyway," she added, when she really should work. But Rosie and Tess had been there for her in every crisis of her life since the third grade. It was the least she could do.

"Do you mind? I can't go to school today with my eyes so red. The little kids would wonder."

Rosie taught kindergarten and adored children. "I don't mind at all. I'm between things right now, anyway," Chloe lied. "By the time you get here, I'll be back with the lattes. A chocolate croissant or an almond-paste one?"

"Both."

"Sounds good to me. I'll see you in fifteen minutes." Chloe leaped out of bed, threw on some sweats, ran the two blocks to Marshall, returned at a more sedate fast walk with the coffees and food. Setting everything out on the small table in her sunporch, Chloe went back downstairs to wait for Rosie outside.

When Rosie pulled up and got out of her car, she burst into tears.

Chloe hugged her tight, helped her upstairs, got her seated on the sunporch, handed her a croissant and coffee, pushed the box of Kleenex closer and said, "Men can be such bastards."

Rosie nodded, tears streaming down her face, her mouth filled with chocolate croissant.

"You'll find someone better, sweetie." And Chloe meant it with all her heart. Markie Mark was the biggest asshole she'd ever met. An up-and-coming lawyer who prided himself on his buff body—hence hers and Tess's derisive nickname—he'd been cheating on Rosie forever—since their first date in college. Mark Olson had brought Rosie, who was already in *luvv*, back to the dorm and then gone to pick up a girl he'd met in the bar. Everyone knew it but Rosie. And his cheating had only escalated as he'd become increasingly successful.

"I have to give back his engagement ring," Rosie said with a sigh, pulling out a Kleenex from the box and wiping her eyes. "I told him I never wanted to see him again."

"Keep the ring. He owes you. I think Miss Manners might okay you keeping it too. We could check if you want, but don't rush into giving it back." Chloe viewed the ring as a partial payment—like five dollars for every time the horse's ass had cheated. Rosie's two-carat diamond was worth maybe twelve–fifteen thousand, which would be just about right, she guessed, at five bucks a shot.

"It was terrible, Chloe," Rosie whispered, her bottom lip beginning to tremble again. "He just looked at me like— what are you doing here? Like I didn't have the right."

"You have every right to be there; you've been engaged for a year. He was just blustering because you caught him in the act. It's not your fault, sweetie." Leaning over, Chloe patted Rosie's shoulder. "No way it's your fault that he's screwing around with another woman."

Rosie sniffed and sighed again. "You're right. I know you're right. He's just been a part of my life for so long. Since sophomore year . . ."

Rosie was a pretty little blonde, one of those curly-haired, petite women who smiled a lot and always said nice things about people and didn't deserve a schmuck like Mark Olson. "Look. We're both single now. I got over Sebastian. You'll get over Mark and we can do a little clubbing now. It'll be fun."

"You didn't even care about Sebastian."

How did everyone know that but she, Chloe wondered. Was it stamped on her forehead—unfeeling, callous female? "I thought I did," she said lamely.

"You just liked his apartment at the lake and his boat."

Why was everyone so damned insightful? "I was always nice to him," Chloe said in way of defense.

"I know. You're nice to everyone. You weren't mean to him, Chloe. You just didn't look at him like he looked at you."

"Maybe someday I'll find someone who knocks me off my feet." Like last Friday, she thought, with a little lurch of her heart. "In the meantime," she quickly added, "you and I can check out the available men in town. What's your preference? Blonde, dark, short, tall, do you like horseback riding and tennis, long walks in the woods or cozy evenings with a glass of wine," she teased, paraphrasing some of the single's ads. "Personally, I like someone who's good in bed, but if you ask, they all say they are."

"Mark wasn't very good in bed," Rosie said, half under her breath.

Holy shit. And it wasn't as though Rosie had scads of experience with which to make comparisons. "All the more reason to look farther afield," Chloe suggested with the utmost diplomacy. Should she ask for particulars, or run screaming into the night?

Rosie ran her finger around the rim of her latte cup. "He never lasted very long."

"That's not good," Chloe said in the tone of voice a therapist would use, bland and nonjudgmental, leaving the door open for further disclosures should the client wish.

"I hardly ever had an orgasm."

After the hundreds she'd had that weekend, Chloe felt a great sadness—for her friend and in turn for herself. Because she wasn't likely to be that lucky again. "I know phrases like 'it's for the best' aren't very comforting when you feel as sad as you do. But, sweetie, you deserve someone so much better." Chloe had always felt protective toward Rosie. She'd always been so naïve and trusting—probably why she got along so well with five-year-olds. Chloe viewed the world with a slightly more jaundiced—or practical— eye, she liked to think. "Tess and you and I will scope out the dating scene and find us some fine young stuff. It'll take your mind off your troubles."

"Tess is all in love. She's not going to want to go out."

"Sure she will. Haven't we gone out with her when we didn't feel like it?"

Rosie smiled. "About a thousand times."

That smile was a good beginning, Chloe thought. Sayonara, lying, cheating Markie Mark. "For instance," Chloe murmured, with an answering smile, "Tess and Dave are going to some party Thursday at some artist's supposedly stupendous studio on Lake Minnetonka. I say we tag along. You know those artist types. They're always ready for something unconventional."

Rosie's eyes flared wide. "I'm not unconventional, Chloe."

"I know, I know. I meant it should be fun. A great house on the lake, arty talk, drinks—what's to complain about? You love museums."

"I just saw the new show at the Institute. It was wonderful."

"See? You're all set. I'm going to call Tess right now. See what we have to wear." On her serious quest for a man for Rosie, Chloe wasn't about to waste any time. She called Tess at work, explained their plan and hung up three minutes later. "It's a done deal. Casual dress, cocktails at five, a buffet at seven, boating in the moonlight if you're so inclined. A yacht, no less. This artist must have a trust fund. I have the address. I'll pick you up at four-thirty."

Rosie sat up a little straighter and offered Chloe another tentative smile. "You always go after what you want. I've always admired that in you."

"Sometimes. Not always," Chloe replied, thinking of the man she desperately wanted, who she couldn't have. Even for sex. "But hey, we're going to have a good time Thursday night. Now what do you want to do today? Should we go shopping, go to a museum, drink away our troubles at Chino's, watch old movies and eat truffles? You decide."

They sort of settled on a combination, ending the day at Chino's happy hour where Tess joined them. It was girls' night out, although they made it an early night since everyone had to work in the morning.

TEN

ON WEDNESDAY MORNING, CHLOE WAS IN her office by seven. Her voicemail was overflowing, several messages from Bill Martell in the mix, which had come after she'd left yesterday. His tone had sounded a little desperate by the last message. Diversified was adding a contest to their Crunchies web site and needed her to come in and talk to them ASAP.

She immediately called him; he was in his office at seven-fifteen.

An hour later, dressed in a black linen skirt suit—not too short—and simple black pumps—not too high—she was pulling into the parking lot at Diversified Foods. Bill and several colleagues explained what they needed and the urgency of their timing and asked how soon they could expect a mock-up.

The money was good. She could shift her other projects. "I'll have something for you by Friday."

They were definitely beaming when she left. Not only

lost in her thoughts with several ideas for the web site jostling in her brain, but digging in her briefcase for her car keys, she accidently bumped into someone as she walked out of Bill's office.

"Sorry." She spoke automatically before she looked up, her smile of apology half-formed on her face where it froze. "I wasn't . . . looking—I mean—" Her voice trailed off. She'd never seen Rocco in a suit; he could have graced the cover of *GQ*. Navy-blue pin stripe, white shirt, a tie in a gorgeous shade of celadon, the soft silk melting into a Windsor knot, and of course, his handsome face—now wearing a shocked and/or wary expression.

"If you think I'm following you or stalking you, I'm not," she said quickly, his silence intimidating.

"I didn't say anything."

"That look. I could tell."

"What look?" Rocco's expression went completely blank.

"I just had a meeting with Bill Martell. He called me yesterday for a rush order. Otherwise I wouldn't be here."

"Bill never mentioned it."

The "or" was left unsaid, she thought. "The meeting went well," she blurted out and immediately wished she'd not spoken.

"Good."

Feeling clumsy and maladroit, particularly before the polished executive who was a complete stranger from the man she'd known this weekend, she half-lifted her hand in a wave. "Well—nice seeing you."

"Sure."

The awkwardness was palpable; he hadn't moved.

"See ya." Clutching her briefcase, she turned away, wishing she could disappear into the floor and not have to walk all the way to the elevator under his gaze. She'd taken two steps when she remembered his money clip. Swinging around, she said, "You forgot your money clip at my place."

"That's all right."

"There's quite a bit of money in it. Would you like me to send it to you?"

He didn't answer for another awkward moment. "No. Just forget it."

Well, that was a brush-off if she'd ever heard one. He was leaving six hundred dollars behind because he didn't want anything more to do with her. "Okay." She could be blasé too, and turning, she strode away.

If she would have looked back, she would have seen him watching her.

But she didn't, because she was saying "fuck you" in a heated undertone all the way to the elevator.

He waited until the elevator doors closed on Chloe before he moved, as though needing a three-inch steel barrier to keep him from giving in to temptation. He should have been more cordial, less stiff. He should have said, "Sure, send my money clip back," like it didn't matter. But the last two days had been so harrowing, he hadn't dared relax his guard or have the slightest contact with her.

Since Monday morning, he'd thought of Chloe nonstop. He'd picked up the phone a hundred times to call her. His mind had been so distracted by memories of their weekend together, by the torment of his yearning, that his secretary had asked him more than once whether he was coming down with something when he didn't respond to her. He'd made some vague response about feeling a little under the weather. What the hell could he say? That he might be in love with a woman he'd met four days ago? That he was as mixed up as an adolescent with a first infatuation? That all he could think about was making love to a woman who viewed sex with the same degree of casualness as he? He hated that thought most because it made him wonder who she was with—now. Or who she might be with tomorrow. He was eaten up with jealousy and there wasn't a damned thing he could do about it.

Anthony and Mary Beth were counting on him. He couldn't jeopardize their or his huge financial commitment for sex with someone he'd met last Friday.

He wasn't that stupid.

He wasn't that desperate.

He had enough self-control to stay away from Chloe.

Because, let's face it, even if it was love—and he wasn't willing to admit something so really fucking bizarre—this wasn't the time to indulge himself.

ELEVEN

 THURSDAY WAS ONE OF THOSE DAYS.

First, she had to get Bill's web-site contest screen more-or-less finished because he wanted it Friday. And if she was going out Thursday night with Rosie, she might not feel like getting up at the crack of dawn to put any finishing touches on it.

Which meant she'd gotten up at the crack of dawn today.

It was now three in the afternoon, and Tess had only called twenty thousand times about the evening ahead. You'd think she was the hostess. But apparently she was concerned about impressing Dave—not much of a problem there, Chloe would have thought, considering the guy never wore anything but jeans. Nevertheless, Chloe had to assure Tess that she and Rosie would not only dress properly, but behave properly. She promised not to hang from any chandeliers or take off her clothes—hardly in her repertoire . . . well, maybe that once when they'd skinny-dipped at a college party, but Tess had been right behind her—or discuss her mother's propensity for collecting salt-and-pepper shakers from every state in the Union. Which reminded her; her mother had also called twenty thousand times today. Something about Aunt Grace and the pool boy at the club which almost made her want to say to her mother, "Good for Aunt Grace." But of course, she wouldn't say that when her mother was so upset.

So it had been a day from hell.

But she'd finished the contest page for the web site, and if she said so herself, it looked damned good.

And as an added bonus, she'd been so busy working and taking phone calls that she hadn't had time to think of Rocco more than, say, a hundred eighty-two times.

Really—practically—hardly at all.

She glanced at the clock.

Now to peruse her wardrobe and select something suitable to pass Tess's stringent standards tonight.

She chose a chartreuse pique halter-top dress, utterly simple in design. Not a ruffle or button or bow anywhere. She picked out a pair of lavender strappy heels and placed a bunch of silk lilac flowers at her waist. No earrings, no jewelry, she debated a bag and decided against it. The evening was casual. What the hell did she need that she couldn't leave in her car?

Rosie was ready at four-thirty when Chloe picked her up.

She was sort of stiff-upper-lipped, but not crying, and dressed in a white linen pantsuit with braid trim that made her look suitably nautical for boating.

"I'm in a good mood," Chloe said. "I finished my web page today. I'm allowing myself to have two drinks tonight. Tess has given me orders."

Rosie smiled wanly. "Thanks for taking me."

"You look like you could use a drink, and I'll bet Tess didn't call you and warn you about overdrinking."

That brought a real smile. "I never overdrink."

"Perhaps, therein lies the problem," Chloe said facetiously. "Although, I'm afraid tonight such behavior is verboten. Orders from Tess Carlson and her newly acquired moral code. Doesn't she know Dave drinks like a fish?"

"Everyone else knows."

So Rosie wasn't a complete babe in the woods after all. Chloe had never quite understood whether she chose to overlook Mark's infidelity or didn't realize he was unfaithful. "It's so hard to find that perfect man, isn't it," she teased.

"We'll see what's on the market tonight," Rosie said, with a new lightness to her voice. "I might have more than one glass of wine after all."

"Tess said this artist's house is huge so he throws really big parties. We should be able to find someone interesting in a crowd that size. And there's always the band. Tess claims he knows every musician in the Cities. You play the piano better than anyone I know. Maybe the piano player will be cute."

Rosie sat up a little straighter. "I met a piano player at Nye's one night who was really good and sooo handsome." She grimaced. "But Mark made us leave early."

"Because you were having fun—that's why. You and I can have fun tonight and do whatever we like."

"I'm not the same do-whatever-you-like type as you, Chloe."

"I'm not saying we have to do the same things. But freedom's nice—you have to admit. No one to tell you what to do. No one to please. No one to say, 'Do you really want to see *that* movie?' when you do."

Rosie smiled. "You're talking about Sebastian, aren't you?"

"No kidding. I love movies, and all he ever wanted to see was special-effects science-fiction shit. If I went to his movies, you'd think he could have gone to mine."

"Mark wouldn't even go to a movie. He couldn't sit still that long."

Which might have accounted for his short attention span with women. He continually needed new conquests. "We should go and see some of the foreign films at the Lagoon."

"Any time. They have real butter on their popcorn too."

"And dark chocolate bars with espresso beans."

"And espresso."

Chloe laughed. "Sounds like a plan. Are you going out on the boat tonight? You look stylishly ready."

"I hate boats. You can never get off."

"So you're not cruise material."

Rosie shuddered. "Torture."

"But we *are* going to check out the merchandise tonight, right?"

Rosie smiled. "Oh, yes. Although, I'm going to stay away from lawyers."

"After your experience with Mark, that might be wise. You need a change of pace—say a—"

"Piano player," Rosie interposed.

Chloe grinned. "You took the words right out of my mouth."

"You know, I *am* in the mood to have fun. It's been so long, Chloe, I'd forgotten how it feels." Rosie sort of wiggled in her seat. "It feels good. By the way, I decided to take your advice and keep the ring. I'm having it put in a new setting."

"Good girl. Courageous, confident"—Chloe smiled—"kick-ass assertive."

"Kick ass, that's me." But Rosie pronounced the slang with two long syllables, like someone using English as a second language might. "Do you know low long it's been since I danced?"

Since you met Mark, who didn't like to dance. "It's been a while, hasn't it," Chloe said instead. "I'll bet we'll have dancing music there tonight."

"Tess said so. I wore good dancing shoes." Rosie lifted her feet slightly, her navy blue flats practical work shoes. "Leather soles."

Rosie was always so efficient; even her classroom cubbies were neat as a pin, and that took some doing with five-year-olds. "Me too. Leather soles," Chloe said as though she'd planned it. Four-inch strappy heels generally didn't come with rubber soles, so she was safe. Inadvertently, she'd fallen into the efficient category tonight. "Do you think they'll play any polkas? I'll dance with you if they do."

Rosie gave her a look of disbelief. "Of course they won't."

"I'll ask the band. Remember the fun we used to have up at the lake when we were in high school? There always were wedding dances at the country halls—and polkas."

"That was a long time ago."

"They still polka at Nye's."

"I forgot about Nye's. We could always dance there." Rosie gave Chloe an assessing glance. "You're definitely in a mood tonight."

"I need a change of scene. Like you."

"Any special reason?" Rosie had that soothing kindergarten-teacher tone that solved issues of sharing toys and missing Mom and wanting to be first in line.

"I met a guy last weekend who's hard to forget. And I want to forget him."

"Anyone I know?"

Chloe laughed. "Not really. I barely know him—discounting the hot sex, of course."

"Was he good?"

"Oh, yeah, definitely good. But already taken."

Rosie's mouth formed into a shocked O. "You mean he's married?"

"I don't think so."

"That doesn't sound good. He's probably as bad as Mark."

No one's as bad as Mark, Chloe wanted to say, but on such short acquaintance, she couldn't be absolutely certain where Rocco stood in terms of badness. "I don't really know much about him. Nor will I. He's gone." She blew out a breath of discontent. "So I'm out looking tonight."

Rosie giggled. "Like we did in high school—at the dances."

Not exactly, Chloe thought, not anywhere near exactly. She nodded and smiled. "Just like that."

TWELVE

 WHEN ROCCO CAME TO PICK UP AMY FOR
dinner on Thursday, Marcy Thiebaud met him at the
door. "Come in and have a drink with us. Amy's still
getting ready. And Jim's celebrating today. He just bought
part interest in the baseball team."

Rocco smiled. "Sounds like something to celebrate."

"I know; isn't it exciting? It's been hush-hush for a
month or so, but it's official today. Come," she said, waving
him to follow her. "Jim's in the library."

"Congratulations," Rocco said as he entered the large
sun-filled room, wishing Amy wasn't their daughter; he
really liked the Thiebauds. "Marcy told me the good news."

Jim was grinning from ear to ear. "We've been dickering
for weeks and the lawyers finally got all the i's dotted and
t's crossed. The announcement will be on the six o'clock
news. A little bubbly to celebrate?" He held up a champagne bottle.

"Of course. The team's hotter than hot. You must be pleased."

"It's a pretty good feeling, no doubt about that." Jim poured champagne for them and handed out the flutes. "Sit. Amy'll be down any minute. I suppose she's trying to decide what to wear." He winked. "You know women and their clothes."

Rocco had every intention of not getting to know Amy that well. "How did you decide to get involved with the team?" he asked, preferring not to discuss Amy.

"I knew most of the owners already. Have for years. I think we first talked about it over a golf game last spring. In fact, *next* spring Marcy and I will be going down to Florida for the training camp. I suppose I'll get in the way and make a general nuisance of myself, but, hey—"

"Jim's like a kid with a new toy," Marcy interposed, smiling fondly at her husband. "It's all he talks about."

"It's a damned nice toy. I don't blame him."

"It's an old man's indulgence," Jim said with a grin. "I don't feel like sailing around the world or climbing Mount Everest or even buying a sports car. My pickup suits me just fine. But enough about my midlife crisis plaything— how are the new product lines shaping up? I talked to Anthony a couple of days ago and he said he hoped to start up the first run of shampoos by the end of the month."

"That's my understanding. With our accelerated schedule in mind, I gave notice at work. I'm going to be out of town a fair amount making sure we have the orders we need."

"You always were such a hard worker, Rocco. Remember, Jim, when the boys decided to sell vegetables that summer they were ten? I never saw such a neat, well-tended garden."

Rocco laughed. "We made about fifty bucks for all our

hard work, but you couldn't fault the flavor. That home-grown stuff is good."

"And then you and Steve decided to repair motorcycles when you were in junior high," Marcy said, reminiscing.

"I still do occasionally for my friends; it's my mental zen."

"Have you hung on to your XLCH sportster? I remember that machine tore up the road," Jim remarked. "What was top end again?"

"One forty, one fifty. Not that I have much time anymore to take it out and open it up, but maybe someday." Rocco's gaze flicked to the doorway and his smile stiffened.

"Did you hear about Daddy's newest amusement?" Amy cooed, strolling into the large cherry-paneled room dressed in a pale blue Chanel dress.

"Yes. Great news," Rocco replied, watching her approach, overwhelmed—as always in her presence—by an urge to flee.

"Rocco's going to have to come with us to the games, won't he, Daddy?" Amy dropped onto the couch beside Rocco, sitting so close her thigh touched his on a leather sofa that could easily seat six.

He would have liked to move, but he couldn't.

And she knew it.

"You're welcome to come to a game anytime, Rocco," Jim offered, leaning across the coffee table to hand his daughter a glass of champagne.

"Thanks, Daddy. You and Mommy are the best," Amy said in a breathy little-girl voice. "We'll have *so* much fun."

Marcy and Jim gazed at their daughter with doting smiles.

Amy was undeniably beautiful, Rocco reflected, taking in the expressions of parental pride opposite him, but that didn't make up for her manifold faults, and that childish tone was one of them. It always sounded so phony, it made him wince—but then, she wasn't his daughter. Maybe the phoniness became charming when you were related.

"Amy tells me you two are going to Zinc's tonight," Marcy noted, shifting her fond gaze to Rocco. "It's such a lovely place."

"Then we're going to Andy's party later." Amy smiled at Rocco like she'd actually told him before—knowing he couldn't take issue in front of her parents. "Andy's having a band and moonlight boat rides. I just adore the lake at night."

"His mother told me he's thinking of settling down," Marcy said with a small conspiratorial smile. "He might have an announcement to make tonight."

"Humph. It's about time," Jim grumbled.

"Young people don't get married as early as they did in our generation, Jim. It just isn't the same."

"Seems to me when you find someone you want to marry, you don't have to wait until you're forty."

"I don't think Andy's quite forty."

"Well, I'm certainly not going to wait that long." Amy tilted a flirtatious glance at Rocco.

"Good. I'm not getting any younger," Jim said, "and Steve seems more interested in dating *Playboy* playmates than settling down."

"L.A. is way too fast for me."

Amy's prim tone set Rocco's teeth on edge. This was the girl who was asking him or Steve for pot or drugs or booze when she was thirteen. "Steve's work schedule is pretty brutal, I hear," Rocco said in defense of his friend. "I don't think he's dating all that much."

"Call me old-fashioned," Jim muttered, "but that Hollywood tinsel town glamor seems fake as hell."

"Steve has been seeing that nice girl from San Francisco

who works with him too, Jim. Remember? Her parents teach at Berkeley."

"Well, that may be, but Steve's already made it clear he's not interested in the business. We sure could use a son-in-law in the family," Jim added with a wink at Rocco. Jim and his son had butted heads over the business for years. That was part of the reason Steve lived on the West Coast. "One of these days someone's going to have to take over the business." Jim's voice was gruff, his gaze on Rocco. "I'm hoping a son-in-law might be willing."

"You're so sweet, Daddy." Amy cast the full power of her baby blues on Rocco. "Isn't Daddy just the sweetest, Rocco?"

At that particular moment Rocco was finding himself hard-pressed not to bolt from the room and run until he reached an ocean, at which point he'd dive in and start swimming.

"Don't embarrass the boy. Hell, you've got that deer-in-the-headlights look, Rocco," Jim said with a chuckle. "Been there myself once. There's plenty of time for talk of weddings. We don't have to do it now. Here, have another drink." Leaning over, Jim handed Rocco the bottle. "Now tell us about the advertising firms you've been looking at. Mary Beth said you like some better than the others." Jim Thiebaud knew when to change the subject. His people skills were a natural gift and largely responsible for his rapid rise to millionaire status.

After talk of weddings and son-in-laws, Rocco needed a moment to find his voice. Fear did that to you. "I'm leaning toward McGillicutty and Perth," he finally managed to say.

"Didn't they do that great ad for Volkswagen—that funny one with the couch?"

"Right." Rocco's mind was practically blank—the wedding march a crescendo, drowning out everything else in his brain.

"Ed McGillicutty's a good guy—his golf handicap's not bad either." Jim nodded, as though satisfied with those two criteria. "When can they deliver if you decide on them?"

"Ah . . . a month . . . well—maybe five weeks." Distracted by the organ music in his head, Rocco hoped whatever he'd just said sounded reasonable.

The moment their conversation had shifted from her and her marriage, Amy's interest had waned. "You two can talk about business some other time," she announced, rising from the couch. "We're going to be late for dinner."

Coming to his feet, Rocco politely offered Amy his hand although in his current skittish mood, it felt like too literal a gesture.

"You two kids have fun," Jim proclaimed, lifting his champagne glass.

"We always do, Daddy, don't we, Rocco?" Amy replied, leaning into him.

Using all his willpower to keep from jerking away, Rocco said, "Thanks for the drink," in lieu of lying. Moving toward the door, he was mentally counting down the hours until his torture was over.

"We'll call you when the next game is in town," Marcy called out as they walked from the library. "There's plenty of room in the owner's box, isn't there, Jim?"

"Sure is, honey. They're a great-looking young couple, aren't they," Jim Thiebaud added in a stage whisper.

Amy smiled a contented little half-smile as they walked down the hall.

A chill ran up Rocco's spine.

He was beginning to understand how a trapped animal would gnaw off his foot to get away.

THIRTEEN

THE NOISE LEVELS AT ANDY'S PARTY WERE
morphing into call-the-police stage, and if the house
hadn't been set on ten acres, the explosive sound
might have been a problem. The bartenders were having
trouble keeping up with the thirsty, raucous crowd. The
band, set up on the ground floor of the four-story lake
home, were playing a combination of way-early U2 and get-
your-ass-on-the-dance-floor rock and roll, the music vibrating through the house like a centrifugal force.

Andy, obviously high, had just announced his engagement, hoisting his fiancée over his head and twirling her
around like John Travolta in *Saturday Night Fever*. Although, with reflexes considerably impaired by illegal sub-
stances, Andy's coordination didn't quite match Travolta's
fine-tuned precision. On the third revolution, he and his
fiancée, Tiffany—if her boobs were real, Chloe would eat
her nonexistent hat—fell onto a section of an enormous

sectional taking up a half acre of the living room. They were currently trying to get untangled, not unlike a scene from the Three Stooges.

"Dave said this is Andy's fourth fiancée," Tess hissed into Chloe's ear.

The two women were out on the balcony viewing the scene through floor-to-ceiling windows.

"Maybe four's his lucky number." The girl looked happy—and young. Andy looked like he'd been around the block a few times, but obviously had money, so maybe it was one of those proverbial matches made in heaven.

"Have you seen Rosie lately?"

Chloe turned to Tess with a wide grin. "You're going to seriously believe in miracles when you hear this. She found another *kindergarten teacher* among the guests. How many kindergarten teachers have you ever *met* in your life other than Miss Engle at Bass Lake Grade School? Exactly. He teaches somewhere out here, an ex–Peace Corps philanthropist type who wants to give back to the world. She's all starry-eyed and smiling."

"So screw Markie Mark."

"Figuratively speaking, of course. You heard about his less-than-stellar performance in bed."

Tess's eyes sparkled like the glitter on her T-shirt. "I'm telling everyone I know."

Chloe's smile was one of satisfaction. "I've beat you to it."

"He deserves every word of bad press."

"You don't have to convince me. He deserves a lot more payback if you ask me. Think how many years Rosie's suffered. Although, speaking of suffering, I'd say those days are over. There's Rosie over there by that lamp made from someone's car bumper. The tall, sandy-haired man gazing at her like he's just found the lost treasure of the Incas is the kindergarten teacher-slash-philanthropist."

"He's good-looking."

"And right out of central casting in those khaki shorts and rumpled shirt and espadrilles. He was in Peru last."

"Rosie looks happy. He must be nice, because she's not the type to hug a man she's just met."

"Or maybe he's just charming as hell. But who cares? She's enjoying herself, and right now with the Markie Mark debacle so recent, she needs entertainment."

"He has that look of enchantment, though—staring into her eyes like that. Wouldn't that be nice after all the shit she put up with from that prick Mark? And a philanthropist? That would be just be the coolest thing to piss off Markie Mark, who talks about how rich he is within three seconds of meeting him."

"I'd pay money to see Markie Mark's face when he hears. This guy with Rosie has some foundation for underprivileged children. I forget the name. So it sounds pretty real."

"Not that money's everything."

"Actually, it's not much of anything unless there's something to go with it."

"How're you doing?" Tess's voice changed, her gaze turned kindly and she patted Chloe's shoulder. She knew Rocco had been more than a weekend guest.

"Fine." Chloe smiled her well-honed social smile. "Absolutely fine. The food's good, the drinks are perfect and the band is beginning to sound pretty hot. I think I'll go downstairs and listen."

Tess gave Chloe a hug. "You're sure you're okay?"

"I'm sure. Go find Dave. I don't need a baby-sitter. My heart isn't broken. Really."

"I don't want to leave you alone if—"

"Go," Chloe said, giving Tess a shove that jiggled her short black curls. "I don't need company."

*   *   *

JUST AS CHLOE stepped into the small elevator connecting the floors of the lake house, Rocco and Amy arrived at the line of valets in the car court.

As Rocco exited the car and handed his keys over, he glanced up at the blaze of lighted windows, heard the music drifting out over the lake and checked his watch.

CHLOE FOUND A secluded spot on the terrace, away from the crowd, but near enough to enjoy the music. Sitting on the fieldstone wall that marked the eastern boundary of the terrace, she sipped her drink. The night was peaceful, the stars ablaze in the sky, the band playing some plaintive/electro version of a song about love and loss. How appropriate, she thought dismally—as appropriate as the perfect summer night just made for love.

Having begun the second drink of her two-drink quota, the irrepressible longings and lovesick musings that a completely sober mind could curtail were beginning to infiltrate her mind. Potent, sexy, tall, dark and handsome images of Rocco floated in and out of her consciousness, and no matter how many times she tried to tell herself he was just another guy, she knew she was lying. She knew it as well as she knew the fabulous, very talented length of his cock. Damn.

Looking up, in a weird juxtaposition of eyes-wide-open and ingenue hope, she wished on a star like she had as a child—asking for something she couldn't have, because she wanted Rocco more than she'd ever wanted anyone before.

But a pulse beat later, reality intruded as it did from time to time, even into the most intense longing, and she questioned whether it was only his leaving that made her

want him more. Had he been available, would she have felt
as deprived? If he was in hot pursuit, would she even be
interested? She didn't, as a rule, like men who panted after
her. So was it the challenge she found alluring?

All caveats aside, though, she understood with crystal
clarity that the sex had been so fine she wasn't likely to find
that perfection again. Or at least, not very likely. And on
that inauspicious, damnably depressing note, she told herself to get a grip—silently screamed at herself to get a grip;
her northern European background constrained her from
actually screaming in public.

Because, let's face it, she thought with her new-found
sense of grim reality, men like Rocco had to beat off women
with a stick, and delusional fantasies aside, he wasn't likely
to change his interest in casual sex for her. Had he once
said anything about going out on a actual date? Okaaay.
We know the answer to that one. As for all his sweet talk,
hell, that was de rigueur in the bedroom. Most guys had
figured that out even before their first lay.

So if she had an ounce of sense—becoming more difficult
to dredge up with the increasingly maudlin direction of her
thoughts—she'd dispense with the really senseless and utterly useless yearning for something she couldn't have and
concentrate on the damned fine music. The amps were
cranking out a wild, battery-acid rock and roll she could
feel coursing through her body even at thirty yards.

And on that optimistic, upbeat note, she reminded herself that Rocco Vinelli wasn't the only man in the world
with a golden cock. There were men aplenty out there.
Didn't she always manage to find someone who interested
her? Yes, yes, *yes*, she confirmed with the pointed surety of
a highly independent woman. And lifting her glass to her
mouth, she took another sip of her Mojito just as a shadow
flitted into her peripheral vision.

Footsteps crunched on the sand-strewn flags, but she kept her gaze on the calm surface of the lake, definitely not in the mood for small talk tonight, preferring her own astute observations on the state of the world. Perhaps if she sat very still, whoever it was would go away. Perhaps if she sat real still the music would lift her up and carry her away to another shining galaxy.

"I didn't expect to see you here."

She shut her eyes. That voice. She must be hallucinating. Obviously, her drink and a half was too potent, which also accounted for her drivel about shining galaxies.

"Are you an artist groupie?"

So much for hallucinating. "Are you?" she snapped.

"We keep bumping into each other," he said mildly, ignoring her response. "You wouldn't be following me, would you?"

"Right. I hired a detective to check out your schedule because I can't live without your dick." She looked back at the lake, hoping he'd leave.

He wanted to soothe the set line of her jaw, brush away her scowl, apologize for his sarcasm—take her home and fuck her for a month. But useless dreams aside at this juncture in his life, he'd settle for what was possible. "Can we start over?" he said, softly. "I've really missed you." If he'd not spent an evening with Amy, he might have said it with less feeling. Or maybe he would have said it exactly the same way regardless of the circumstances because he was thinking, screw reality—pick her up and take her away to anywhere—a desert island, a hotel room on the Ile de la Cité, the backseat of his car.

Chloe turned her head, incapable of resisting those heartfelt words, and saw him half-smiling like he did so you wanted to kiss him forever. "Are you here alone?" Obviously some bitch inside her head wasn't in the mood for Hallmark sentimentality, heartfelt or not.

He shook his head.

Great. "With her?" Definitely a bitchy tone.

He pretended not to care about her tone for a three count and then, half-resentful because she shouldn't be at a party like this, she should be home knitting or baking pies or doing something wholesome, in a terse and taut manner, he said, "Yes. Is cocaine-head Andy a friend of yours?"

"No. He's a friend of Dave's—the drunken artist on Saturday. I'm hiding out."

He smiled then, as though she'd been vetted by his jealousy-and-purity brigade—brand new members of his psyche. "Saturday was nice."

She didn't mean to smile back, no more than she meant to be so gauche as to speak the truth in a situation like this. "Sunday was nice too. I shouldn't say that when you're pissing me off. Your ego is more than adequate already."

"You should talk." She looked gorgeous in the moonlight—barely dressed in that halter top and short skirt—pale skin everywhere.

This problem they had wasn't about her, she reminded herself. It was about his commitments elsewhere. "Are you still on your leash tonight?"

The smile was wiped from his face.

"Will she find you talking to me and give you ten demerits?"

"That's not funny."

"I didn't intend it to be funny."

"Fucking bitch." Half-resentful, half-seductive, schizoid—like his current mood.

"You're confusing me with someone else," she said, super-sweet.

"I don't think so. I know who you are," he murmured, advancing on her, his faulty, skewed resentment finding focus, his libido one step ahead. "You're the lady who likes to fuck anytime, anywhere." Sliding his finger down her cleavage, he slipped his hand under her halter top and cupped her breast.

She should move. She should object. She should cut his hand off at the wrist. She should do anything but press into his palm and ache with longing.

"I'll bet you're getting wet right now." Brushing her skirt upward, he eased his other hand between her thighs and, smooth as silk, his fingers glided inside her. "I was right," he whispered. "Nice and wet . . ."

Maybe it was his tone, the soft gloating, the arrogance and assurance that restored her sanity. "Go back where you belong," she hissed, trying to pull away. "Go fuck your girlfriend."

But his hand tightened on her breast and her squirming only allowed him to penetrate deeper, making her voice turn breathy at the last.

"I don't want to fuck her." He'd heard her hushed neediness. "I want to fuck you." And he forced his fingers in all the way, so his palm was jammed against her clitoris, so she moaned and melted inside and drenched his fingers.

Her flame-hot reaction was wildly familiar and so damned arousing, he was instantly rock hard. Quickened by lust, spurred by umbrage, lush memory a critical goad, he scanned the immediate area, looking for privacy, someplace he could take her and ram himself inside her and do what he'd been wanting to do ever since he'd left her Monday morning.

Neither was thinking clearly—chafing and provoked, their emotions fueled by absence, frustration and a hardcore, heart-pounding urgency that was careless of all but ravenous desire.

She was panting, so close to orgasm he was wondering if he'd have time to get his cock in her before she came. He was reaching for his zipper when he heard Amy's voice in the half-second interval between the band's driving beat. She was asking for him inside.

It was one of those galvanic moments of decision.

Or perhaps, in his current fanatical frenzy, decision wasn't the right word.

Scooping Chloe from the wall, indifferent to consequences, ruthlessly focused, he carried her, kicking and punching, into the darkness—barely into the darkness—away from Amy.

"Damn you," Chloe whispered, struggling in his grip. "Put me down. Go back to her!"

He didn't respond; it didn't matter. This was far enough, some rash, improbable sensibility observed, and he lay down with her on the cool grass no more than a dozen yards from the house, indifferent to detection, indifferent to her wishes and her pummeling fists. Unzipping his trousers, he pushed her skirt aside and stripped away her thong, bristling at the thought that some other man might have seen that small scrap of silk tonight.

Moving between her legs, impelled by resentment and need, he held her hips in a crushing grip, plunged into her without preliminaries, and launched into a selfish, pounding, hard-driving rhythm.

She swore, kicked, punched.

His grip only tightened.

She finally sank her teeth into his shoulder, and shocked by the pain, he stopped mid-stroke and looked at her, startled.

"Get the hell off! Off, off, off!" she grunted, shoving against his immoveable weight.

He shook his head as though he'd surfaced from thirty feet of water and, looking around, took in the shore, the house, the people milling on the balconies. "Jesus," he whispered, sitting up. "Sorry." He zipped up his pants, but he held onto her wrist; he wasn't so sorry that he was going to let her go.

Scrambling up into a seated position, trying not to feel the warmth of his thigh against hers, she pushed her skirt down. "Let go," she muttered, glancing around to see if anyone had taken notice.

His fingers tightened.

"Damn you." She tried to pull away. "Let. Me. Go."

He dipped his head faintly in apology and half-shrugged. "Not just yet," he murmured, holding her securely. "I need to talk to you—see you—" He stopped short of saying what else he wanted to do to her. "You're making me crazy." His eyes were shadowed, moody. "I'm going fucking nuts thinking about you."

"I know." She knew what crazy was too. It was not making him leave, right now, this instant. "That's no excuse for what you did, though," she said with a scowl.

"I know. I'm sorry—really." And he was. Although it was tempting as hell to point out to her that she'd been as ravenous as he a couple of minutes before. "I've thought of you, of this"—he shut his eyes briefly—"a lot. Could we go somewhere—anywhere . . . maybe—to—"

"Fuck?" Sarcasm, condemnation, a little huffy sniff at the end.

But he'd seen what he'd seen, felt what he'd felt, knew the level of her neediness. Knew his. "We don't have to do anything you don't want to do."

"For the record," she said, curtly, "I don't want to do anything with you."

He took a chance and spoke the truth, which wasn't always wise when a woman was looking at you flinty-eyed like that. "Yeah you do."

"Then I'll overcome my inclinations," she said coolly.

"What if I beg?"

Her sudden smile matched his. "This I gotta see." She could hear the Helen Reddy song, "I Am Woman," begin to tune up in her brain. The numbers on her side of the scoreboard were definitely clicking upward in a major way.

He grimaced. "The fucking pathetic thing is that I'm almost willing to do it."

"Almost? You're going to have to do better than that." She cupped her ear and raised her brows, waiting.

In hindsight, that might have been the moment of bitchy overkill.

He lightly touched her nipple through the fabric of her dress. "I will if you will."

"No way. Let go of me."

"In a minute." He leaned in and kissed her before she could jerk away. Or maybe the fact that he gently tugged on her nipple at the same time, causing a spiking pleasure to rush downward between her legs, was in the way of a shameless distraction. As she softly moaned, he slid his tongue into her half-opened mouth and demonstrated in leisurely pantomime what he wished to do to her somewhere else.

And effectively shifted the balance of power.

It became much harder after that to deal with issues of reproach and reproof. With each plunging thrust of his tongue, with every fine-fingered caress of her nipples, Chloe found herself less able to compartmentalize good and bad, right and wrong, the substantive virtue in restraint. Flame-hot longing blurred those edges, scruple gave way to ravenous desire, and when his hand slipped between her legs, she was more or less lost.

"What do you think?" he whispered after a small heated interval, his mouth lifting just enough to say the words against her lips, his fingers staying right where they were—deep inside her. "Feeling better?"

"I'd hate you if I could." Breathy words, tainted with bliss.

"I'd walk away if I could."

She tried desperately to rein in her scandalous eagerness, to ignore the gentle stroking massage, the exquisite sensations rippling outward from where he was touching her. And failed. "What are we going to do?" she breathed.

"You're going to tell me you missed me as much as I missed you, and then we're going to see what we can do about—"

Amy's shrill cry sliced through the pulsing beat of the music, shattered the moonlit night, jarred like a hammer blow.

"Her?" A cold as the grave utterance.

You'd think someone had said "If you don't pull out your fingers in one second you're a dead man"—that's how fast he withdrew them.

"Feeling guilty?" she sneered.

"No. I don't want you embarrassed."

"Go. Your girlfriend's waiting." She was surprised she could speak in such a temperate tone when she'd been seconds from orgasm and the throbbing between her legs was wildly undiminished, when she couldn't decide if she was about to explode from passion or anger.

He looked around, gauged the degree of their concealment.

It was questionable but he didn't move. He didn't have a gun to his head yet, although in his current state of arousal, he wasn't sure it would have mattered.

"Rocco, I can't walk on this wet grass with my heels!" Amy cried. "Rocco! Where are you?"

Chloe stared at the woman silhouetted against the house lights. "Is she for real about her shoes?"

He shrugged.

"You ruined my dress. I've grass stains everywhere. I should put in a claim."

He was watching the figure on the terrace. "I'll buy you a new one."

"You'd better go."

"She'll manage. These are her friends, not mine."

"You're going to have to pay big time for escaping from your keeper."

He shot her a glance. "Don't fuck with me."

"A shame, when that was my plan."

He looked at her again, this time with riveting attention. "If you're serious, I'll come over later."

She shook her head, nervy and pissed and damned near out of her mind with longing. "Now or never."

Maybe it was the hand of God. Maybe it was something more mundane like Andy calling her in for another drink, but Amy suddenly turned around and walked back into the house.

Rocco's smile lit up the world. "Now looks good."

It was an outrageously generous offer considering Amy might be looking for him again soon, or maybe just outrageous—like Chloe's demand.

She smiled back. "I'll say thank you in advance in case you have to leave in a hurry."

"Cute. Keep in mind who can make you come in the

next two minutes," he warned with a teasing light in his eyes.

"The perfectly focused sensual receptors in my brain, you mean?"

"Are you saying you don't need me?"

She hesitated a moment. "What if I said yes?"

He laughed, and coming to his feet, held out his hand. "I'd say bring me along for the ride."

"Well, maybe just this once."

"Since when did you only want to come once?" Scooping her up into his arms, he murmured, "We wouldn't want you to ruin your shoes," and began walking across the wet grass toward the boathouse.

How sweet of him to care. How darling and dear and charming, she thought with the delirium of excessive in-fatuation. But in the next second, she reminded herself this wasn't about sweetness or charm. With a man like Rocco, sex was sex was sex. And point advantage in this tennis match went to the person who remembered that casual mantra. "What about my dress?" she asked drolly.

He smiled down at her. "Buy a new one. Send me the bill."

"Don't you want to come shopping with me and help pick it out?"

"No."

"Then maybe I don't want to make love to you."

"I'll come shopping."

"You do know how to please," she purred.

"You're not so bad yourself," he whispered back, reach-ing the boathouse, shoving the door open with his shoulder.

They stood in the shadowed interior, the smell of gaso-line and motor oil pungent, slivers of moonlight visible through the louvered gables, the quiet enveloping them in a soft cocoon of isolation.

"So," he said in a deep murmur.

"If you're having second thoughts . . ."

"God, no. I'm looking for someplace to set you down"—
he smiled—"or for me to sit." He dipped his head. "Like
that workbench over there."

"You *are* going to owe me a dress," she teased. Not that
she really cared. This rendezvous was definitely about mutual satisfaction.

"The way I'm feeling right now," he said, moving toward
the bench, "you can buy out the fucking store."

"How nice."

He stopped and looked at her, the faintest frown furrow-
ing his brow. "I'm serious—about this—us . . . everything."

The implication was she wasn't. "I'd like to be too."

He inhaled and nodded. "Later, then."

She smiled. "My dance card will be ready for you to write
in your name whenever you want."

He grinned. "So we're just testing out the dance floor
tonight?"

"Something like that." How do you say you can have
anything you want and still be whole? She couldn't and she
didn't and she wouldn't. "You talk too much," she whispered. "Kiss me."

He kissed her then, and then again, as he gently lowered
her onto the workbench, as he wrapped her legs around his
waist, and slowly entered her. His kisses were sweet and
soft; his erection, in blissful contrast, was hard and not in
the least bit soft. And she came the first time like he knew
she would, when he buried himself so deep she gasped and
panted and shut her eyes tight. "You're crammed full," he
whispered, his hands cupping her bottom, cushioning her,
holding her impaled. "Tell me you like it."

Her orgasmic scream ricocheted around the cavernous

space in answer, brought a smile to his face, added libidinous dimension to his erection and he waited for her cries to die away before withdrawing slightly. "Now what?" He already knew the answer, but he wanted the decision to be hers.

"Stay," she whispered, exerting pressure with her legs, drawing him back. "God, I missed you . . . this . . . you," she breathed as he slowly slid back in, as he filled her. "Don't ever—ever . . . ever go . . ."

He felt himself swell larger, gratified, his own indefensible cravings vindicated, his fanatical need balanced, compensated. His no-holds-barred desire returned in equal measure.

He stayed hard no matter how many times he came; she did that to him. Made him insatiable.

And she'd whisper, "Please, more, more, more," coming over and over again in wave after wave of unbridled passion.

She said once, "We should stop. You should go. We shouldn't—"

"Hush," he whispered, kissing away her protest. He'd been wanting her, this, the feel of her engulfing him, the warmth of her body touching his, since he'd left her.

She'd tried, she thought, as salve to her almost nonexistent conscience tonight. But how could she resist when he made her feel on fire and half in love and all aglow. When she was as near to addicted as she'd ever been? How was she expected to turn away from this veritable candy store of lush sensation?

But finally—and strangely, she thought—beginning to feel light-headed, the sustained intensity of sexual passion was affecting her.

Or he was affecting her.

Or maybe it was the cloying gas fumes.

As another orgasm began to peak, as she panted and cried

out in ecstasy, as he raced to meet her, the heat of her body melting around him—enchantment and lust and, more curiously, love, a tumult in his brain—she suddenly went limp in his arms.

Terrified, his pulse rate spiking in fear, he quickly checked to see that she was breathing. Yes, yes, good. Stripping off his shirt, he swept it through the water in the empty boat stall and returned to gently wipe her face.

Moaning, she twisted away from the coolness, and relief washed over him.

But he should have had more sense, he thought, even as his panic lessened. He should have known better.

As she slowly came awake, he slid his arm under her shoulders and lifted her slightly. "How do you feel?" he whispered.

"You're way too good . . ."

"I'm so sorry. I should have stopped."

"Let me be the judge of that," she whispered, half-smiling.

"I don't think so. I'll be more careful next time."

"When you fill my dance card you mean."

It was always there—the ten-ton albatross hanging around his neck. "Yeah . . . then."

She touched his cheek. "Look—whenever next time is will be fine—I'm fine—don't look so worried. And you know what?" she said, pushing herself up into a seated position with his help. "I'm going to remember Andy's engagement party with great fondness."

He frowned faintly, not in the mood for flirtatious repartee, wanting her to be as deeply affected as he, as messed up and needy. "It's going to take a month or so to sort out my situation," he said gravely. "But, I'll find a way."

"I understand. In the meantime, come and see me when you can."

He shook his head. "I can't." He grimaced. "Everything's fucked up."

"Then maybe you shouldn't be with her," she said, more snappish than she intended.

"It's not her." He sighed. "It's my family."

"Whatever." That shrewishness again. Straightening her dress, she remembered her discarded thong with a twinge of embarrassment, knew it was too late to do anything about it and began lowering herself to the ground.

Quickly lifting her, he set her on her feet, smoothed her skirt, brushed her hair away from her face like he was sending her off to her first day of school. "I'll fix things. Promise."

"Sure you will." She adjusted the top of her dress so nothing showed that shouldn't show.

He hated that brittle, sardonic tone. "It's just business—okay? It's complicated. Give me some time."

"Take all the time you want," she murmured, trying to fluff up the scrunched silk flowers at her waist, walking toward the door without waiting for him.

He felt like punching something. But she had the right to sound that way; she had every right to walk away too. Beating down his temper, he slipped on his wet shirt and followed her. "It shouldn't be more than a month."

Pulling the door open, she glanced back. "Why don't you give me a call when you own your life again." And she stepped out into the night.

Buttoning his shirt, he caught up to her as she started down the path leading to the dock. "Are you going to go out?" He had no right, but he had to know.

"Are you?"

"Not really." He shoved his shirt into his trousers.

"What does that mean?"

He took a deep breath. "I'm not having sex with her."

"Don't lie. Jesus, Rocco." Chloe started walking faster, not sure she could deal with someone so shamelessly dishonest.

"It's the truth."

She swung around. "Fine, that's great. Thanks for the orgasms. They were terrific as usual. Better than terrific. Let me know if there's anything more I can do for you," she said, each word dripping with sarcasm.

"There you are! Rocco! Rocco!" Amy waved frantically from the dock. "I've been looking all over for you!"

"I believe you're being paged," Chloe purred. "That tone sounds like you're going to have to soothe some ruffled feathers. You're lucky I'm easygoing about sharing your dick."

Amy was standing on the edge of the dock where it met the path to the house, a scowl marring the porcelain perfection of her face as they approached. "What the hell are you doing with *her*?" she screamed, looking daggers at Chloe.

"Since this isn't my idea of fun," Chloe said in an undertone, "I'll say good night."

"He's engaged to me, you bitch," Amy spat, grabbing Chloe's arm as she passed. "You keep your hands off of him!"

Shaking her away, Chloe kept walking.

"Tell me what you were doing out there with that slut!" Amy shrieked.

A little shiver went up Chloe's spine at the grating sound.

"Don't scream at me," Rocco growled.

"I'm going to tell Daddy!"

"You do that." It had been a long, difficult evening; his balls were in a vise, had been for a long time and he didn't know if he was capable of enduring the pain much longer.

He wasn't the right candidate for martyrdom. "I'm leaving now if you want a ride." And at the moment, he didn't give a damn if she came or not, if she told her father or not, although he supposed in the cold light of day, he'd be thinking a little more clearly. Or perhaps even before then, he thought, disgruntledly. "Come on, Amy, I'll give you a ride home," he said in a kinder tone and braced himself for the inevitable tirade all the way back into town.

But he knew this ball-breaking situation had to be dealt with.

He'd talk to Mary Beth and Anthony tomorrow.

FOURTEEN

 CHLOE WOKE IN A BLUE FUNK. TESS HAD found her current true love—not that Dave would necessarily last any longer than Tess's previous twenty true loves, but she was at the moment real busy having her heart beat in double time. And Rosie had gotten a ride home from Ian Price, her wish-on-a-star come true. This morning, Chloe hadn't received a crying phone call, so she was guessing Rosie had had a pleasant ride home.

She, however, who never even worried about men because she'd always subscribed to the philosophy that there were lots of fish in the sea, found her love life hostage to some bitchy little blonde with a high-pitched scream that could peel paint from the walls.

Whatever little Miss Amy had over Rocco must be nuclear serious.

And she was supposed to wait patiently while he: one, continued to lie to her about everything; two, struggled to break free of his ball and chain; three, only lied to her about minor issues; four, pretended he'd never met her and forgot her phone number and address.

In the mood she was in at the moment, all of the above seemed most likely. And as if her life wasn't sufficiently in the doldrums, her mother called, still dogging her about Aunt Grace.

"You have to come to dinner tonight and help me talk some sense into Grace," her mother insisted. "This new affair of hers is embarrassing the entire family."

"Will Aunt Grace come to dinner if she knows you're going to harangue her?"

"I'm not going to tell her that, for heaven's sake. I'm going to tell her her brother misses her."

"Jeez, Mom, you'll have to do better than that. Dad barely talks to her. He thinks she's flaky. He calls her a hippie."

"Well, that's exactly what she was."

"Is, Mom. She still wears paisley skirts and Earth shoes."

"She has a very good job, a very responsible job."

"Just because she manages the arts council doesn't mean she thinks like an accountant."

Her mother sighed. "I'm afraid you're right. And that's exactly why I need your help tonight. If you have plans, bring your nice man friend for dinner. Another place at the table won't be a problem."

If she wanted to scare away a nice man friend, that's precisely what she'd do. Her mother really did collect salt and pepper shakers, and while she was pretty normal in other ways, she had a propensity for expecting others to share her views. Everyone did not subscribe to the wetlands projects, nor agree with her concern for migrating water-fowl. And when she handed out her postcards with the local congresspeople's addresses, admonishing her friends to take responsibility and actively participate in their government, Chloe always found the recipients' expressions amusing.

While her mother was always heartily supporting one cause or another, her father preferred tying flies in his study when he was home, or mowing the grass—his summertime pride and joy. He was a research scientist, so his penchant for solitude and order was understandable.

They were a perfect example of opposites attracting.

How Aunt Grace had ever emerged from the Chisholm family of scientists and engineers was one of those mutant enigmas. She'd studied at the Rhode Island School of Design and the Beaux-Arts in Paris, wandered through Southeast Asia before it was fashionable, lived with no visible means of support in Japan for five years, although Grace spoke of a certain Japanese businessman with great fondness. When she returned to the States, she enrolled at Stanford, and spent another five years in graduate school; Chloe suspected the same Japanese businessman had funded that. When Grace had received her PhD in philosophy, she'd heard of the arts council job in Minneapolis and apparently knew someone who knew someone who'd hired her.

She'd been the bane of Chloe's mother existence ever since.

"You have to come. I won't take no for an answer," her mother said, in that tone that she knew she couldn't ignore.

"Okay. But I'm not staying long. I've got plans."

"Dinner's at six. You know your father. Grace will probably be late. I'm having ribs and potato salad and lemon meringue pie—oh—and homemade Lowell Inn rolls."

Her mother was bribing her. All her favorite foods. It must be serious. "Okay. I'll be there at six."

Chloe spent the day in her office, moving from one project to another. She was finding it difficult to focus on any one thing for long, her mind obsessed with you-know-who.

He didn't call, of course. She hadn't actually expected he would after his cryptic disclosure about his commitments. Although, she found herself more and more intrigued by the odd relationship between Rocco and the blonde. Amy, the heiress, didn't seem his type, although in all fairness, he probably didn't have a type. Men who looked like Rocco probably never heard a woman say no.

Not a comforting thought when she was equivocating about her lots-of-fish-in-the-sea that had always been her old standby.

It was also not comforting when Tess called several times, gushing about Dave, nor when Rosie stopped by after work and practically drew pictures of the hot and heavy ending to her evening.

But Chloe said all the appropriate things, never once complaining about her fucked love life. When Rosie finally left and Tess stopped calling because she had to get dressed for a date with Dave, Chloe was able to silently grumble and grouse to her heart's content. As she dressed for dinner with her parents, she pictured Rocco getting ready to squire his fiancée somewhere trendy.

Ugh. Life was so unfair.

She was spending her Friday night with her parents. It was pathetic.

FIFTEEN

ROCCO WASN'T WITH AMY. HE WAS MEET-
ing with his brother and sister in their communal
office at the factory.

"What's so important that it can't wait until I see you
tomorrow morning?" Anthony asked, coming in and sitting
on the edge of his desk. "Make it fast. I have to be home
for dinner."

Mary Beth was more perceptive. "Whatever it is, we have
time, Rocco. Sylvie won't mind if you're a few minutes late
for dinner," she said, giving Anthony her hex-sign scowl.

"Okay, okay. I'm not in a rush," Anthony grumbled.
"What's up?"

"I'm thinking about saying something to Jim about
Amy. She told someone last night we were engaged. And
worse," Rocco added, "when I picked up Amy last night
for dinner and had a drink with Jim and Marcy, Jim spoke
of me as his son-in-law . . . you know—as in taking over

the business someday." He sighed. "He meant Thiebaud Homes."

"Oh, dear," Mary Beth murmured.

"And you're against becoming a millionaire?" his brother inquired, his voice bereft of mockery.

"Anthony, for God's sake. You know how Rocco feels about Amy."

"Jim's offering you a pretty good life," Anthony noted, ignoring his sister.

Rocco's gaze narrowed. "I don't want it. I'm not for sale."

"Am I supposed to say I don't care if you piss off Jim?" Anthony countered. "That I don't care if we lose our financing and my house in the bargain? Is that what you want?"

"You can at least be sympathetic to his plight," Mary Beth admonished.

"Everything doesn't always work out perfectly," Anthony said, bluntly. "We've been struggling to develop this business for almost five years. I'm not sure who you want me to sympathize with. Sylvie and the kids, who might lose their house? Or Rocco, who doesn't think he wants to marry Amy because she's not his type. I didn't know you had a type, Rocco. I thought you screwed anyone and everyone. That's been your pattern. Since when do you have scruples about the type of woman in your bed?"

Rocco wasn't angry with his brother. Everything Anthony was saying wasn't far off the mark. And Anthony had a lot more to lose than either he or Mary Beth. They were both single. They didn't have a wife and kids to worry about.

"Sylvie's expecting again," Anthony said brusquely. "I hadn't mentioned it before because it's early yet and I didn't think it mattered. But if Rocco's going to rock the boat, it's beginning to matter."

"Never mind. It was a bad idea," Rocco said. "Go home. I'll see you tomorrow morning for our meeting with Jim. It's not the end of the world. I'll survive."

Anthony came to his feet, frowning. "We're starting up the first line next week, Rocco. It's just so fucking late . . ."

"I know. Forget I said anything. Tell Sylvie congratulations. I'll bet she's hoping for a girl this time."

Anthony smiled. "She painted the spare bedroom pink."

"That's a clue," Rocco said, grinning. "Now, get going and you won't be late for supper."

"I wish—"

"Don't worry about it. I'll deal with it."

But when Anthony left, Mary Beth said, "Why don't we try and get financing somewhere else?"

"We need too much. And it's not as though we haven't tried."

"I'll send our financial statements around again. It won't hurt. We're much closer to opening than we were on the last go-around with the banks."

"Thanks," Rocco said. "But the chances aren't very good and you know it."

"I'm going to restart the process anyway. Don't scowl at me. I'm the accountant. Do I tell you how to market?"

"Okay, okay." Rocco smiled. "Thanks for trying."

"Did Amy actually say you were engaged?"

Rocco grimaced. "Oh, yeah."

"Where? To whom?"

"At a party last night, to this woman I've been seeing."

"The one in the elevator."

Rocco smiled. "That one."

"I don't suppose she was pleased to hear it?"

"I doubt it. She didn't stick around."

"What did you say to Amy?"

"I took her home and listened to her bitch the entire way."

"Do you really think Jim is serious about this engagement and marriage?"

"It sure as hell sounded like it to me. I have no idea what Amy's saying to them. She could be telling them anything. The little twit always was a first-class liar, starting in grade school. Her folks have always thought she's pure as the driven snow—no drugs, hardly any booze, I'm not sure what they think about her sex life, but I doubt they understand the extent of it."

Mary Beth wrinkled her nose. "I've never liked her, but then she was so much younger than I, I didn't have much contact with her until . . . well—"

"I made the mistake of going out with her."

"Yeah, that. She started calling me up, asking me about you. It was creepy. Like a stalker."

"She likes to have her way. She's been used to it. Both Marcy and Jim are buffaloed by this Miss-Goody-Two-Shoes persona she affects with them. Look, it doesn't matter what I say or how I feel. She has her agenda and I've got to find a way out."

"Because of this woman? Does she have a name you care to divulge?"

"I don't know if it's because of her. All I know is she's on my mind twenty-four seven. Yeah, no shit, you can look at me like that. It's a first." He smiled. "Her name's Chloe and she excites the hell out of me. Whatever that means."

"You're not calling this love."

"Don't ask me. What do you call your relationship with Doug?" His sister had been seeing a local senator who couldn't leave his wife without jeopardizing his political career.

"If he ever leaves his wife, I might call it love," Mary

Beth said, her brows raised in skeptical arches.

"What if he doesn't?"

She shrugged. "If he doesn't, I'll look around. Did I tell you I'm thinking about having a child?"

"Nooo. I would have remembered that. With him?"

She shook her head. "I was thinking about adopting or using a sperm bank. I still haven't decided. I'm going to wait until we have everything up and running nicely here. And I don't mean to put any added pressure on you. I can always go back to my job at Finnley and Katz. I've an open-ended offer. So if this venture flies or not isn't as important to me . . . as, say, to Anthony."

"I know. You and I are slightly more flexible—although if you're talking about a child . . ."

"I can support myself, Rocco. Absolutely do not worry about me. You've got your hands full with Amy and her machinations."

"I'm going to pass on our meeting with Jim tomorrow morning. Will you give him my excuses? Tell him I'm out of town checking on some buyers."

"Were will you be?"

"Out of town, trying to get away from Amy. And trying to sort out this mess. I asked Chloe to give me some time to figure this all out."

"Was she amenable?"

"She was until Amy started screaming. After that"—he grimaced—"fuck if I know."

"Go up to the cabin."

He nodded. "I was thinking of doing that." Their grand-parents had left them a cabin on Vermillion. "Do you know if Anthony's going there this weekend?"

"I think Sylvie's family is having a picnic."

"Perfect." Rocco smiled. "At least something's going my way."

SIXTEEN

GRACIE WAS THERE WHEN CHLOE ARRIVED at her parents' house.

But then, Chloe was late.

"You're late," her father said from the easy chair he called his own—the one even the cat didn't dare sleep in. "We've already had a martini."

"Then make me one and I'll try to catch up."

Her father rose from his chair and went to the small bar they had in their living room and measured out a martini with the precision that made him the world's most dependable bartender. He used lab beakers with the measurements in millimeters on the side and always held the container at eye level to make sure he was on the mark.

Chloe hugged her aunt and mother and took a chair in the bow window with the cat who was still living after twenty-seven years. Tiger had the markings of her namesake and the personality to match. Only certain people were allowed to touch her, although since she'd come to them the day Chloe was born, Chloe was one of the anointed few allowed that privilege.

Tiger hopped into her lap the moment she sat down.

"So tell me how rich you're getting in your own business," Gracie said with a smile. "We in the arts have no pretensions to make money, so I always view those who do with fascination."

"I'm holding my own nicely. Perhaps I can pay off the mortgage on my building in three years, and my client list is increasing to the point where I might have to consider hiring a helper next year."

"I'm impressed."

"We're all impressed," her father said, handing Chloe a martini. "Lizzie most of all, who didn't think our baby girl could get a client with her pink hair."

"I never said that, Harold."

He gave her a narrowed look and a grin.

"What I said, was *some* business managers *might* look askance at a woman with pink hair. *Some* and *might*, Harold. It was no more than a mother's concern."

"They don't care, Mom, as long as the product works for them. They're not buying me, they're buying my talent."

"And didn't you always get such good, good grades in college," her mother said proudly.

"I had to, Mom, or you wouldn't pay me," Chloe teased.

"We never did. Harold, tell Grace, Chloe's joking. Grace, really, I don't know where the child gets her sense of humor." Chloe's mother worked part-time as a social worker; she saw enough misery and poverty and lack of opportunity to be more proud than most of her daughter's accomplishments. And even though she'd never understood her daughter's blatantly arty lifestyle, she took most of it with as much grace as a practical person could.

"She gets her sense of humor from our grandfather, who was the world's most persistent practical joker. Remember, Harold? You'd hardly dare shake his hand for fear of something going off. So how's your love life, Chloe?" Gracie said with a grin.

"I thought we were here to discuss yours," Chloe replied with an answering grin.

"Chloe! For heaven's sake," her mother protested. "Are you drunk? Harold, do not make her another drink."

"It's perfectly fine, Lizzie. I'm perfectly fine. The pool boy is perfectly fine, and he's not a boy at all. He's twenty-six, finishing up his doctorate and working at the club for the summer to make some money."

"He's still too young for you, Grace. Tell her he's too young, Harold."

"The last time I told Grace what to do, she left the country and didn't come back for seven years."

"Don't blame yourself, Harold. Father was the real culprit. He threatened to put me in a nunnery."

Her father looked at his sister over his martini glass. "Are there any convents left?"

"There were a few at the time. And Lizzie, you needn't be concerned that I'm embarrassing the family, because young Tom is sleeping with any number of women at the club. So there's embarrassment enough to go around. Would you like me to name names?" She grinned. "You might be surprised."

"For heaven's sake, no. How could I look those women in the eye if I knew?"

"He's just a bit of fun for me. Nothing serious. So don't be alarmed."

Elizabeth Chisholm exhaled loudly. "I don't know whether to be relieved or not. Does the club steward know?"

"I certainly hope not. His . . . well, enough said on that score. But I'm afraid there would be a great outcry from a number of women if Tom were to leave before the end of the summer."

"Well . . . I never," Chloe's mother exclaimed. "And it's not as though I don't understand the ways of the world. In my profession one sees it all, but"—she waved her hand ineffectually—"it's just a little surprising, that's all."

"But no big deal, Mom. Really."

"I must be getting very old-fashioned."

"That's okay, Lizzie," her father said. "Old-fashioned suits me just fine. Please don't ever come home with a motorcycle or a yen to travel the world and tell me you have to find yourself."

"Why would I ever do that, Harold?"

Chloe liked the warm smile that passed between her parents. Home was always safe and secure. It was nice that some things never changed.

She and Gracie exchanged smiles, too. Their smiles were different; they had always had an understanding about a world where one took chances from time to time.

But both worlds were good.

After dinner, Chloe and Gracie had a chance to talk privately when Chloe's parents cleared the table together like they always did and loaded the dishwasher before Chloe's father brought out his twenty-five-year-old Dalwhinnie.

"So tell me about this new stud at the club," Chloe murmured.

"He's nice, he's good in bed, he's so busy pleasing his harem he's not demanding. I can't complain about a thing."

"Is he really sleeping with, like, tons of women?"

"Sort of."

"You don't mind?"

"It's just sex, darling. Why should I mind?"

"Is he really sleeping with Charlie Mercer's wife?" Charlie was the club steward.

" 'Fraid so. That one's a bit more dicey than the others, but Heather won't take no for an answer. She threatened to have him fired if he didn't. Another little blonde prima donna did as well. So it's not all fun and games for poor Tom."

The words blonde prima donna set up a very loud ringing of bells in Chloe's head. Nah. It couldn't be. The Thiebauds didn't belong to the club. She shouldn't even ask. It was ridiculous. "Was the blonde prima donna Amy Thiebaud?" So much for reason and constraint.

"How did you know?"

"Unlucky guess," she muttered. "How the hell did she cross Tom's path?"

"She came to play tennis with some friends and zeroed in on him like a heat-seeking missile, apparently. How do you know her?"

"I've had a few run-ins with her lately. She really threatened to have this Tom fellow fired?"

"She has a temper, he says. Apparently she's a randy little tart, busy sleeping around with just about everyone."

"Really." Chloe's mouth set in a grim line. Not having sex with her, Rocco said. How likely was that with *his* reputation and little Amy's propensity for fucking?

"She's affecting you in some way?"

"Nothing serious," Chloe said with a feigned calmness.

"That's just as well from what I've heard about her. She's not someone to be trifled with, according to Tom." Gracie smiled. "I shouldn't be telling tales out of school, but she likes to give orders in bed, and kinky suits her best—handcuffs, leather, that sort of thing."

"Jesus." It just came out; she couldn't help it. Kinky? Fuck. So much for her fantasy world centered around Rocco

Vinelli. She could kiss that dream good-bye.

"She knows someone you know?" Gracie didn't have to be prescient to recognize Chloe's ashen face.

"Yeah. I guess."

"Someone you care about?"

"I don't know—probably. Nah—not really. I'm just surprised about all this with Amy. I just found out Rocco's engaged to her." She grimaced. "The guy's one smooth talker."

"When you've reached my age, darling," Gracie said with a commiserating smile, "you'll find out that most men are smooth talkers. Just don't expect too much and you won't get hurt."

"Good advice," Chloe said softly. "Thanks."

SEVENTEEN

ROCCO WAS SITTING ON THE DOCK AT LAKE Vermillion, smoking a spliff, drinking a beer and trying to figure out how to get himself out of Amy hell. It was a perfect summer day, the sky cloudless blue, the sun warm but not too warm, the lake like a mirror. He'd gotten there late the night before and it was mid-afternoon on Saturday and he was no more near to a solution to his problem than he'd been before.

It was a no go, getting that square peg into that round hole no matter how he tried to wedge it in. He'd reached the stage where he was thinking about staying up here the rest of his life and fishing for a living.

The cordless phone rang.

Paranoid, he checked the caller ID. He wasn't taking any phone calls from Amy. He smiled when he saw the name and hit the button. "Howzit goin'?"

"I was about to ask you the same thing," Steve said. "How's the lake?"

"Great. Peaceful. How did you know I was here?"

"I tried your house. No luck. I thought I'd give the cabin a try, seeing how it's the height of the summer. Got any news?"

"Not much. The factory's firing up. We're pleased about that. I saw your folks the other night. Your dad's helping us out, you know."

"Yeah. I heard. Good."

"So are you coming home this summer?"

"I don't know. I might if there's reason. Anything you can think of might bring me home . . . some occasion?" Steve's voice had taken on a teasing tone.

The hair on the back of Rocco's neck began to rise. "What the hell are you talking about?"

"Amy called me."

"Yeah?" Rocco tossed his spliff into the water and sat up straight.

"She told me you two were engaged."

"She's psycho."

"I know, that's why I thought I'd better check it out with you. She's got big plans. Just a warning."

"I'm up at the lake to get away from her. She's driving me nuts."

"That's the Amy we all know and love," Steve said sardonically. "I wish you luck."

"I'm going to need more than luck. Apparently she's feeding your folks some crap about us. Your dad made some pretty pointed allusions to son-in-laws when I saw him a couple of nights ago."

"If I could talk to my dad without the conversation turning into a shouting match, I'd say I could try and give you a hand. But my interference won't be much help."

"Thanks. I'll manage. So how's the job going out there? I always see your name on the credits after the games. Impressive, dude. Are the ladies keeping you busy?"

"I'm sort of dating someone."

"Sounds serious."

"Could be. We'll see."

"Is she from out there?"

"San Francisco."

"Hey, your mom mentioned a girl from San Francisco."

"I told Mom about her. Anyway, Sarah's keeping me home at night."

"No more *Playboy* babes?"

"Nah. You go through a phase. I suppose you're still turning the ladies away." Rocco had always been a magnet for women.

"One in particular," Rocco muttered.

Steve laughed. "Tell Amy she has to go and get a job if you marry her. That will scare her off."

"I wish. I'm sure she could probably talk your parents into some suitable alternative. And I met someone, too—so Amy's more of a pain in the ass than usual."

"No shit. I figured you'd be the last one to give up bachelorhood. Who is she?"

"Her name's Chloe and she's hotter than hot."

"And?" That wasn't a new style of woman for Rocco.

"And she's on my mind—a lot."

"Bring her out to L.A. sometime. We'll go clubbing together. Sarah knows everyone. She helps produce the entertainment news for Fox."

"Maybe later—if she's still talking to me after this Amy fiasco. Your sister screamed at Chloe the last time I was with her."

"You used to do a better job of keeping the ladies in separate rooms."

"Your sister's not normal."

"True. Do you want me to talk to my mom?"

"Not yet. If I can't find a way out, I'll consider it."

"Hang in there, buddy."

"That's my plan. Thanks for calling."

"I figured you needed a head's up. I haven't believed anything Amy's said since—well . . . since never. See ya."

"Yeah."

Rocco set the phone down and lighted up another spliff to block out the huge black cloud of unease coming his way. That was one fucking ominous head's up.

Lord—all he wanted to do was call Chloe, tell her to come on up and well . . . maybe do a few other things too, come to think of it.

But, dammit, he couldn't. Not until Amy was off his back.

EIGHTEEN

 CHLOE SPENT SATURDAY WORKING. TESS and Rosie weren't home. She'd tried calling them a dozen times. So much for friends in need. It was a gorgeous summer weekend and everyone who walked by her office windows seemed to be hand in hand or pushing a baby stroller while smiling at their significant other or with a friend—roller blading, running, bicycling, carrying a picnic basket. She was the only sad, solitary, significant other-less woman in the entire city.

She could have gone to Chino's and hung out. Their terrace looked out over the city and was always packed on a Saturday afternoon, and that cute bartender who'd been giving her the eye would be available, she knew. He looked like Colin Farrell. How good was that? But her recalcitrant libido decided it was only interested in Visnjic types this weekend, and there her libido sat—unbudgeable.

It was shocking, really . . . her inability to get past wanting a man who slept with everyone including kinky little heiresses and lied and cheated and in general was the playboy of the western world. Every reasonable brain cell understood that Rocco Vinelli was not the kind of man to get involved with—let alone crave.

It was like craving cocaine.

It wasn't good for you; it was bad for you; it was *very* bad for you.

It would leave you, figuratively speaking, in the gutter, like in *Reefer Madness*. Which meant she had to keep those reasonable brain cells wide awake and on full alert.

But between *trying* to design a snappy, upbeat web site for one of the new car dealerships, craving the no-good, rotten-to-the-core Rocco Vinelli and gnashing her teeth over being alone when every other twentysomething was out having fun this weekend, Chloe was so ready for a drink by five o'clock that she bitch-slapped her obstinate libido into compliance and headed for Chino's.

"Hey, nice shorts," her Colin Farrell look-alike bartender murmured, giving her a long, low whistle as she walked up to the sunny terrace bar. "And that top." He winked. "Even better."

She suddenly realized she was still wearing her raggedy cut-offs, purple tube top and Adidas flip-flops. "Shit, I forgot to change." She grinned, finding the physical act of smiling less difficult than she thought, feeling good about feeling even mildly good. "My brain's fried. I need a drink."

"One mango tango coming up."

When she tried to pay for it, he shook his head.

That first sip helped—like instant calm—or his smile helped and it helped too that she realized she wasn't the only one chained to a job on this summer Saturday. She watched him work the bar, his movements deft and sure, the muscles in his arms and shoulders smooth, taut, rippling gently as he swiftly made the drinks and handed them off. And when he'd look up and smile at her from time to time, she began feeling more like a normal twentysomething.

She watched the women hitting on him, one after another, saw how he laughed with them and joked, how he made them all feel good, how he turned them all down with a small shake of his head and an excuse that still left them smiling.

God, he was smooth. Like another man she knew.

She was on her second mango tango and thinking about calling Rocco. During the entire time she sipped on that drink, she curbed her impulse, telling herself her Colin look-alike was just as sexy and more available. Or at least available—the more part was debatable, of course, but not relevant at the moment. As she started her third drink, however, her restraint began to slip. "I'll be right back," she said with a wave to the bartender and made a dash for the bathroom, where they had a comfy couch by the phone.

Don't, don't, don't, the little voice inside her head implored, but ignoring it, she dialed Rocco's number. One ring, *please, please answer,* two rings, *she thought about offering something to the gods,* three rings, *maybe he had to get up from his chair where he was reading some highly literate book,* four rings, *dammit, he was in bed with someone,* five rings—his voicemail came on and she slammed down the receiver.

Oops. Not on the table. There. And she slumped down on Chino's sleek Italian couch and gave in to all the paranoid, disturbing visions flooding her mind—the ones where Rocco was with other women—and yes, she meant plural, because she was extra paranoid after two-plus drinks—and he and his harem were all having a fabulous time like everyone else on this blissful Saturday. She almost called back and said something stupid about missing him and adding her to his harem, but two women came into the bathroom just then, gave her a look like where did you get that outfit and started fixing their perfect makeup and talking about their boyfriends and making her feel even more pathetic because not only didn't she have a boyfriend, but she looked very much like a particular type of street person.

Her dispirited feelings served as further deterrent to calling Rocco and leaving him a message begging him to come and see her. These two beautifully dressed, coiffed and madeup women were sure to look at her and snicker.

Rising from the couch with as much grace as she could muster after her mango tangos and the non-skid properties of rubber sandals on cork tile, she walked from the bathroom with the refined posture of a convent-bred lady who had been taught to walk with a book on her head. When she reached the bar, she immediately drank down the dregs of her drink and asked for another.

"You sure?"

The bartender was giving her one of those looks clearly questioning her capacity for liquor. "What's your name?" she asked because she was having trouble saying "my Colin Farrell look-alike" in her brain after three drinks. It took too long. And if they were going to argue about her wanting another drink, she didn't have time to run through that long tongue-twister of a name while explaining to him— very nicely, of course—that three drinks were not too many for her.

"Colin."

"No way!"

"Word of honor."

"You must know you look like Colin Farrell."

His dark brows rose in a quick flicker. "I've been told."

"You can't be related."

"Nope. Last name's McCarthy."

"Well, then, Colin McCarthy, another mango tango please, and don't give me any shit." She could be infinitely subtle in her arguments when drinking.

"You're not driving, are you?"

She hesitated. "I'll call a cab."

"I get off at seven. I could give you a ride."

She couldn't continue to act like an infatuated teenager over Rocco, pining over him, mooning over him, practically lighting candles before his picture. He had no redeeming qualities—except one, of course—but that didn't count because he shared that with everyone. She would have to consider those other fish in the sea. Really. Seriously. Seriously, seriously. "Okay," she said. She also had the ability to make quick decisions when drinking. "Now, may I have a drink?"

"Sure can." His smile was boyish, like he'd gotten a present he'd wanted.

"How old are you?" A libido was so much more tractable when tipsy.

"Old enough."

"Okay. How young are you?"

"Twenty-one."

She softly groaned.

"You can't be much older, and it doesn't matter anyway."

He said it so casually, like a twenty-one-year-old would, like the world doesn't have any rules. And, she supposed, she'd never played by the rules anyway. But it was more about her being older than about his youth. God, she wasn't used to this—being the older woman. It was like a weird milestone. Was wrinkle cream the next step, and men calling her Ma'am?

"You're the hottest babe that's ever walked in here. Word of honor," Colin said, soft and low, pushing another drink across the bar to her. "I've been having wet dreams about you for months."

She smiled. Maybe she wouldn't have to buy wrinkle cream right away.

Maybe her Saturday had just taken a great big U-turn for the better.

NINETEEN

IT WAS A GORGEOUS PINKY-GOLD SUNSET lighting the horizon on Vermillion, and maybe it triggered something in his brain, or maybe eight beers and too much ganja jump-started the cosmic concept. Whatever—the idea came to him like the proverbial flashing lightbulb over the character's head in a cartoon, and he picked up the phone.

"Good, you're back from your picnic," Rocco said, and proceeded to describe exactly what he wanted.

"It's not that easy," Anthony muttered when the lengthy description came to an end. "You know how long it takes me to mix something like that?"

"Take your time. I don't need it 'til Monday."

"Screw you. I have a life and you're loaded."

"I didn't say I wasn't. Are you going to do it?"

"Not by Monday."

"By when?"

"This is just going to make more trouble. You're supposed to figure out how to placate Amy for a few more weeks, not have her go ballistic."

"She won't know."

"If you market it the way you're talking about, she sure as hell will. Unless you can keep her inside her house, she will."

"Okay. So my idea needs a little tweaking."

"It needs a shitload more than a tweaking."

"I'll figure it out. You just do your part."

"This chick must be some piece of ass."

"Yeah, I guess." The chrysalis stage of male commitment. "Don't fuck with me, Anthony. I really want this."

"I'll have something for you to look at by the end of the week. This isn't a simple process you can do in a hurry. Even loaded, you should remember that. Friday, I'll give you a couple to choose from."

"Thanks. Now, you know what I want."

"Yeah, yeah. You want the fucking moon on a platter."

Rocco laughed. He was feeling better; he was almost feeling good. At least he was going somewhere he wanted to go . . . somewhere in the right direction. Or maybe just in the opposite direction from Amy.

TWENTY

"SHOULD WE GO TO MY PLACE?"

They were sitting in Colin's pickup, his crotch rocket bungee-strapped in the back of the truck, the cab floor a jumble of motorcycle paraphernalia—boots, a couple of helmets, jacket, tools that he'd just swept off the seat so Chloe could sit down. He was leaning on the steering wheel, looking at her, waiting for an answer.

"Sure."

He smiled. "Got it." Turning on the ignition, he shoved the gear into reverse, pulled out of the parking spot and squealed rubber as he accelerated out of the ramp onto the street.

He'd mixed her one last drink because she'd asked him to, and he'd snuck it out of the bar under his shirt. She was holding her umbrella drink carefully between her hands as he drove south on the freeway, taking a sip now and then when no one could see her, enjoying the lingering sunset through the opened windows, listening to the music he'd flicked on, half over the worst of her longing for Rocco.

But his image would still appear from time to time in her brain like one of those holograms that shimmered and faded depending on your viewing angle. The intensity of her response had lessened, though. She was glad, considering the futility of wanting something you couldn't have. And when Colin said, "Wanna go for a swim first?" she nodded and said, "Love to," and really meant it.

"Have you been bartending long?" She half lifted her glass, lazily making conversation, feeling the wind blowing through her hair, liking his taste in music, wondering if all those tattoos on his arms had hurt when he'd got them.

He flashed her a smile. "I just turned twenty-one in May. This is my first job bartending. They said I could stay on part-time when school starts again."

"School?" She was almost zoning out from the sun and the heat and the music, complete sentences beyond her grasp.

"The U—electrical engineering."

"Good for you." It just went to show—all engineers weren't geeky. Some could look like sexy street punk movie stars.

"I like numbers," he said simply. "And hot babes," he added with a wink.

She smiled. She would have liked to tell him that he'd renewed her faith in the merits of growing old gracefully, but couldn't muster the necessary brain synapses to explain the complicated pattern of male–female relationships that had brought her to Chino's that afternoon. "Are we almost there?" she said instead.

"Ten more minutes." He hit another button on his CD changer. "Do you like Ben Kweller?"

They drove to a small lake south of Eagan, traveling

gravel roads at the last before turning into a driveway of an abandoned farmhouse and parking between the house and what was left of the barn. He pulled a blanket and a small cooler from behind his seat, then came around, opened her door and helped her out.

"This is my grandpa's land, so we're cool. No one's going to come and run us off." He nodded. "The lake's over there."

She said, "Wow," in astonishment when they skirted the ruins of the barn and stood on the crest of the hill behind it. The grassy slope swept down to a jewel of a lake, bordered on the opposite side by an apple orchard, the site hidden away like a green glen in the depression of hills, the sunset illuminating the horizon in a glorious gold. "It looks like an illustration from *My Secret Garden*."

"It's a great place. Quiet," he said. "Secluded," he added in a softer tone of voice. He held out his hand. "Watch your step going down."

She kicked off her flip-flops and felt the cool grass between her toes and began thinking she'd made a very good decision saying yes to Colin. Not that she hadn't thought that before, but now—in this romantic, sylvan glade—it seemed like she was surrounded by some potent magic.

He spread the blanket on the ground when they reached the lakeshore and helped her sit down. Kicking off his sandals, he stripped off his shirt, tossed it aside and lay back with a sigh. "Ah . . . peace and quiet. I must have made a thousand drinks this afternoon." He smiled up at her. "But it was worth it, 'cause you came in."

"I almost didn't. I was working."

He grinned, ran his finger down her arm. "I was praying hard."

She laughed. "Then I'm glad I showed up. I wouldn't want you to lose faith."

"No way, now." He rolled over on his side, picked up

her hand where it lay on the blanket beside her leg and slid his fingers through hers. "I'm almost believing in miracles."

She could see the bulge in his jeans, and smiled. And after the mango tangos, his enthusiasm was charming, more than charming, interesting—even a little bit exciting. And she was seriously in the mood to get on with her life . . . put aside all that teenage infatuation stuff that was utterly ridiculous at her age and engage in some sex with this darling, sexy young man.

He seemed to understand, because he rolled upward in a smooth, effortless display of honed muscle and took her face between his hands and kissed her with the kind of enthusiasm she'd expected from him. He was boyish and impetuous and deliciously strong as she ran her hands over his shoulders and down his back and not inclined to wait, she discovered as he pushed her down on the blanket and reached for the zipper on her cut-offs.

"Do you know how long I've been wanting to do this?" he whispered, sliding the zipper down.

It wasn't a question that required an answer, and she wasn't sure he would have heard it had she replied.

Foreplay wasn't on his agenda, his hands swift and sure as he pulled her shorts and panties off, his jeans and boxers discarded a second later, the sound of crickets and frogs melodic adjunct to his fierce impatience.

But she didn't care, preferring a mindless intoxication, disposed to unequivocal passion, just wanting to feel and not think. Just wanting to climax and feel the pleasure. But he was in a profession that made her more nervous than usual and she said, "You have to use a condom," in the tone of voice that meant, "If you don't, I'm leaving."

He rolled off her, rummaged through his jean pockets and was back almost literally a split second later, having done as she'd directed.

She felt a warm, little frisson at the level of his enthusiasm, and when he entered her a second later, she felt more
than a little frisson.

Ummm . . . he was fierce and wild, ummm . . . and
large. She liked that. Call her selfish, she didn't care. When
it came to sex, she wasn't altruistic. And so far, she hadn't
had any complaints. Wrapping her legs around his hips,
she met his unbridled, tumultuous rhythm and they both
took and gave in equal measure, coming in a roughshod
convulsive burst that almost—*almost* matched.

"Next time," he panted, dropping a kiss on her shoulder.
"I couldn't wait."

"Next time sounds good," she breathed, having to race
at the end, but gratified and content.

"Wanna swim and cool off?" His grin was very close, his
forehead sheened with perspiration, the weight of his body
the merest brushing pressure as he held himself up on his
forearms.

She nodded and he kissed her again and rolled off with
a long, low sigh.

Disposing of his condom like he'd done it once or twice
before, he pulled her up into a seated position and lifted
her tube top over her head.

"Va-va-va-voom," he whispered, touching her nipples
with the tip of his finger. "Definitely a wet dream come
true." And bending his head, he kissed first one nipple and
then the other with a gentleness that sent a new spiraling
heat downward between her legs.

It was a delectable, nice, felicitous heat, not the kind
that blew your mind, but definitely the kind you wouldn't
refuse. And it wasn't Colin's fault that the level of her rapture was less than mind-blowing. It was someone else's
fault.

Someone who probably had a decade more experience

fucking than sweet young Colin. Someone who knew all the ropes and everything in between. Someone who had a natural talent that no amount of practice could match.

Damn him anyway for setting up unattainable goals.

They didn't wait until they cooled off from a swim as it turned out. But they swam afterward and then lay on the blanket and basked in the sensual bliss of sexual satisfaction, a golden sunset and two imported beers that tasted better for the gratifying orgasms that had preceded them.

The stars came up after a time, and they indulged their senses yet again and then once more before swimming one last time and dressing.

Then they walked back to the truck, hand in hand, and when he dropped Chloe off at her house, he said, "May I come in?"

She felt the smallest twinge of guilt when she answered him. "Next time," she said. "I'm so tired now, I'd be poor company."

He smiled. He was a polite young man. "Okay. Next time."

And he kissed her sweetly and walked her to her door and kissed her again.

Why didn't she feel anything but his sweetness when he kissed her?

Why didn't the earth move when she came with him?

Why didn't she crave him like she craved Rocco?

She had no answers.

Maybe there weren't any answers even if she hadn't been half-drunk and dead tired.

"Thanks. I'm going to call you."

"Okay," she said. She brushed her palm over his cheek, turned to punch in the numbers for her lock and smiled at him one last time as he held her door open for her.

She heard the roar of his truck pulling away as she climbed her stairs.

And she wondered who Rocco was fucking right now.

TWENTY-ONE

CHLOE WOKE UP SUNDAY MORNING AND called both Tess and Rosie, needing someone to whine to. She struck out. Answering machines at both places. Which meant her friends were abed with their lovers while she was sharing her Sunday morning with George Stephanopoulos and two arguing political pundits.

Throwing on some clothes, she walked to the coffee shop for two double iced lattes and two croissants that would in some small measure give a kick-start to a morning that didn't appear to be one of her better ones. Then she started working because if nothing else, she at least could make some money.

Small recompense for a broken spirit and heart, but at least she could buy a neat sports car to ride around in looking for happiness.

*   *   *

FOUR HOURS NORTH, Rocco woke in similar low spirits, not to mention hungover. The sun shining through the porch screens was hurting his eyes; he'd obviously not made it to the bedroom last night, he decided, turning over on the couch to get away from the excruciating light. And if he wanted a latte, which he did, it was a half-hour drive to Tower.

That half-hour drive was a real deterrent in his current physical state, and if someone would have delivered him a latte even for an exorbitant sum, he would have phoned in an order. But Betsy, who owned the shop, worked alone. He'd already tried to bribe her on previous occasions and failed.

An hour later, he was sitting in Betsy's coffee shop, nursing his head and half listening to the steady stream of customers who came and went in the only espresso spot on the north end of the lake. The south end of the lake was an hour by boat and two hours by road, so Tower was a busy place. Everyone seemed happy except him; he took personal affront at their happiness. Had he asked for a crazy woman to target him for her fiancé? Was he responsible for a spoiled princess's skewed view of the world? Could he help it if he'd taken Amy out in a weak moment? Well, yeah, he guessed he could have helped that. But how could he have known she was going to turn out to be a marriage stalker?

A latte and a triple espresso later, he was almost ready to face the world. Or at least the world four hours removed from any danger of running into Amy. Returning to his cabin, he spent the day chopping wood. It wasn't a task for a summer day; it was fall work, when the weather was cool. But he practically filled the whole woodshed, sweating and working like someone on a southern chain gang, needing

the physical torture to keep his mind off his mental torment.

But he drove by Chloe's late that night on his way home
and saw a pickup truck with a motorcycle in the back
parked at the curb near her door and almost stormed in and
beat the shit out of the guy.

But he didn't.

He didn't have the right.

She was free to see anyone she wished.

Like he was—if he'd felt the urge.

Like he was—if he even felt like looking at another
woman.

Like he was—if he wasn't going nuts over a woman who
was obviously entertaining some guy who rode a damned
nice motorcycle.

He parked across the street like some idiot and stared at
Chloe's windows and wondered if she was coming every ten
seconds like she liked. He almost called Anthony and told
him he couldn't wait until Friday, but his car clock was
brightly shining the midnight hour. Sylvie would blow a
gasket if he called at midnight.

Shit.

He put the car in gear, pulled away from the curb and
drove home.

ONE WOULD THINK when one was having multiple orgasms that all was right with the world.

One would think when some really sexy, handsome
young guy was saying and doing really sweet, endearing
things to you that life couldn't get any better.

One would surely think that one wouldn't be thinking
of some other sexy, handsome guy at the same time.

Oh, God, she was coming again.

Oh, God, she hoped she screamed the right name.

But Colin was smiling when he kissed her a moment later, so she must have. And when he said, "I think I just blew off the top of my head—thanks," she figured she must have been discreetly silent about her shameless fantasies.

So she smiled back and said something flattering to him because she was feeling guilty and then wished she hadn't been quite so flattering because he said, "Then I'll stay and make you feel that way a few more times."

He'd been wanting to stay.

She'd been politely evading his requests.

And now she'd done it—he was going to stay, and unfortunately, great sex aside, she was blatantly cognizant that something was missing. Who would have thought? Who would have seriously thought that romance or love or affection could screw up sex in any way, shape or form? She was astonished and stupefied and now sadly wiser.

Rocco Vinelli had a helluva lot to answer for.

He was fucking up her perfectly good sex life; her really supremely good sex life; the sex life that had brought her great joy and comfort for many years.

And he was going to marry a beautiful heiress, like in a fairy tale.

And she was going to measure every damned sexual encounter against his expertise and end up disillusioned and incapable of that unalloyed pleasure she'd always enjoyed.

Oh—that did feel good, though . . . the sweet boy could last for hours—not that someone else she knew who would remain nameless couldn't as well. Ummm . . . that was nice—he was strong too, lifting her like that . . . um-um-um and she decided if she was going to have a houseguest all night, she might as well take advantage of him.

Not that Colin McCarthy felt as though he was being

taken advantage of. Not that he had any complaints at all.

And when he left in the morning, he was trying real hard to come back right after work that night.

"Call me," Chloe said, smiling as she stood at the door with him. "And I'll see how much I get done at work today."

"Work hard. I want to come over later."

He was barefoot, dressed only in jeans, his shirt and sandals in his hand, looking fresh and young, like he'd slept all night when he hadn't. She grinned. "I'll try."

"I'm gonna pester you." He pulled her close, held her hard against his body and said, softly, "I can't get enough . . ."

"Thanks, now go home," she whispered, pushing gently against his bare, muscled chest. "I've tons of work."

He released her and stepped away. "I get off at one." He grinned. "Take a nap."

Her mouth twitched into a smile. "Don't get pushy, kid."

"Yes, Ma'am."

But she didn't mind when he said it like that.

TWENTY-TWO

ROCCO WENT INTO HIS LAST DAY OF WORK
very early because he hadn't slept well. Or at all—
unless his daydreams about Chloe counted. After
clearing out his desk, he made the rounds, saying his good-
byes, was polite to everyone at his going-away party and
flew out of town at two for his first sales trip as Marketing
Director for Vinelli Enterprises. He'd scheduled four cities
in four days, hours of meetings in each city, and he hoped
like hell he could get his mind focused on what it needed
to be focused on—making a success of their business.

CHLOE WAS IN dire need of a sounding board for the
botched muddle of her life, and at last her friends came
through. Tess and Rosie both called her Monday morning.
They decided to meet for drinks at five.

"You look tired," Rosie said as Chloe slid into the banquette at Zelo's.

"With good reason."

"How good?" Tess inquired with a grin.

"That's what I wanted to talk to you about." And over
drinks, Chloe went on to explain her new revelation and/
or bewilderment apropos of sex and romance.

"I fall in love with everyone I ever go out with," Tess
said, "so don't ask me to define the difference between sex
and romance."

"And I thought I was in love with Mark." Rosie grimaced. "So how much do I know about anything?"

"Well, that was helpful," Chloe muttered.

"And I'm in love *again*." Tess grinned. "I'm the person
all those touchy-feely cards are written for—you know, the
ones where a barefoot couple is walking hand-in-hand on
the beach with a dog running along beside them and the
inscription is all about eternal love and devotion."

"Ian certainly is making *me* believe in love again," Rosie
said softly.

"You just never put sex and love together before, Chloe,"
Tess pointed out. "You're a seriously liberated woman."

Rosie nodded. "You're like a man."

Chloe sighed. "Why has it all changed, though? That's
what I'd like to know. I'm obsessed with Rocco in a way
that's really screwing up my life. He's the last man in the
world I should be dreaming about. He wouldn't recognize
love if it came to his door dressed in black leather and studs.
Although, come to think of it, that might work for him
after what I heard about his fiancée's kinky fetishes."

"What? Hey." Tess held up her swizzle stick. "You can't
say black leather and kinky without an explanation."

Chloe's filled them in on Grace's tidbit.

"Jeez, that should be an interesting marriage—oops,

sorry. I'm sure there's never going to be any marriage," Tess quickly said. "She's all wrong for him. He'll discover she's a huge mistake any minute now."

"But if he's engaged to her," Rosie noted, "maybe he likes black leather and, oh dear." She caught sight of Chloe's expression.

"That's okay, Rosie. You're probably right." Chloe sighed. "And if I'm going to try to calibrate love, I'd better not put Rocco in the equation. He's totally indifferent to the concept; in fact, the last time I saw him, we screwed about ten feet away from his fiancée."

Rosie said, "Eww," with her nose all wrinkled up. "How could you?"

"I wasn't thinking too clearly at the time." Chloe ran her finger up the stem of her martini glass. "He makes me so hot, my brain melts."

"I've never felt like that."

Chloe looked up and grinned. "There's a good and bad side to the feeling."

Tess leaned her elbows on the table and gave Chloe a hard stare. "You want him to call, don't you? Love or no love."

"I guess. That's the point. I don't know what I want. And since he's engaged to Miss Heiress, he's not likely to dump her for anything more than a series of quickies. I'm not so sure I'm interested in that kind of sex."

Rosie eyes opened wide; Chloe hadn't been so scrupulous in the past. "You're really *serious* about this Rocco."

"See—that's the problem. I don't know what serious means. I miss the sex. That I know. But whether it's *more* than sex escapes my obtuse or callous, or maybe cold-as-ice sensibilities—although I've never seen myself as cold-hearted. Nor does that cute bartender from Chino's whom I spent the weekend with think that I'm—"

"The bartender who looks like Colin Farrell!" Tess squealed.

"That one. His name's Colin, too, and he's really nice."

"*Nice!* Jesus, he's God's gift to women! I'd strip naked at the bar if he asked me to!"

"Well, fortunately, he didn't ask me to, as I'm not sure I would have. Correction. I wouldn't have. He doesn't turn me on the same way as Rocco. Even though he's really good in bed."

"He's good in *bed!*" Tess's squeals were beginning to draw attention to them.

"Keep it down, Tess," Chloe hissed. "And there's another thing, too," she murmured. "I need you guys to help me make up my mind about Colin. He wants to come over again tonight, and I'm not sure I want him to."

"Are you crazy!" Tess exclaimed in a stifled squeal.

"Not about him, I'm not, which is why I'm beginning to think about all this stupid love stuff and how you can't always make things work out. He's hotter for me than I am for him, and I'm hotter for Rocco than he is for me, and everything's really mixed up and confusing. So tell me what to do."

"Tell Colin to come over, FOR CHRIST'S SAKE!" Tess practically shouted which made everyone in the bar swivel around.

"Jesus, Tess, get a grip." Chloe tried to pretend she was unaware of the intense scrutiny, of everyone leaning forward a little like at a tennis match.

"Have I seen this guy?" Rosie was clearly perplexed by Tess's violent interest.

"Obviously not," Tess retorted with an exasperated look, "if you can't remember what he looks like. He's a *god.*"

"He's also twenty-one," Chloe supplied.

"So, who cares as long as he's eighteen?" Tess fluttered

her fingers in a dismissive gesture. "He's legal. My God, Chloe, tell me everything . . . every little thing from the minute he asked you out until he left your place. Don't leave out a single detail."

"I guess I should have let him videotape it after all."

"Really? He wanted to? Oh, God, why didn't you?"

Chloe leaned over and patted Tess's hand. "I'm kidding, okay? Nobody wanted to videotape anything. And don't get any ideas," Chloe warned. "Or I'll take my key back from you right now. And what ever happened to *I'm in love again*? What about Dave?"

"This has nothing to do with love. That bartender, Colin, is pure fantasy."

"He's also damned young."

"And that hurts the fantasy—*how?*"

"May I say a few words about Ian now?" Rosie's one-drink limit had been passed, her hands were no longer clasped in front of her on the tabletop, her cheeks were flushed and a small frown creased her brow. "I'd like to talk about Ian."

"Talk away," Chloe offered. "There's no answer to the tumult in my life anyway. Tell us about Ian."

Rosie smiled and sat up a little straighter like she was talking to her pupils. "He likes puppies."

"Any special kind?" Chloe wasn't sure where this was leading since none of them had or ever had had puppies.

"Little puppies." Rosie held up her hands and measured a very small space. "We saw some puppies in the park on Sunday. They were teeny, tiny and ever so cute and Ian said he was thinking about getting a puppy now that he was back home. Isn't that sweet? Mark didn't like dogs. He said they were troublesome."

Ah . . . that's where this story was going. "The only thing Mark knows about is lying," Chloe said. "Obviously

Ian is a much nicer person. I'm glad you found him."

"I'm glad too. Did I tell you he likes Italian food?"

"I thought you didn't like Italian—"Tess abruptly curtailed her comment when Chloe kicked her under the table.

"You've always liked D'Amico's desserts," Chloe pointed out with a smile. "I'll bet Ian would like them too."

"I know he would. He likes everything I like."

Chloe was hoping Rosie wasn't going to use the phrase soul mates, but braced herself just in case.

"I'm probably a little drunk." Rosie leaned back against the padded leather banquette, her smile curving upward slowly, as though her reflexes were half asleep. "But I don't care. Ian kisses really, really nicely, too. Mark never kissed much. I like that Ian likes to kiss. It makes me feel all cuddly and cared for and wanted. I know that's different from all the hot passion you like, Chloe, and you too Tess, but it's just perfect for me. Ian's sooo perfect. And he's coming over to take me out to dinner, so . . ." She sat up and fumbled for her purse. "I really have to go. If it's okay—I mean . . . if you know what you're going to do and all, Chloe," she said, half-apologetic, already sliding off the banquette.

Chloe nodded. "Everything's figured out." It wasn't as though she'd actually expected an answer to her unsolvable problems anyway. And after a couple of drinks they seemed a whole lot less pressing. "I'll drive you home. My car's outside in the valet lot."

Chloe and Tess saw that Rosie had something to eat on the way home, to temper some of the alcohol coursing through her hundred-pound body. Although if Ian was as perfect as Rosie described, he wouldn't care if she was a little tipsy.

"I talked to a couple of my Vinelli cousins," Tess said in a cautious tone, as she and Chloe drove away from Rosie's.

"And they wouldn't recommend taking any bets on Rocco's settling down. I debated telling you, but," she sighed, "you seem to be vaguely aware of the situation already. He's been a babe magnet for most of his life." She made a moue. "Not exactly the white-picket-fence kind of guy. Sorry."

"That's okay. I already knew. I had a gut feeling from the beginning. I was just trying to work around the cruel, harsh reality. I know enough to be sensible about a guy like him. And if his reputation wasn't enough, let's face it, he's engaged. End of story."

"Fortunately, you have Colin to amuse you," Tess said with a grin.

"True. He's definitely entertaining. Thanks for checking out Rocco with your relatives." Chloe pulled up to Tess's house. Her friends lived a block apart in arts-and-crafts bungalows they'd restored. "Have fun with Dave tonight."

"We're taking in a gallery showing somewhere—wire sculpture I think. Are you going to see Colin?"

Chloe shrugged. "I don't know . . . probably—maybe. It depends how much I want to be amused, I guess."

"If you do decide to see him," Tess said with a wink, "take notes."

"If I decide to see him, I'm going to have to go home and take a nap. I barely slept the last two nights."

"If you want me to feel sorry for you, that's not going to do it." Tess gave her a narrow-eyed look. "And don't give Rocco another thought." She opened the car door and stepped out. "He's not worth it."

"Right," Chloe murmured as the car door slammed. That should be as easy as making water run uphill. Maybe she *did* need Colin as a diversion tonight. Otherwise she'd mope and eat too much ice cream and then really feel sorry for herself for eating too much ice cream. Which would drive her to the cookie jar, which would—

She picked up her cell phone and dialed Chino's.

TWENTY-THREE

WHILE CHLOE WAS LISTENING TO COLIN say "cool" about a thousand times on the other end of the phone connection, Rocco was trying to decide how to answer the buyer from Neiman Marcus, who had just asked him out for dinner and was smiling at him now, waiting for an answer.

The cosmetics buyer was a small, petite, expensively dressed brunette and very attractive. He was debating how she'd respond to a no. Intellectually, he knew better than to turn her down. "I'd like that," he said with an inward groan. "The Mansion at Turtle Creek?" he offered, since she'd suggested it.

"That's perfect. Shall we?" She put out her hand.

It was the strangest feeling he'd ever had—not wanting to touch her. He'd never experienced a squeamishness like that before, and in compensation for his curious reluctance, he grasped her hand a little too hard. He smiled. "Sorry."

Having read her own meaning into his strong grip, Sarah Lu Bonner smiled back and said, in a soft Texas drawl, "Don't be sorry, darlin'. It feels gooood . . ."

Oh Christ. Would she still honor the large order she'd just given him if he didn't sleep with her? Although this wasn't the first time a buyer had hit on him, it was the first time he'd be losing his own money if she took offense when he said no. Shit. He needed a drink. Or better yet, he'd see if she'd have a drink and shift her focus from him.

It wasn't much of a plan, but it was all he had.

In hindsight, he wouldn't have had to worry. Sarah Lu had a mighty thirst for champagne. When she asked for a third bottle, he said, "Maybe we should have coffee instead."

She'd given him one of those clear, direct looks that said without words, "You must not have heard what I said," and he waved the wine steward over and ordered another bottle of champagne. So dinner cost him eight hundred bucks because she like Grand Dame Veuve Clicquot. It turned out to be a bargain.

She ended up talking about herself pretty much exclusively—her childhood, her schooling, her two marriages that had foundered. At which point he'd had to express the necessary concern when he couldn't remember if it had been Jeb or Buck who had driven her crazy by wearing cowboy boots with his shorts. She'd gone on to discuss in great detail her rise through the ranks at Neiman Marcus, and all he had to do was nod on occasion or say, "How interesting," or smile at appropriate intervals while he surreptitiously checked his watch.

But she seemed not to notice, and in reality, Rocco was more than willing to listen in lieu of having to rebuff possible sexual advances—a fact he was more than aware separated him from the Rocco of old who hadn't actually understood the word "rebuff."

Then again, since he'd met Chloe, nothing had been the same.

He hadn't been in the habit of turning down sex before.

He definitely hadn't pined for a woman like some love-sick troubadour or country-western singer.

Nor had he thought about counting the minutes until he saw any certain woman again.

While Sarah Lu declined coffee, he ordered some for himself. His level of interest was beginning to fade as she launched into a long list of her husbands' emotional defects. Not that anyone could fault him for that. Men weren't good about discussing feelings or listening to discussions about feelings. The coffee definitely helped.

She was still marginally awake on the cab ride to her place, but he was able to withstand her advances with deftness and flattery as they traveled through Dallas. But he truly believed in miracles when she passed out just as they reached her apartment building.

Carrying her into the lobby of the building, he gave the doorman a handsome tip to open the door of her apartment and stay with him while he deposited Sarah Lu on her couch. He wanted a witness—just in case.

"Thanks," he said to the man as they took the elevator back down to the lobby. "She had a little too much to drink at dinner."

"Veuve Clicquot?" the doorman said with a grin.

"Lots of it."

"Mansion at Turtle Creek?"

Rocco smiled. "You must be a mind reader."

"You're a real polite young man," the older man said as the elevator came to a stop on the ground floor.

"I'm getting married," Rocco said, the words tumbling out compliments of his obsession and the Veuve Clicquot.

"Congratulations."

"I haven't actually asked her yet. What day is it?" It seemed as though he'd been away from Minneapolis for weeks.

"Monday"—the doorman looked at his watch—"almost Tuesday."

Rocco sighed. "I gotta last 'til Friday." He blew out a breath and looked around. "I suppose the cab left."

"I'll get you one."

Rocco started adding up the minutes until Friday as he waited for his cab.

If you're hooked, you're hooked. He gave in.

TWENTY-FOUR

IT WAS THE LONGEST WEEK OF CHLOE'S life.

Rocco would agree, although for different reasons.

Colin was persistent, determined and unwilling to be deterred. On those evenings when Chloe told him not to come over, he came over anyway and banged on her door until she let him in. It was either that or have the neighbors call the cops, and he wasn't unruly, just wistful and eager and bearing gifts—little things like books and those touchy-feely cards and stuffed teddy bears, bigger things like a barbecue grill because he noticed she didn't have one. It had never occurred to him that she didn't have one for a reason. But she thanked him politely and let him grill steaks for them that turned out really delicious and altered her thinking about barbecue grills. He brought over flowers and eggplants too, putting the first in vases and cooking the second in a ratatouille that was truly fabulous. The boy was talented in more than bartending and bed.

But it didn't seem to matter how talented he was or how solicitous, Chloe couldn't find it in her heart to return his passion in equal measure. Or even in lesser measure. And she was seriously beginning to wonder if there was something wrong with her—what with Sebastian and Colin and other suitors too numerous to recall—that she couldn't seem to get past the good sex to something more meaningful and permanent.

Did she have some emotional blank in her genome band?

Or had she just made some bad choices?

Should she have gone out with more staid, conventional men? "Not in a million years" came to mind when she asked herself that question, but still she wondered. . . .

And she was beginning to feel nervous too, wondering what she was going to say to Colin, how she was going to tell him that she didn't want to see him again. Because she didn't—not really—even with the fabulous sex.

She was worried about how he'd react—whether she'd hurt him long term.

She worried about herself—whether she had the capacity to love or whether these great feelings during sex *were* a kind of love and she just didn't know it.

Although if she was in search of the Holy Grail of love, Rocco—who figured rather largely in her thoughts—couldn't really be considered a candidate in her quest. Even semi-bereft of reason as she seemed to be of late, she wasn't that gullible or disingenuous.

Which brought her back to the same old question.

Was what she felt for Rocco love or something else?

Or didn't she have a clue?

Her friends were no help. Tess kept telling her she was the luckiest woman on earth to have Colin in love with her. Rosie was so involved with Ian and their new puppy that she was living in some zoned-out nirvana where wishes came true, the sun never set and dogs were named Toto. Seriously. They named their puppy Toto.

So Chloe was on her own. Her friends were as clueless as she.

ROCCO WORKED HIS ass off that week, sold tons of product—his new, rather good plan, if he said so himself, having to do with paying off Jim as soon as possible. He worked twenty-hour days on the road, made a series of phone calls back home to an advertiser he knew, made more calls to Mary Beth, who was ecstatic with his sales, made a few too many to Anthony, who finally said, angrily, one night at ten, "Don't call me again. I'll have your stuff by Friday."

Some people were more cranky than others, Rocco cheerfully reflected, hanging up, his mood having lightened considerably as the orders kept coming in, as he began to see some light at the end of the tunnel, as Friday approached.

CHLOE FINALLY TOLD Colin on Thursday morning, after several nights of sleepovers, that she needed some time for herself. "Sweetie, I'm not getting enough sleep to make it through the day. My projects are piling up, and much as I enjoy your company, I need a few days off." She was never good at saying good-bye. She always figured she'd think of something in a few days.

"How many days?" He was lounging on her bed, nude and virile and scowling just a little.

"Two days. Call me Saturday."

"I'll come over Saturday."

"Fine. Come over Saturday." She was such a coward.

"Don't go out with anyone else."

"Hey." She turned from her closet and gave him a look.

"Sorry . . . I'm just jealous as hell."

"I don't want you to be jealous."

"You're going out with someone."

"I'm not going out with anyone, but if I were, I wouldn't have to get permission from you. Understood?"

"Sorry." He rolled off the bed, came over to her, pulled her into his arms and held her for a moment. "I'm really sorry. I have to go now, right?"

"I have to get to work. I have a client coming in at nine."

He brushed a fall of hair from her forehead. "I'm crazy for you."

"You can be crazy for me on Saturday." She just wanted him to go; she wanted to have some time to sort out the chaos in her brain. Mostly, she wanted to meet her client in more than her underwear.

"Saturday," he murmured, dropping a kiss on her cheek and stepping away. He picked up his jeans, slipped them on, grabbed his sandals and shirt and left with a smile and a wave.

Life was less complex at twenty-one, she thought, watching him walk through her bedroom door. He traveled with a pair of jeans and a shirt and lived for the moment.

When had she stopped living that way?

When had she started to think about a future—not in terms of a career or paying off her mortgage or buying a new car . . . but in terms of wanting to be with someone for more than a night or two or ten?

Unfortunately she knew the answer to that question when so many of her other questions went unanswered.

Now if only the man she wanted wasn't engaged to someone else.

*   *   *

WHEN THE PHONE rang just as Robin Williams was finishing his interview on *Leno,* Chloe was still chuckling as she said, "Hello."

"Do you have company?"

Oh my God, oh my God, oh my God, an excited little voice inside her head cried. But a second later, she responded to the gruffness in his voice instead. "I should be asking you that. It's more likely, isn't it?"

"I'm in Chicago."

"So? There are plenty of women in Chicago."

"There's no woman here. I'm alone."

His voice was low, neutral and even then her heart was beating in quadruple-time. *Come over and make love to me, come over and let me touch you, come over so I can chain you to my bed and keep you forever.* "What do you want?" she asked instead.

"You're still mad."

"I'm not mad. I'm realistic. What do you want? Besides a quick lay when you're in the mood and away from your fiancée?"

"That's not what I want. I've been thinking about you. I've been on the road all week, selling product so we can get out from under our financial obligations sooner."

"Good for you. Does that mean getting out from under little Amy too, or does she like the missionary position?"

She could practically hear him count to ten in his head, but she didn't care.

"I already told you nothing's going on."

"I hear she likes black leather and cuffs. I wouldn't think you'd turn that down."

"I don't care what she likes."

"Yeah, yeah, yeah and this is my real hair color."

"I don't want to fight. I didn't call you to fight."

"What the hell *did* you call for?"

"I wanted to hear your voice."

"Pul-eese."

"Even when you're a bitch." Which just added another building block to his fucking tower of love. Now he knew how Waylon Jennings felt.

"You're still not free and clear, babe. Maybe I'll stop being a bitch when I hear those chains snap."

"And maybe I'll tie you up again and make you beg like you did before."

"Fuck you." But a rush, a ripple, a violent spasm of arousal vibrated up her vagina when she remembered what they'd done with the whipped cream; she could feel the flush rising on her cheeks. "I'm going to hang up if you talk like that."

There was something in her voice that gave him hope. "Don't hang up."

"Then, be good." *Oh, God, she shouldn't have said it like that.*

It was amazing how he could recognize the nuances in her voice. "I wish you were here with me."

"I wish a lot of things, but most of them aren't going to happen. Like world peace and equality for women and hair straightener that doesn't leave goop on your hair."

"The Chicago shoreline is all lit up. I'm on the fifteenth floor."

"I don't care about the Chicago shoreline."

"I think I'm in love with you."

"I think your fiancée won't like that." But she was having trouble breathing and all her stupid hopeful dreams came rushing back without regard for harsh, nitty-gritty reality.

"I'm going to straighten all that out when I get back."

"I'm not a virgin in case you hadn't noticed; I don't like to be snowed just for the sake of a lay. Also, in case you hadn't noticed, I can be persuaded to make love to you without a lot of unnecessary lies."

"No lie. Tomorrow when I get back. It's second on my agenda after seeing you."

"Jeez, Rocco, I wish you wouldn't do this to me. Let's not start any of this until—well . . . until—you do whatever you have to do and it's done."

"Do you love me?"

"No." Unless thinking of him every waking minute counted.

"Maybe later you will."

"Don't talk in such a reasonable tone." He made her sound like a petulant child.

"I've had all week to think about this. Hotel rooms are damned empty and cold. It gives one time to reflect."

Now she really felt immature. While he was reflecting, she was sleeping with practically a teenager and whining about it, even. Although she reminded herself that Rocco still had a fiancée. He wasn't completely mature and virtuous and pure. She sighed—because none of that mattered when she thought of him lying all alone in his hotel room. When she wanted more than anything to be there with him. "Sometimes I wish I'd never met you in that elevator. You've really fucked up my life."

"I'm going to fix everything."

She sighed again. "Like Dr. Seuss's fix-it-up chappy?"

"Better. I know how much you like whipped cream. I'll fix some of that too."

Maybe there were times when you just had to go with the flow. Maybe she'd lived her life that way for twenty-seven years and there was no point in changing things now. Maybe she wanted to see him more than she wanted to be right. "A man who knows his way around the kitchen definitely gets points in my book."

"How about a man who knows his way around your sunporch?"

"He gets double points."

He heard the smile in her voice.

"And just for the record, you didn't actually tie me up. I don't like to be tied up. I wouldn't let anyone do that."

"I know." Her wrists had been tied for maybe twenty seconds with a pink ribbon before he'd seen that look in her eyes and untied it.

She wanted to separate herself from Miss Handcuffs and Black Leather. Call her bitchy. Call her jealous as hell. Call her so messed up with wanting him she found herself saying, "How big is your bed?" Like it mattered when he was four hundred miles away.

He laughed. "Too damned big without you. Come closer."

"You come here."

"Have you moved the hassock yet?"

She almost didn't answer; she shouldn't have answered. It was just going to make her wanting him go off the charts. "No."

"Perfect."

"It's not perfect."

"I thought it was. I thought it was about as near to heaven as I'd ever been."

Silence. A lengthening silence. He was all set to apologize.

"Maybe it was," she softly said, unable to lie about something so fine.

"No maybe," he said as softly. "I remember. You were shaking; we both were."

"Don't. Okay? Are you still dressed?" Lust was better, easier—safer. The rest was too hard, unfathomable, bitter and sad.

Until he had his life back on track, he was more than willing to play instead of pay. He understood. "Uh-uh, no clothes," he said in a deep, husky murmur. "I'm sitting on the hassock in the middle of your sunporch, waiting for you to come closer."

"I didn't invite you in."

"Yeah, you did. You left your shoes on the stairs and your dress in the hallway and from where I'm sitting, you look inviting as hell."

"Maybe you misunderstood."

"I don't think so. The words 'come fuck me' got my attention."

"So you got a big hard-on."

"It usually works that way. If you come closer, I might let you touch it."

"If I come closer, I'll be doing more than that."

"If I let you."

"You're not the boss."

"Sometimes I am. Are you coming?" he whispered.

"What if I want to give orders?"

"Maybe you can—later . . . after we see how you like this whipped cream someone left here. After I take off that thong that's barely covering your hot little pussy. Come here, babe . . . let's try out this cream . . ."

She remembered everything—every touch, every whisper, every scent and taste that day on the sunporch. Her body remembered too. She was wet and aching—no longer sure she was angry with him. "I shouldn't let you."

She hadn't said that, then. "Just come a little closer—here, take my hand," he whispered. "That's a good girl,

that's the way . . . you're almost here—here . . . stand between my legs so I can reach you. And we don't need this
thong."

She could practically feel it slide down her legs, the
throbbing deep inside her a hard steady rhythm, her skin
so heated, the air felt cool. "I want to touch you," she
breathed.

"Don't worry—you'll be touching me in just a little
while. We don't want to waste this whipped cream, now, do
we? Bend over a little so I can put a dab on your nipples—
that's the way—can you feel it? Is it cool? Your nipples are
really hard. Does that mean you're ready for cock? Answer
me, darling," he whispered, "or you can't have it."

"Yes, yes . . . oh, God, yes . . ." She was panting, her eyes
shut, feeling as though she were teetering on the brink.

"Bend over a little more. I can't quite reach your nipples
with my mouth—umm . . . perfect, sweet when I lick it.
Give me the other. Put it in my mouth. Can you feel me
lick you? Can you feel me holding your breasts—they're
soft and cushiony and really big. The more to eat, right,"
he purred. "Like your pussy. Bring it closer—so I can fill
it with cream . . . here we go—one dollop—all the way up
. . . another—stand still or I can't get it far enough in.
Stand still, darling," he said more sternly. "I want to eat
more than two spoonfuls. Hey, hey . . . don't come yet, Jesus . . ."

"I'm sorry," she whispered, gasping.

"Then we'll just have to start all over again," he said,
half softly, half firmly, like the most tolerant of masters.
"And we'll just keep doing it until you get it right . . ."

"Don't say that," she breathed, holding her hand between
her legs as though she could protect herself from wanting
what she shouldn't have.

"I've barely started," he said, his voice mild, constrained.

"There's a big bowl of whipped cream to deal with and I haven't even begun to think about seeing if I fit inside you—or how far I fit inside you—whether you can take me all."

"Hurry home, hurry, hurry, hurry home—please, please, *please* . . ."

"I'll be home in the morning. Sleep tight."

And then he hung up as though he wasn't leaving her frantic.

As though he were made of ice.

As though it really had been just a game.

She screamed in frustration—the echo of her cry pricking up the ears of Mrs. Gregorich's cat sitting on Mrs. Gregorich's front porch railing. And then she rolled over, jerked open the drawer of her bedside table and pulled out her vibrator.

Rocco didn't dare scream in his hotel room with the heavy security nowadays, but he would have liked to. Just like he would have liked to keep talking to Chloe if he wasn't afraid he'd lose his mind.

And he didn't need an appliance when he had two strong hands.

But he swore under his breath at the end because he wanted more.

He wanted her.

TWENTY-FIVE

FRIDAY MORNING STARTED OUT TO BE A pretty fine day. Chloe had actually slept eight hours the night before—orgasms were supremely relaxing. It helped that Rocco had said he was coming home. Not that she expected a Cinderella-story happy ending tied with a bow, but he'd sounded serious about making things work. Yesss and thank you God and she was keeping her fingers crossed.

The sun was shining as though in harmony with her mood, her web site for the car dealership was ninety-nine percent finished and when she had the little dancing cartoon bears singing their jingle, it *would* be done.

She even ate breakfast as would a mature woman concerned with her health and nutrition. Although Count Chocula perhaps didn't count toward any actual food group. But the milk did.

She'd also decided last night in a kind of post-orgasmic

calm that she was getting too stressed-out about men. Colin, Rocco or whomever—none of them should unduly disrupt her life. Maybe the two chapters she'd read in the Zen book were rubbing off. She hoped Rocco would be a part of her life, but she'd never allowed a man to complicate her existence in the past and she didn't want to begin now.

A shame she hadn't extended that decision to include their fiancées because Amy Thiebaud was standing at her office door when she arrived downstairs.

"Your office hours say ten. It's after ten," Amy said pettishly.

"Feel free to leave." And for a second Chloe debated leaving herself, her Zen calm evaporating on the spot. But she refused to look cowardly in front of this woman. She didn't know why. It was simply one of those unassailable facts.

"I have a few things to say to you before I do that."

That blue-eyed glare was not a pretty sight, Chloe reflected, punching the numbers on her lock. Should she open the door, slip inside, quickly shut it again and lock it? A fleeting thought, instantly rejected when Amy said, "What a tiny little office. But I suppose you can't afford anything else."

"My bed's pretty small too, but Rocco doesn't seem to mind," Chloe retorted, because she liked her office and whether Amy Thiebaud did or not was irrelevant to just about everything in her life—or in the universe for that matter. She pushed the door open and walked in.

"He probably was drunk or wanted to see if you had any pierced body parts," the heiress said in her best put-someone-in-their-place tone of voice as she followed Chloe in.

If malicious intent was contagious, Amy Thiebaud would be the Typhoid Mary of the affliction, Chloe thought. But the last thing she wanted was to prolong this encounter by trading insults. Her list of grievances was long, and she didn't want to waste a week of her time. "If you came here to say something, say it and get the hell out. You're blotting out my sunshine."

"I came here to this shabby little place," Amy said with a disdainful glance about, "to let you know that my fiancé is not available to sluts like you."

"Shouldn't you be telling Rocco this? He's the one shopping around."

"You don't understand. I'm telling you for your own good. I can hurt you, and I will."

"You mean like *Fatal Attraction* in reverse? This isn't Hollywood, if you haven't noticed."

"You're a real smart-ass, aren't you?"

"Not smart enough to wear pearls in the morning, but what the hell, we're not all fashionistas." And she supposed pearls went with that sleek pink suit.

"Just don't sleep with Rocco again. I'm only going to warn you once."

"Come on," Chloe murmured. "This is ridiculous. If you don't want your boyfriend to sleep around, talk to him, not me. Now, if you don't mind, I'm busy."

"My father has considerable influence in this town. I can see that your business is shut down."

"No, you can't." But Amy's expression was a little scary and Minneapolis wasn't that big a town. In fact, when it came to the business community, it was a relatively small town.

"Try me."

Her certainty was even more scary. "Thanks for the warning. Shut the door when you leave." Never show fear. That was her motto.

"Listen, you mouthy little bitch, just stay away from him. I mean it. I don't care what kind of lies he's been telling you, but he's mine. He's always been mine regard-less of the sluts who've thrown themselves at him. I have my wedding dress picked out and the country club is booked for the reception, so stay the hell out of my way."

Chloe thought of all that Rocco had said last night. God, was that only last night? "His story's real different from yours. I talked to him last night."

"I don't care if you screwed him last night; he's marrying me."

Such finality, such indifference to Rocco's extracurricular activities. Maybe Amy was more European, more sophis-ticated—certainly richer. Maybe her father had a wife and a mistress and two families like that French premier who'd died a few years ago. The one that had a little out-of-the-ordinary state funeral. "Well, congratulations, then. I'll tell Rocco I'm not interested in marrying him." Not that he'd actually suggested marriage, but he'd said he'd loved her—she was allowed a body blow.

"You stupid cow. You didn't actually believe him? You did." Amy's smile was so arch the Romans could have built an aqueduct on it. "I suppose he said he only had to break up with me first."

Along with a couple hundred other lies, Chloe reflected, forcing herself to show no emotion. Damn she was dumb. And Rocco had used the same smooth talk so many times, he had it down pat. Fucker. "If you come back here again, I'll call the cops," Chloe said. "Get the hell out." There was no way she had to deal with Rocco's fiancée. Or any more shit from him. "I don't want to sound dramatic, but if you're not gone on the count of three, I'm picking up the phone and calling the cops." She was amazed at how calm she sounded—like a zombie—like she felt. Dead inside.

"No need for that, darling," Amy drawled, as though she could smell defeat in the air. "And tell Rocco I stopped by if you wish. He won't bat an eyelash." Turning away, Amy swept Chloe's flat-screen monitor off her desk with a swipe of her hand. "Oh, dear, how clumsy of me," she purred, stepping over the broken glass as she walked out of the office. "I hope you have insurance."

Shit. Rocco owed her a new monitor. Not that she was likely to collect. His girlfriend looked as though she was going to be keeping a close watch on him. And in her new frame of mind, she didn't want the grief. She was finished with Rocco and his cheating heart. In fact, all the men in her life were getting to be too high-maintenance. She glanced at the mess on the floor and then at the clock. Almost ten-thirty. A ray of sunlight shining through her plateglass windows led her eye outside, reminding her of the beauty of the day.

Screw it. The dancing bears could wait until Monday. So could the insurance man.

She was getting out of town, escaping all her problems like any well-adjusted, discerning, mature adult would do when faced with the train wreck of their life.

Rocco was never going to call again. Nor did she want him to, considering his truckload of lies.

Colin would be calling too much and she was relatively sure she didn't care to take on the role of girlfriend to a college student who said "cool" a lot.

As for sex. She always had her vibrator. And electrical appliances were blessedly undemanding.

So she had only to leave a message for Colin, canceling their Saturday night. She conveniently left a voicemail for him at Chino's because he wouldn't be in to work before noon thus eliminating pointless argument.

It took her less than ten minutes to pack an overnight bag, leave a message for Tess and Rosie and hit the open road. She had no idea where she was going other than up north where everyone went on the weekend. She'd find a motel or bed and breakfast somewhere when she felt like stopping.

And right now, she didn't feel like stopping until she was far away from any and all men currently messing with her brain.

She'd meditate, put some balance back in her life.

She'd read something philosophical and enlightening.

She'd clear her mind of all emotional disorder.

Or then again, maybe she'd get a good bottle of wine, some videos and cookies and chips and lie in bed and indulge in said items until she had to drive back home on Sunday.

TWENTY-SIX

ROCCO HAD CHANGED HIS FLIGHT TO AN earlier one and arrived in the cities from Chicago at eleven-thirty—just prior to the time Colin got his message from Chloe at work.

The men's trajectories converged on Chloe's place within seconds of each other.

Colin had arrived first and was pounding on Chloe's door, as if her message hadn't said she was going out of town but into seclusion at home. Perhaps it was more a reaction to his frustration than a rational impulse.

Rocco recognized the pickup truck with the motorcycle in back when he pulled up to the curb. And suffice it to say, his reaction was no more rational than Colin's.

He came out of his car as though the building was on fire, strode up to Colin, who was so engaged in his pounding the door down that he'd not noticed Rocco's arrival, and tapped him on the shoulder. Hard.

Colin spun around. "What the fuck are you doing?"

"I could ask you the same thing." Rocco's glare matched Colin's growl.

"None of your damned business."

"If she's not answering, she must not be home."

"Maybe, maybe not."

"You do this often?"

"What's it to you?"

"I'm a friend of hers."

Rocco's tone brought a belligerent gleam to Colin's eyes. "How friendly a friend?"

It was Rocco's turn to say, "What's it to you?"

The two men measured each other with sulky looks, and then Colin said with a lovesick sigh, "She was supposed to go out with me tomorrow."

"Supposed to?" Rocco was surprised he was able to keep his tone so mild.

Colin sighed again. "She left me a message at work saying she was going out of town."

Rocco felt an immoderate relief that Chloe wouldn't be going out with this young man with tattoos and a Chino's ID hanging round his neck. "Should you be working?"

"Screw you."

"Did she say where she was going?"

"I wouldn't tell you if I knew."

He obviously didn't know. Another reason for relief—along with a small niggling fear. He'd come home early because she'd asked him to last night. So why was she gone?

"Jesus God, I'm just crazy about her," Colin murmured, unable to restrain his unhappiness, his heartache spilling over. "I suppose she's going out with you too."

Rocco didn't know if going out was the right term.

Fucking their brains out, maybe, but he didn't think this young man would appreciate such frankness. "Did Chloe say when she was coming back—where she was going?"

Colin shook his head, sighed a long wafting sigh and then looked up as though struck by a sudden thought. "Wanna go have a beer and talk about her?"

No matter how lovesick the sentiment, Rocco understood perfectly. "Louie's is just around the corner. I'll buy."

Colin looked at the well-dressed man and frowned. "I can buy."

"We'll take turns," Rocco replied diplomatically.

They walked in silence to the small neighborhood bar that opened at eight in the morning for the regulars who needed that first eye-opener before breakfast. Louie was behind the bar where he'd been for nearly fifty years, setting them up for a few of his customers who were leaning their elbows on the century-old bar. Four old codgers were playing cards at the table in the window and an elderly couple in one of the booths was having their lunch with a couple of beers.

They all looked up when Rocco and Colin walked in.

"Afternoon, fellows," Louie said. "What can I do you for?"

Rocco was going to ask what their choices in beer were, but decided against it. He looked at Colin.

"A tap." He shoved his hand in his jean pocket and pulled out some crumpled bills.

"Same here," Rocco said, taking a seat in the first booth and loosening his tie.

Colin brought them two tap beers, set them down on the scarred surface of the booth table and slid into the seat opposite Rocco. Lifting his glass, he said, "To Chloe."

Rocco raised his glass and nodded.

Colin drained his beer and set the empty glass on the table.

A challenge any man would recognize.

Rocco did the same and waved at Louie for two more.

In earlier centuries, they might have saddled their destriers, taken up their lances and charged each other, or perhaps met at dawn for a duel. This wasn't a contest to the death, but it was confrontational, and as so often in the past, it was over a woman.

Men were like that.

Possessive.

Quick to appropriate territory.

Unwilling to relinquish it.

"She's unbelievable," Colin softly said, lifting his refilled glass in both praise and challenge.

"Yeah."

Two glasses were drained and refilled.

"How long have you known her?" Rocco asked, watching Colin closely for any minute clue his words might not reveal.

"A week."

Colin's answer hit him like a jolt. He knew that instant covetous feeling.

Colin dipped his head. "How about you?"

"Two weeks."

"Fuck."

"Yeah."

Both men drank down their beers, consumed with jealousy.

Louie was waved over, Rocco gave him a fifty, said, "Keep them coming," and gazed at Colin with the piercing scrutiny of a forensic scientist. "How old are you?"

"What the fuck's the difference? How old are you?"

"Older than you."

"Then that makes me younger than you." The beer was beginning to work its wonders.

Rocco sighed. "You're right. It doesn't matter. She goes out with everyone."

"Fucking-A and that's the problem."

"Our problem. Not hers."

"I'm not in the mood to be reasonable."

Rocco thought about it for a minute. "Me either."

"I'll arm wrestle you for her."

"I'm not sure she'd acknowledge the winner."

"Are you saying you won't?"

"No, I'm not saying that."

"What *are* you saying?"

Rocco slipped off his suit jacket, rolled up his shirt sleeves, set his elbow on the table and looked Colin square in the eye. "Let's say loser backs off."

Some things never change—flinging down the gauntlet has been the male equivalent of problem solving since time immemorial. On the current world stage, nuclear weapons were involved; here at Louie's, a less cataclysmic option was operating.

Colin moved the beer glasses out of the way and took his position, flexing his fingers once or twice to limber up.

The men carefully grasped each other's hands, adjusting their grips.

"Someone has to give the signal," Colin murmured.

"Hey, Louie," Rocco shouted. "Come over and give us the go-ahead."

Louie was thin and wiry; he didn't look as though he drank any of his beer or ate any of his greasy grill food. He rarely smiled, talked less, but his drinks were the best price for name brands in town, so he'd always made a good living even though he lacked personal charisma.

He tipped his head as he arrived at the booth. "Ready?"
Both men nodded.

He looked at Rocco, then at Colin, raised his hand, held
it upright for a three count, then dropped it and walked
back to the bar.

Both men were powerful, well-muscled, their biceps
bulging as they strained for advantage in that first initial
thrust.

Colin's teeth were gritted and he was breathing hard after
fifteen seconds, the tattoos on his arm shifting as he threw
all his weight into maintaining his position.

Rocco was holding steady, looking for that first small
muscle of his opponent's to inadvertently disengage. A thin
sheen of sweat broke out on his forehead as he held firm.

Twenty seconds.

Neither man had fluctuated from center.

Rocco's nostrils flared.

Colin grunted.

Thirty seconds.

Then it happened, that minute recoil when a muscle
yielded for a fraction of a second.

Rocco shoved hard and Colin's arm smacked into the
tabletop.

"Two out of three," Colin growled, his jaw set.

"That's it, then. Loser backs off."

"Yeah, yeah." Colin scowled. "Put it up." He set his
elbow on the table again.

"You give the go this time. Louie isn't too sociable."
Rocco got into position.

The men grasped each other's hand, Colin said, "Go,"
and Rocco slammed Colin's arm down on the table.

He wasn't in the mood to fuck around—or lose to Colin.
He particularly wasn't in the mood to waste any more time

when he'd just thought of a way to find out where Chloe might have gone. He was sliding out of the booth before Colin had finished swearing.

And he was out the door and running two seconds later.

TWENTY-SEVEN

ROCCO WOULD HAVE LIKED TO KNOW what had happened between Chloe's plea for him to come home and her subsequent disappearance, but first things first. He had to find her.

It's not all that easy to find a phone book anymore. They're all ripped off from the phone booths and bars, even restaurants. He found one at the Super America gas station on Central, discovered there were twenty-two Chisholms in the phone book; four of those had addresses that could be Chloe's parents. It would have helped if he knew her parents' names, but he didn't. It would have helped if he knew someone they knew, but he didn't. It would have helped if everyone wasn't so freaked out with serial killers and child molesters and harassing telemarketers so a phone call from a stranger was cause to call the cops.

Mostly, it would have helped if it wasn't a workday with few people at home. Which is how phone calls one and two turned out. Three hung up on him, so that was a problem. He changed his story a little for phone call number four, deciding to call himself a friend from college.

Chloe's mother answered on the fifth ring because she was just coming in from the garage with groceries.

Rocco had been just about ready to hang up.

She listened politely to his story. In her line of work she'd even seen a serial killer once, so she wasn't as freaked as most people who only read about the problem people in the papers. But when he was finished with his explanation of why he was looking for Chloe, Lizzie said, "Are you the Rocco who's engaged?"

It wasn't a good start, but he was desperate, so he said, "Yes and no, let me explain."

Maybe it helped that Lizzie had been dealing with other people's problems for years. Maybe it helped that the young man sounded so desperate and his explanation was succinct but telling. Perhaps the fact that Gracie had given her a heads-up on what appeared to be Chloe's first real passion—because anyone who knew Chloe had discounted Sebastian despite the fact that she had lived with him—tipped the scales in Rocco's favor. "She never tells me anything, but if I were to guess where she's gone, I'd say the North Shore. She likes the cabins right on the lakeshore. Which isn't very helpful, I realize, with a zillion resorts, but that's all I can suggest." She thought of saying, *Maybe you should disengage yourself, first,* but decided she wasn't in a position to tell this stranger what to do. Although, she intended to put her two-cents worth in to Chloe once she returned. Engaged or semiengaged men did not make the best boyfriends.

Rocco thanked her profusely, said something cryptic about meeting her soon and hung up.

Lizzie immediately called Grace, for despite their differences of opinion on issues of age and dating, politics, opera, books and the occasional artist, they shared a love of Chloe. "He called," Lizzie said.

Grace didn't need to ask who. The ladies discussed Rocco's conversation in great detail.

A S I T HAPPENED, Chloe wasn't on the North Shore. She'd driven up 94 and, on reaching Alexandria, decided to look up an old friend from college who'd married another friend of hers and settled back in their hometown. She'd sort of lost touch with them, because they'd picked up on small-town life, had three children and didn't do much clubbing anymore. Barry had joined his father's law firm, Lia had become a wife and mother, and even as she exited the freeway Chloe wondered why she was stopping.

She knew *why* she was stopping. She'd been overcome with an urge to see Lia's babies. But what she didn't understand was the underlying urgent motivation when babies had always seemed infinitely more interesting from a distance.

It was all Rocco's fault, of course, like everything else that was going wrong with her previously self-indulgent, amusing, vastly contented life. And even Amy's visit that morning hadn't been sufficiently dampening to her inexplicable compulsion. Now she wanted to see babies and actually hold babies and, God help her, maybe even *have* a baby—specifically with a person who shall remain nameless. There was really no accounting for the maternal instinct, she realized. Even bitchy Amy hadn't been able to quash it.

She took a deep breath, because even thinking about something so outre was causing her pulse rate to accelerate dangerously. Pulling over to the shoulder, she talked to herself very seriously for a moment, questioning the raving delirium that had overtaken her somewhere between Elk River and the Alexandria exit. But when a police car drove by very slowly and the officer stared at her with more than a little scrutiny, she quickly put her car into gear and pulled back onto the road.

If she was going to do any further soul-searching, the Holiday station up ahead would be a much safer venue. But her demented baby craving persisted, through two small bags of salt-and-vinegar chips—really nowadays a bag held no more than three chips, barely a mouthful—a Coke to wash down those three chips and an ice cream bar—again, very small—to balance off the saltiness. Then truly, as though the hand of God had intervened, Barry drove by in a smart black BMW convertible that had caught her eye before she saw him. *Barry*. Can you imagine? There was no longer any question whether she should go or stay when divine intervention was involved.

But he accelerated away from the red light like a sixteen-year-old driver trying to impress his girlfriend and was out of sight before she had maneuvered through the cars at the gas pumps. Parking her car again, she called information on her cell phone and dialed Lia.

A small note of panic underlay Lia's invitation to stop by, but the screaming children in the background no doubt contributed to that nuanced tone. She had said, "You're in *town*?" in a kind of high-pitched shock, like the Russian sentries might have said on first seeing the charge of the Light Brigade coming across that valley near Sebastopol. Chloe hoped her visit went better than that charge.

But she was just slightly tense as she pulled up to the large brick colonial house with a curved driveway up to the front door that was decorated with a Smith and Hawken wreath of dried hydrangeas and surrounded by a variety of brightly colored plastic wheeled vehicles for children. And she sat in her car for a moment after turning off the ignition, not sure she wished to go in.

But Lia opened the door just then and waved; in one arm she held a plump, hairless baby. A toddler of indeterminate sex clutched one leg and a thumb-sucking little girl in braids scowled on her other side. My God, had it been that long since she'd seen Lia? That little girl looked old enough for school.

She had to go in, of course. She'd been seen.

Chloe almost turned and ran, though, when the scowling little girl threw her doll at her as she approached. Lia said something snappish, curtailing the imminent discharge of the dart gun her daughter held in her other hand, and added, in a more artful, hostessy tone, "You know children—do come in, Chloe. It seems ages since I've seen you."

The baby cooed just then, held out her little pudgy arms toward Chloe and only someone with a heart of stone could have resisted. Chloe only winced slightly as she picked up the baby and felt the drool dribble down the front of her silk shirt.

And Lia was genuinely pleased to see her, which partially alleviated the loss of her favorite Marc Jacobs silk shirt that she'd bought on sale after it had been marked down three times.

They reminisced about their college days over coffee, the baby—it turned out to be a girl—absolutely perfect, just sitting on Chloe's lap and cooing like a little bird. The older children—the toddler was a boy, she discovered when Lia addressed him as Michael (Lia had always hated her ethnic-sounding name)—were less adorable—screaming and throwing things until their mother had to placate them with ice cream and cookies. Which really worked very well; they sat at their little painted table on their little painted chairs that Lia had bought in New York at some adorable shop and ate their ice cream and cookies with considerable mess, but quietly. Lia said she had a housekeeper so the mess wasn't an issue. And the quiet *was* very nice.

Chloe put Lia's clever way of maintaining order with ice cream into her memory bank for future reference.

They exchanged information about their lives in edited versions, neither quite willing after six years to be completely candid. But Lia did say, once, that she might come down and spend some time with Chloe. She missed the clubs.

And Chloe said in an offhand way that she'd been thinking about having a baby someday . . . in the very distant future, she'd quickly added. And the baby had cooed again, as though encouraging her, and Lia had spoiled it all by saying, "I'd think about it if I were you."

It wasn't that she was unhappy, she quickly added, but one lost some of one's identity, she pointed out. She was thinking about going back into teaching once the baby was weaned.

Chloe couldn't say that she was surprised. Lia had never struck her as someone who adored children, although she supposed everyone adored their *own* children. But Lia had always talked of traveling the world and writing for *National Geographic* or something. Her degree was in anthropology and she'd interned with Jane Goodall for a semester. Chloe couldn't imagine living in the jungle anywhere, but then she didn't like being bitten by bugs that could kill you. But Lia had loved every minute of it. And now she was in a brick colonial in Alexandria juggling three children instead of chimpanzees . . . *do not even go there*, Chloe's inner voice urged.

When the two older children were full or bored or both, they began throwing their ice cream. Another handy ref-

erence for the future: children had a short attention span.
When a splat of spumoni ice cream joined the drool on her
shirt, Chloe said with complete dishonesty, although she
seriously tried to think of something less untrue, "I'd better
go or I won't reach Brainerd by nightfall." Which then
meant she had to make up further lies about meeting someone at a specific resort so she had to leave right that very
moment.

But her visit had been useful. Her own life looked less
stressful—very much less. And if her love life wasn't completely to her liking, at least she didn't have the
responsibility for anyone but herself. She was feeling, really . . . much more optimistic and heartened. She was almost back to her old standby about fish in the sea.

Travel was indeed enlightening. Whoever had coined the
phrase was quite insightful. She was truly grateful for what
she had and what she didn't have—in this case, three children under age five.

She found a lovely cabin at a lovely resort on Gull Lake,
ordered a great many items from the room-service menu
and lay back on the bed with the remote control in her
hand, counting the blessings of her solitude.

Screw Rocco.

Screw Colin.

Double screw little Amy and her threats.

She was free and untrammeled, the wine was very good—
she took another sip—and *The Forsyte Saga* was on cable . . .
all five episodes. She'd even remembered to bring her vibrator. So when that actor who played the part of Soames
Forsyte with so much intensity and utter constraint began
to get to her libido, she could enjoy his really fantastic,
masterful maleness in her own fashion.

TWENTY-EIGHT

 BEFORE ROCCO COULD THINK ABOUT DRIV-
ing up to the north shore, he had several stops to
make—one significant and some merely essential.

The most serious was going to take every ounce of cour-
age he possessed and perhaps a good amount of brash stupidity as well. But he was going to do it. He'd made that
decision. He was going for broke.

That's not to say he wasn't apprehensive as hell as he
walked into Jim Thiebaud's office. The term cold feet took
on pertinent meaning; he had to overcome the urge to flee
by sheer will.

"Come in, come in," Jim cried, rising from his chair and
moving around his desk to greet Rocco. "Tell me about
your trip. Mary Beth's ecstatic about the numbers."

The large office overlooking the Mississippi River
seemed larger today, ominous in its size, like crossing two

football fields, Rocco thought, each step bringing him closer to disaster.

The two men met near the model of Jim's latest townhouse and green-acres development and shook hands.

"Come on, sit down." Jim waved Rocco into a chair. "A drink? Some good single malt?"

"No thanks." Rocco took a seat, feeling tense and unsure. But then, he had a lot to lose.

"So tell me about the orders. You were stupendous, I hear."

Rocco cleared his throat, then cleared it again, unable to find his voice. "I've something to ask you first," he finally said.

"Ask away. We're friends." Jim smiled, conscious of Rocco's discomfort. "Look, Rocco, I've known you all your life. You can say anything to me."

Rocco almost changed his mind. He thought of Mary Beth and her wanting a baby, of Anthony and his family, and wondered if he was being unreasonably selfish. Then he reminded himself that if need be—if Jim went apeshit, he'd become the sacrificial lamb. Not a role he'd ever considered before, but on the other hand, there'd never been so much money at stake before, nor so many people's lives.

And sometimes you did what you had to do.

But not before that last Hail Mary pass.

He took a breath. "It's about Amy."

"Is something wrong?"

"There could be. It depends."

"Rocco, obviously something's up. You look like you did the time you and Steve took my truck when you were kids and put it in the ditch out on the farm." He smiled again. "Just tell me. Whatever it is, we'll deal with it."

Rocco tried to smile back but couldn't, not certain what he was doing was right, not sure his willingness to be sac-

rificial would ultimately placate Jim if he were to take offense. "Okay, here goes," he said quickly, plunging forward.
"I don't know what Amy's been telling you, but we're not
engaged. In fact, I haven't taken her out for over a year and
when we did go out"—he half-lifted his hands—"it was
only a few times. I don't want her angry with me. I don't
want you and Marcy angry with me. But, the thing is"—
Rocco shifted in his chair—"the thing is," he said again on
a long, low exhalation, "I want to marry someone else. And
that's so weird I can't even explain it to myself."

"You've told Amy this?"

"I've tried, but she doesn't always listen. I have no idea
where she got the idea we were engaged, but in case I
missed something somewhere and she's part of our deal,
well"—he took a deep breath—"then, I guess"—another
deep breath—"she'll have to be part of our deal."

"You'd marry her, you mean?"

Rocco gripped the chair arms, every muscle in his body
tensed for flight. But he didn't flee, he said instead, terse
and low, "We can't afford to lose your financing. Anthony
would have a heart attack if he even knew I was talking to
you about this. He's nervous as hell about losing his house
with his family and all. Sylvie's expecting again—it's all
pretty dicey . . . although I was thinking if I stayed on the
road selling for the next six months, maybe we could pay
you back sooner, say—a third of what we owe you in six
months and the rest in two more six-month installments."

Jim hadn't moved, not an eyelash, not a finger, not a
flicker of emotion betrayed his thoughts. "Let me get this
straight. Amy says you're engaged. You say you're not. But
if I'm thinking about jerking my financing, you'll marry
her?"

Rocco's grip on the chair arms turned white-knuckled.
"I don't know. I thought I could." He looked out the win-

dow, as though some solution would appear streaming out behind a small plane in little puffs of skywriting smoke. But the sky was empty of advice. "It seemed like a semi-reasonable solution when I walked in here," he said, while every nerve and cell in his brain was screaming NO! "But, now"—he suddenly shook his head—"no . . . I can't."

"I'm gratified to hear it," Jim said with a faint smile.

"Really?" Rocco felt like the guy in those old grainy black-and-white movies strapped in the electric chair who gets the governor's last-minute reprieve. But his relief was short-lived, quickly replaced by renewed apprehension. "What about your financing?" he asked, not sure he wanted to hear the answer.

"Look," Jim said, gruffly, "I didn't decide to put money into your company just for the hell of it. I expect to make a profit on my investment. So, this isn't about Amy. Although, don't get me wrong, she's going to be disappointed. Marcy and I will be too." Jim half-smiled. "I would have liked you for a son-in-law. But this is business, Rocco." His voice suddenly took on an edge Rocco had never heard before. "I don't put my money in start-up ventures on a whim. I'll get a good return on my investment or know the reason why. Is that clear?"

"Yes, sir."

"Good. Just so we don't have any misunderstandings."

The office shrunk back to normal—only half a football field. "I'm really sorry about—well . . . all the rest—how everything got out of hand."

Jim's gaze was warm once again, familiar. "What the hell—we can be business partners anyway. Although you know I do have to talk to Amy about this. Hear her side of the story." He smiled. "She can be a little high-strung and demanding at times. Hell, I can be too . . . and maybe Marcy and I have been a little too indulgent. But she can be a sweet kid. And I'm her dad. You see my point."

"Yes, sir. Of course." Shit. As if the words "sweet" and "Amy" were within missile range of each other. He knew it had been going too damned easy.

"Now, tell me about this woman who's swept you off your feet," Jim went on as though he'd not just put the Holy Toledo fear of God into Rocco. "I hope she's not going to take your mind off our business."

"No, sir. I'm pretty focused." He took a deep breath, debating how much or how little to say. Then he went with his what-the-hell-more-did-he-have-to-lose play. "But Chloe's something else. If I knew what it was about her that was rocking my world, I could put it into words. Let's just say, I was willing to take a real chance to keep her."

Jim smiled. "I know the feeling. It's pretty much put me where I am today. I wish you the best."

But there was that caveat Jim hadn't mentioned—his talk with Amy. "Thank you, sir." Rocco wasn't about to open any can of worms when he'd gotten his conditional okay, though. "I appreciate your understanding," he said.

TWENTY-NINE

"YOU DID *WHAT?*" IF EYEBALLS COULD actually spring out of people's heads like they did in cartoons, Anthony's eyeballs would have hit the wall. "You fucker!"

"It all worked out. Calm down. Everything's copacetic." Okay, he was lying a little, but it was mostly good—save for the loose cannon Amy.

"You're in love and I almost lose my fucking house! I should nail your cock to the fucking wall!"

"Jeez, relax. No one's losing anything." Rocco was the youngest in the family. He was used to being hollered at and told what to do. He was pretty much immune. He was also more of a gambler than his brother. "Jim's happy as a clam. He wished me the best with Chloe. He wouldn't say that unless he was cool with everything. Have you got those two samples for me?"

"The way I feel right now, I'd rather throw them down the drain! It would serve you right, asshole!"

"Come on. Lighten up." Rocco was counting on Jim's business sense trumping Amy's lies. "Look at it this way. None of us will have to see Amy at our meetings anymore. She'll have to find someone else to harass."

"She could still come." Anthony wasn't in the mood to be mollified.

"She won't, believe me. She was always bored as hell."

"She's still going to want to be in the ads."

"Mary Beth can take care of that."

"Take care of what?" Mary Beth walked into their small lab.

"Tell her what you did, dipshit. How you almost made us all into street people because you're in *luuuuv*."

"I would have married Amy. I told Jim that. I was going to sacrifice myself for your stupid house."

"*My* stupid house? And maybe this stupid business and all the stupid employees we have working for us and your and Beth's stupid houses too!" Anthony snapped. "I could fucking kill you."

Mary Beth calmly took a seat. Her brothers regularly disagreed, but their arguments were always short-lived. "You talked to Jim?"

"Yeah. And everything came up roses." So he had his fingers crossed against the lab table; anyone would. "I don't know why Anthony's going nuts. Jim's still onboard. I don't have to pretend to be engaged to Amy. I don't have to marry her, and if Anthony will get over his tantrum, I'd like to get those perfume samples he made for me so I can decide which one I want. Sam at McGillicutty is doing an ad for me."

"Really, no repercussions at all?" His sister watched him closely.

"No, I swear. Jim's interested in our company as an investment. He doesn't require any pound of flesh."

Mary Beth smiled. "Good, because I didn't have any luck with financing."

For a flashing moment Rocco experienced a terrible sinking feeling, like suffering an aftershock after you've survived the worst earthquake of the century. He braced himself on the counter top. "Holy shit." He wasn't able to suppress his outburst. Maybe he'd better go to church and pray this week.

"No kidding," Anthony said curtly. "I hope like hell she's worth it. Here's your fucking perfume." Scowling, he shoved two small vials across the white counter top toward Rocco and stalked out of the lab.

"He's just worried about his family," Mary Beth murmured.

"I know. In hindsight, it's pretty scary just thinking about worst-case scenario. I probably was too rash." Rocco hoped like hell not.

His sister shrugged. "It wasn't as though you didn't know Jim. He's always been reasonable. And the possibility of being married to Amy for the rest of your life might have caused anyone to take a few risks."

"Thanks. But, I'm feeling a little shell-shocked."

"Try out the perfumes—see which one you like. I like the first one. The second is a little too citrusy for my taste."

Mary Beth had always been the voice of reason in a family of hot-tempered people. "Let's see," Rocco said, picking up a vial, grateful for her diversion. He could feel his pulse rate lessen as he uncorked the first sample. Holding it under his nose, he inhaled a heady mixture of attar of rose and jasmine with a soft underlay of lily of the valley and an unmistakable let's-get-naked touch of musk and bourbon vanilla. He looked up and nodded. "Perfect."

"I like the hint of lily of the valley. It's playful in contrast to the more potent, sensual scents. Try the other one."

Rocco tested the second sample and then smelled it again. "Light, sweet, you can smell the freesia, but it doesn't remind me of passion."

"It's a day fragrance—delicate, with a transparent lemony base . . . for work or shopping."

"Let's keep it, though. It's good. But I want this one." He smiled. "This one is just like her—memorable, sexy, reminding you of a bed of roses—or any bed."

"So, now what?"

"I have to find her. She left town this morning." While all else might be in tumult, he was laser-sure about his search.

"Where did she go?"

"Good question. I talked to her last night from Chicago and everything was fine. But she wasn't home when I got there. I talked to her mother, though. She thinks she might have gone to the North Shore."

"You talked to her *mother*?"

"I couldn't think of anyone else to call. It's not as though I know any of her friends. I went through the phone book, called up several Chisholms, most of whom didn't answer or hung up on me, and found her mother by chance."

"Did she wonder who you were?"

"She asked me if I was the Rocco who was engaged, so I guess she knew something about me."

"This reminds me of the time you decided you were going to walk around the world the summer you were sixteen. Single-minded."

He grinned. "I got as far as San Francisco before I needed a passport."

"Father and mother were counting on that."

"Did I tell you I arm wrestled her latest boyfriend for her?"

"I thought you were her latest boyfriend."

"I've been gone a week."

Mary Beth frowned. "She might not be the type who wants to settle down. I suppose you thought of that before you went in and talked to Jim."

"If she isn't, I figure I'll change her mind."

"How long have you known her? Seriously, Rocco. I'm afraid you're going off the deep end for a woman who doesn't give a damn. I'd hate to see you hurt." She'd never seen her brother like this—obsessed with a woman. He'd spent most of his life avoiding women obsessed with him. If nothing else, she was curious as hell to meet this phenomenal female.

"I'll just give this my around-the-world attempt. If I get stopped in San Francisco again, I'll survive. I did last time." He grinned. "Don't worry." He didn't want his sister anxious about him when she had enough to concern her, what with the company accounts, her indecisive boyfriend and her baby craving. Anyway, he had no intention of losing on this one. Not a chance. "I've a couple of calls to make and then I'm driving north. Any requests from the North Shore—smoked whitefish, one of Betty's pies, a birch bark basket?"

"I'll take a pie—blueberry. And good luck."

"Thanks." Although, he didn't need any more luck. His major hurtles were behind him. The rest was like coasting downhill.

THIRTY

CHLOE REALLY WOULD HAVE TO FIND OUT
that actor's name on *The Forsyte Saga.* She'd had such
lovely orgasms thanks to him and her handy dandy
vibrator. And she'd forgotten to think of Rocco for vast
minutes at a time—once for almost twenty minutes. Of
course, it was while she was watching a terrible program
on some gruesome murder that had sucked her in like those
semi-documentary programs do, titillating you with little
bits of evidence until you're compelled to find out if the
husband murdered the wife or vice versa, or whether some
man killed five wives in succession before he was finally
caught because he tried to sell his last wife's really fabulous
piece of family jewelry to the jeweler who had originally
made it.

But once that gruesome program was over, she was back
on her emotional, no-win track, desperately wanting a man
who didn't deserve to be wanted desperately by anyone. He

was altogether too selfish and philandering and mendacious to regard with any kind of permanence.

The word "permanence" leaped out and hung in the air, as though she'd exhaled it and it had become a helium word.

Was she really so besotted that she was thinking of Rocco as an object of her affections—permanently? It was laughable, but when she tried to laugh, she found herself crying instead.

Perhaps she shouldn't drink any more wine. It was making her maudlin. As was the continuing unhappiness in *The Forsyte Saga,* she decided, switching the channel to the news. Which was not entirely happy either, she realized, quickly switching to the Home and Garden channel, where some man was building a pergola in only five hours— shown in fast-forward sequences. When he was done, he hung a hammock inside, set a few pots of flowers about and made it seem as though anyone could drill those holes and lift those heavy beams and balance on those tippy ladders. In a way, she found his unrealistic optimism depressing as well.

Or maybe she was in the kind of mood where nothing would raise her spirits.

Surveying the ravages of various meals and snacks strewn on her bed, the crushed packages of chips and cookies, the half-eaten food on the room-service trays, the various wine bottles and dishes of melting ice cream, she found herself dissolving in tears once again.

Was this scene a metaphor for her life?

Discarded food, discarded men, discarded opportunities for happiness?

Maybe she should change rooms.

How typical, she chastised herself. Never facing difficult choices, always moving on, looking for happiness in the next relationship or the next party or the next chance meeting.

Now there was an idea—her mind fixated on it as though it were a life line. Maybe she should go to the bar or the tennis court or the swimming beach and meet someone who would be *entirely different* from Rocco, who had turned out to be disastrous to her peace of mind—or if she wasn't precisely the peaceful mind type, disastrous to her particular style of contentment.

This notable resort catered to people who led serious lives and spent their leisure time in equally serious endeavors. It had three golf courses, a dozen tennis courts, boating, swimming, horseback riding, a complex list of activities for children—all supervised by accredited individuals so their parents could partake in the energetic physical activities they regarded as de rigueur to a vacation without worrying about dirty diapers or childish temper tantrums. No one here actually did nothing—as she had done. All the resort guests worked as hard at their leisure as they did at their upwardly mobile lives.

If she was intent on meeting a serious, committed man, what better place than a resort that catered to that precise type of individual? Particularly when they were currently hosting a convention for members of the pharmaceutical industry.

Glancing at the clock, she saw that it was seven, and if truth be told, found herself just a little bit relieved. She didn't like golf or tennis—and it was a bit late as well for swimming or boating. Even in her serious effort to turn over a new leaf, she couldn't have considered getting on a horse's back and sitting there—well . . . just sitting there. It seemed so pointless unless you were on a mission to map some new territory perhaps, or bring a medicine to areas without roads. But the romance of the west was still a strong thread running through the warp and weave of American culture, and every resort or vacation venue that had pretensions to grandeur offered riding.

Fortunately, she'd had the presence of mind, even after her annoying run-in with bitchy Miss Heiress, to pack her little sequined purple cotton dress that looked like a Guatemalan peasant dress only shorter and cuter. It would be perfect out here in the woods—like back to the earth in a trendy way. And since all the other activities were unavailable at this time of the evening, as fate would have it, she was left with but one choice. The bar.

It was really refreshing to have a sense of purpose once again. Calling room service, she had all the clutter removed from her bed and also had a pile of fresh towels delivered along with a pot of tea. The kitchen even had some of that Dragon Well tea that everyone raved about for its healthful properties, and she managed to drink half a cup. But perhaps her northern European ancestry, evolution and the great distance dividing China from Northern Europe had tempered her body's sensibilities in regard to green teas, because she always felt a little sick after drinking it.

Which slight nausea required just a few very small Famous Amos cookies from the mini fridge and all was well. Could evolution have incorporated Famous Amos cookies so quickly? It indeed made one wonder—what with global warming and frogs with six legs and the rapid depleting of the world's natural resources—whether the evolutionary clock was being speeded up as well. She would have to ask one of the scientifically erudite men she was bound to meet tonight.

A short time later, when she stood in the doorway of the faux rustic bar awash with tartan and timbers, a great number of male heads swiveled to look. Her long legs looked even longer in her spiky heels and short shirt, her spiky hair glistened with rosy highlights in the subdued light, the sequins on her little purple dress further drew eyes that were already staring—riveted.

She always liked those first few seconds when she walked into a room—it gave one such a sense of power. Not that male desire was necessarily terribly discriminating. But for what it was worth, it was gratifying. Now to see if any of these men were able to displace Rocco's image from her mind, she thought, moving toward the bar.

She was literally swarmed with attention. Apparently some of the pharmaceutical-industry types had not brought their families with them to this family-oriented resort. She talked and drank and talked some more to any number of men, waiting to feel some spark, although as the evening progressed, she would have been willing to settle for less than a spark. But she might have been talking to her uncle or her brother if she had one; she might have been talking to a wall for all the excitement she felt.

It was both alarming and consoling.

One, she realized she really preferred less sensible, earnest men.

Two, and this was the alarming part, she came to understand that if she was going to wait for someone to come along and set her senses on fire—as someone who shall remain nameless had—perhaps she was going to have to wait a very long time.

But alarming or not, the experience was significant in terms of setting some new goals in her life. Because, slothful as she may have been this weekend, she was also capable of viewing the world with a mission-from-God mentality.

So she'd investigated the earnest type of man. Check.

She'd eaten just about all the cookies and chips she could eat for a weekend. Check.

She'd surveyed the baby and motherhood scene. And survived it. Check and double check.

Tomorrow she'd actually read one of the books she'd brought along and allow herself to become inspired and enlightened. She might even swim across the lake to burn off some of those cookie calories. And word of God, she'd eat something other than junk food—something fresh, colorful, highly energizing and restorative.

She was going to get on with her life.

THIRTY-ONE

THERE WERE SEVENTY-THREE RESORTS, MO-
tels, hotels, and bed and breakfasts between Duluth
and Grand Marais. Rocco knew because he'd stopped
at each one that weekend—with no luck.

He was hot, sweaty, frustrated as hell and thinking all
the time that Chloe was with some guy somewhere doing
you know what. It was the worst feeling in the world. He
hadn't realized how jealousy could keep you from sleeping,
eating, thinking clearly, thinking at all . . . because his
brain was filled with unpleasant images of Chloe making
it with some nameless, faceless guy.

He just about ran off the road three times, and on the
North Shore that meant plunging fifty feet into Lake Su-
perior, where hypothermia would kill you if the car crash
didn't. He'd pull over each time and shake for a while, then
he'd turn the CD player up real loud to distract his vile
thoughts and drive on to the next motel.

If this was love, it was gonna kill him one way or another. He was miserable.

He didn't dare have a drink, which might have blunted his resentments, because it would have blunted his reflexes as well, and he needed them to stay alive. And let's face it, if he'd drunk, he probably would have only gotten more pissed. Alcohol wasn't known for its overall uplifting properties.

So he stayed sober, the level of his resentment grew and the beauty of the North Shore went unnoticed. He did remember to buy Mary Beth a pie at Betty's Pies on his way back home. By that time he was making alternative plans, and since he planned on parking outside Chloe's house tonight, he bought himself some food to go.

It could be a long night.

SHE SAW ROCCO'S car when she pulled up to her building and all her new resolve to begin afresh instantly vanished. With an iron will and a brief but stern talking to, she restored her sense of purpose, telling herself she'd just come to terms with her life after a weekend of junk food and remorse and she wasn't about to sink again into that calorie-laden, tear-stained pit.

But her hand shook a little as she pulled her keys from the ignition.

He was getting out of his car.

SHE WAS ALONE. Good. He wouldn't have to deck anyone.

He'd never felt this Me-Tarzan, You-Jane bullshit before. He suddenly realized his fingers were curled into fists, quickly opened them and drew in a deep breath. This wasn't the time to make any mistakes.

"I'VE BEEN LOOKING for you," he said as she walked up.

"I was up north."

"Where?"

She paused, debating whether he deserved an answer.

"Your mother thought you were on the North Shore. You weren't. I looked."

She should have given in to the sweetness and warmth coursing through her senses at his admission, at his wanting to find her enough to have talked to her mother and gone looking for her. But the memory of Amy was too recent, the loneliness of her weekend too stark. "Why were you looking for me?"

She said it like he'd better have a damned good reason.

But before he could answer, she added, curtly, "Your fiancée visited me Friday morning. You're going to have to keep her in line. She threatened me."

"I'm sorry." He tried to keep his voice real soft. "It won't happen again."

"See that it doesn't. I've had a long weekend. If you don't mind, I'm not in the mood for any smooth-talking bullshit. Go back to your fiancée."

"I don't have a fiancée."

"She disagrees with you. You two should get together and clear that up."

"It's cleared up. Will you marry me?"

"No thanks. I think bigamy is against the law here. If you'll excuse me, I'm tired." Of bullshit and wanting what she couldn't have. She began moving toward her door.

He stopped her with a hand on her arm.

"I'm not doing that again." She tried to shake off his hand. "Find someone else to sleep with on the side."

His grip tightened, not so he was hurting her, but so she wouldn't leave. "I'm serious about marriage. It's all I thought about last week while I was gone. I talked to Amy's father on Friday when I came back into town and everything's copacetic—fine, perfect in fact." That little white lie again, but he'd been praying a lot. "I was never engaged to her, not really—despite what she said. She's a little nuts as you may have realized. So marry me. I went crazy this weekend looking for you, thinking you were with some one else—like Colin."

Her eyes widened.

"I arm-wrestled him for you on Friday, so at least one of your boyfriends is out of the picture."

She didn't know if she should thank him or not. "You're beginning to freak me out," she said instead, because the whole notion of him and Colin, of marriage, of maybe or maybe not Amy, was way too much to absorb. It was like Chinese torture where you're so worn down and pitiful, the person you should least befriend becomes your friend. Which was way scary after she'd just earnestly and soberly talked herself out of Rocco Vinelli.

"I know it's all kind of sudden." He could have been a hostage negotiator, his tone was so nonthreatening and calm.

"Insane, I was thinking. Let me go."

Her look was the kind that gave him reason to drop his hand from her arm. He wasn't looking for a fight. "Let me talk to you, explain. We could go somewhere for coffee or a drink. I've missed you."

"Seems to me you miss me a lot." Her gaze narrowed. "And we all know how that turns out. I'd get another line."

"I'm serious, Chloe. Dead serious."

She took a small breath because the temptation to believe him was powerful. And had Amy Thiebaud not paid her a visit on Friday, she would have been more likely to listen with an unbiased ear. "Amy threatened to have her father shut down my business. She said she's booked the wedding reception, got her dress. She sounded serious. You two serious people should stay together."

"Do you want a damned affidavit that she's not my fiancée? I'll get you one." A small heat infused his voice; the hostage negotiator tone was gone.

"Look. Maybe you aren't engaged to her. Maybe she's a lying bitch. I'd like for her to be a lying bitch. But I'm getting real conflicting information here. Who do I believe. You? Her? The fucking evening news?" Chloe blew out a small breath. "Do you know what I did this weekend? I drove aimlessly, crying my eyes out because of you, ended up at the Lakeside Inn and ate away my misery. And after two days of that bullshit, I came back to reality and decided a man like you isn't going to make me feel that way again. Okay? So thanks, but no thanks, to your proposal—not that I actually believe it anyway."

"So you don't want to get married?" His voice held a sudden coolness.

"You're not dependable."

"I didn't know you were looking for dependable. I got the impression you were more interested in hot sex and instant orgasms."

"And dependable. Sorry if I hadn't mentioned that before."

"You wouldn't last a week with dependable."

Or a night, she thought, reminded of her night at the Lakeside bar. But she was making a point, not being reasonable. "Yes, I would. Dependable appeals very much to me."

He snorted. "Did you get laid this weekend?"

"Did you?"

"Not likely when I was driving up and down the North Shore."

"Then you'd better go find someone. You're probably going through withdrawal."

"Maybe I found someone already." He held her gaze for a moment and then surveyed the quiet street.

"Don't you dare." But her voice was breathy, his powerful body a potent reminder of the shortcomings of a vibrator.

He took her hand in his and started pulling her toward her door. "I think I remember the code on your lock."

"I'll scream. Mrs. Gregorich will call the cops. She's probably watching right now."

"Good try." He nodded toward the house next door, not slowing his pace. "No lights."

"She doesn't have the lights on when she's looking out at night."

"Then I'll just have to explain to the cops that you haven't quite made up your mind whether to marry me or not and we're going upstairs to talk about it. Is it still four ones?"

"Let me go, damn you." She inwardly groaned at the iniquitous heat vibrating in her voice.

He didn't answer, but he'd heard the nuance of arousal too and held her firmly at his side while he punched in her code. "I won't make you do anything you don't like," he murmured, shoving open the door.

"What a fucking gentleman," she hissed, dragging on his hand, appalled at her body's lack of constraint.

"Or maybe we'll just talk." He scooped her up in his arms to forestall having to haul her up the stairs. "Or you talk and I'll listen," he added, taking the stairs at a run.

"I don't want to talk," she snapped.

"Good, I don't either."

"I didn't mean that. Damn you, Rocco, put me down!"

Reaching the foyer, he set her on her feet so suddenly, she had to wave her arms to keep her balance. "Thank you," she said, huffily, arriving at a motionless state.

"You're welcome." He was smiling.

"This isn't funny. Go." She pointed her finger like a bad actress in a bad movie.

"Uh-uh." He shook his head. "I brought you a present."

"I don't want a present." She was having trouble sounding convincing. She adored presents.

"It's named for you." He dipped his head toward her living room. "In there and I'll show it to you."

"What's wrong with here?"

She hadn't said go again. He was encouraged. "You have a TV in there."

She gave him a funny look, but she walked into her living room and stood in the middle of the room and looked at him with a show-me look this time.

He took a small box out of his pants' pocket and handed it to her.

The box was magenta velvet, a white label rimmed in gold affixed to one side. The words on the label were magenta, the font modern and sleek, the name HOT PINK bringing her gaze up.

"For you," he said. "It's named for you. Open it."

When she opened the small box, a glass bottle lay inside, the bottom green, the top in the shape of a pink flower.

"Smell it."

Lifting off the top, she put the glass stopper to her nose and smiled. "It's gorgeous." She looked up at him. "It's heavenly."

"Like its namesake."

"How am I supposed to stay mad at you?"

"Don't," he said. "This was the worst week of my life."

She held the perfume cupped in her hands and wished the world wasn't so complicated . . . or at least her life. "I don't like to be so dependent on someone . . . needing someone so much my happiness hinges on it."

"We can work that out."

"How?"

He shrugged. "I don't know. We'll figure it out."

"Do you know what love is?"

"This weekend, when I couldn't find you, I was thinking it was abject misery, for one thing."

"You don't know."

"Do you?"

"No. See, that's the problem. Neither one of us even knows what love is. What if it isn't just hot sex? What if we're missing the whole deal?"

"Jeez, Chloe, maybe no one ever knows what it is completely. Hell, Shakespeare wrote about it a dozen different ways. We don't have to dissect every word and breath. Why can't we just enjoy it?"

"I was so unhappy this past week. I don't want a repeat of those feelings. I'm never unhappy. Or I wasn't 'til I met you."

"Thanks."

"I'm not blaming you. I'm just saying maybe we should figure this out before we jump in too fast."

"We'll get engaged first. That's what an engagement is— getting ready for the real thing."

"And you should know," she sardonically murmured.

"Screw you. I was never engaged. She was nuts. Look, we'll go as slowly as you want. I just want to see you."

"Like date?"

"Date, go steady, call it anything you want."

"And we can see other people?"

"No!"

"See. I don't like that already."

"Haven't we both dated other people enough?"

"I don't know about you, but I'm not so sure I have."

He growled softly. "I'm not real inclined to share you."

"But then I'm not yours to share."

"Yet."

"Yet."

A heavy silence hung in the air, a thick, suffocating shroud.

His sigh was long-suffering and afflicted. "Okay. Have your way."

"You don't have to give me permission."

He rolled his eyes. "You're not making this easy."

"But then maybe it's always been too easy for you."

"Give me a break. As if you're a wallflower."

"I think maybe we fight too much."

"I think we wouldn't fight so much if we stopped talking."

"And?"

"Right. And did something else."

"How typically male."

"Jesus, Chloe, I don't want to fight. I must have driven eight hundred miles looking for you and now that I've found you, you're breaking my balls. Look, let me apologize for everything and anything I may have done to make you angry. It wasn't intentional. And I've cleared everything with Jim Thiebaud. He understands—not that his daughter is nuts, because I couldn't tell him that—but that Amy and I aren't engaged and never were. Luckily, he's a sensible man. Lucky for me, he's a decent man." A quick little prayer again and he hoped God was listening. "It's late, I'm tired—you're tired. Maybe we should continue this con-

versation tomorrow," he said, his weariness suddenly
audible in his voice. "I'm glad you like the perfume. I was
hoping you would." He lifted his hand toward the TV.
"There should be ads running—I forgot the schedule—I'll
get you one." He ran his fingers through his hair, stood
motionless for a moment with his hands on his head, his
eyes shut, then opened his eyes, dropped his hands and
smiled. "I'll call you tomorrow." He turned to go.

"Wait."

He turned back. "I'm really tired."

"Me too. Why don't you stay?"

"You sure?"

She nodded. "Sort of."

He grinned. "That's what I like. Enthusiasm."

"You've had way too much enthusiasm in your life.
That's your problem."

His gaze narrowed.

"But I don't want to fight."

A faint smile appeared. "I'm glad." He opened his arms.

When she went to him, he took the perfume box from
her hand, stuffed it in his pocket, said, "We'll look at the
ads later," and kissed her gently. "I think I'm half asleep,"
he murmured, his breath warm on her mouth.

"Come," she whispered, taking his hand.

And they walked down the hallway to her bedroom,
holding hands, smiling at each other, enveloped in a cocoon
of contentment and happiness all the more precious for the
desolation of their weekends.

The shimmering color of her bedroom seemed to welcome him, like her. Or maybe he was becoming attached
to shades of pink for the very best of reasons.

"I didn't pick up before I left," she apologized, pausing
for a moment in the doorway, surveying the unmade bed

and strewn clothing with a small frown. "My mother wouldn't approve."

"Neatness isn't high on my list of priorities," he said with a smile, pulling her into the room and shutting the door.

She leaned into him, slid her hands up his chest and lifted her face for a kiss. "That must be why we get along so well. . . ."

Her thighs were touching his, her breasts cushioned against his chest, the heated desire in her voice doing predictable things to his erection. "Because our other priorities match," he murmured, dipping his head to kiss her.

His mouth rested on hers in a teasing, light caress.

She pulled his head closer and kissed him back—not lightly at all.

After their disagreement downstairs, he was moving slowly, waiting for instructions—like that. His kiss deepened, his hands slid down her back, slipped under her bottom and drew her into his hard, pulsing length. "It's been a long time," he whispered. Colin's face instantly materialized in his brain at his misstatement, and his grip tightened, took on a possessive harshness. He lifted his mouth and met her heated gaze. "Not for all of us though—right?"

"You don't own me," she whispered with a smile. "No one does."

Some women might have been abashed. Some women might have shown a modicum of guilt. But even in the heat of jealousy, he understood he had no right to expect faithfulness. "Maybe I can rent a piece of you."

"Maybe you can. Do you have references?"

"How about this?" He moved his hips.

"Feels like the gold standard to me." She began unbuttoning his shirt. "References checked. Let's try you out."

He stopped her unbuttoning. "Hold it. You're always so impatient." He was having trouble with Colin having been here and everywhere while he was gone.

"Is that a problem?"

"Maybe."

"Let me know when the 'maybe' changes to a 'no.'" Twisting away, she moved toward the bed. If anyone should be questioning anyone's sexual impatience, Rocco was hardly the poster child for the Just Say No abstinence club.

She lifted her blue striped T-shirt over her head, dropped it on the floor, unzipped her white capris, slithered out of them and her bikini underwear, kicked off her blue straw mules and dropped onto the bed in a sprawl. "Should I turn on the TV? Are you leaving?"

Not likely with her lying there naked. He reached for the buttons on his shirt.

"I thought you might stay." Soft sarcasm in her voice, assurance in her smile.

He didn't answer. He kept undressing with swift efficiency, shirt, slacks, boxers, shoes, all discarded in under ten seconds. "You make it hard to leave," he murmured, easing his body over hers. "Real hard."

"I just love when you're hard," she purred, twining her arms around his neck, having him just where she wanted him, between her legs—umm . . . inside her—oh, God, all the way inside her . . . oh, God, just like that. "Don't move, don't move, don't move . . ."

"Just a little," he whispered, pressing deeper. Her blissful sigh warmed his throat, her arms tightened and she started to come like she did, almost instantly. But driven by jealousy, he didn't let her come, withdrawing enough to stop her from peaking, bringing her up again only to leave her hanging, deftly teasing and temporizing and teasing again until she said, fiercely, gazing at him from under the fringe of her lashes, "I'll come with or without you in about a second. You decide what you want to do."

Something about the look in her eyes, the amusement beneath the smoldering heat, reminded him of the allure in mutual satisfaction, tempted him to recall the tantalizing pleasures they'd shared, effectively subdued his mindless jealousy. Suddenly smiling, he drove back in, held himself hard against her womb and softly counted, "One, one thousand, two, one thousand, three—"

She was only off a second and a half.

He was no more than a nanosecond behind.

Afterward, they laughed and kissed, she giggled in delight and he smiled down on her as though he'd just won the lottery. No one mentioned jealousy after that, or Amy, or anything remotely disagreeable. He made love to her like a man who'd gone a week without sex. She returned his passion like a woman who had met the man she most wished to share her bed with.

After the initial frenzy of their reconciliation was over, after they'd reached a level of orgasmic contentment, he leaned over the edge of the bed, reached for his slacks, extracted the perfume from his pocket and rolled back beside her. "Should we test its effectiveness? See exactly how hot Hot Pink can be?"

"I think it's working even from inside the bottle."

"A touch of lavender, cucumber and pumpkin's been added to the formula. It's supposed to increase blood flow to the penis by forty percent."

Chloe smiled. "That's good news." She glanced at his lovely undiminished erection, then at the clock. "Will that little bottle last long enough?"

He grinned. "Greedy. I'll get more tomorrow. How about a test run?" Taking the pink flower stopper from the bottle, he ran the stopper down her cleavage as she lay half reclining on a mass of pillows, then slowly circled the soft mounds of her breasts. Putting the stopper back in, he shook the bottle gently and, lifting the flower again, traced a path up the inside of her legs, drawing the cool glass over her upper thighs with deliberate concentration, stopping just short of her throbbing labia. "I don't want this to sting you . . . the alcohol," he murmured, sliding the forefinger of his left hand up her glistening slit as though testing her readiness.

"It definitely has potential as an aphrodisiac," she whispered, stretching luxuriously, the sultry scent enveloping her, the cool path left by the perfume on her skin tingling slightly, reminding her of what he'd done to her—of what more he could do . . . of the intense pleasure she felt when he was buried deep inside her.

Her eyes half-shut, she felt his hands follow the perfume circuit, his palms warm, the scent rising in the air, sexual promise in his touch, in the fragrance filling the room.

"I think it's working. Look." He came up on his knees so she could see his engorged penis standing hard against his stomach. "That study was on the mark."

The sight of his towering penis always instantly connected Chloe's vision to brain to libido to genitals and now was no exception. Lifting her arms to him, she opened her thighs, arched her hips upward and smiled. "Let's measure. See if you'll fit."

She was slick, gleaming wet, needy and he wasn't sure it was the perfume, his ravenous desire or the thought of trying to fit that was making him so horny. But whatever it was, he was more than willing to test his and the perfume's limits. "This could get out of hand." His voice was deep and raspy as he lowered himself over her, an insatiable lust pounding at his brain.

"I don't care," she said, her breathing erratic, clutching

at his shoulders, trying to draw him in. "Hurry . . ."

He entered her swiftly, a plunging, fierce downthrust.

She cried out in rapture; he felt as though his heart had stopped for a moment and they both understood that no matter how much they might disagree, on this one matter they were in sync.

The sex that time was more perfect than the previous perfection.

Hotter, purer, delightfully aromatic.

It was the honey-sweet prize for a weekend from hell.

It was the candy house at the end of Candy Land Lane.

And they lay in each other's arms afterward as though they'd both discovered the true path to paradise, contentment melting through their bones.

THIRTY-TWO

WHETHER IT WAS THE SHRILL SCREAMS, THE pounding on the door, the ringing doorbell or the neighborhood dogs barking that woke them, they both opened their eyes at the same time.

"Rocco! Rocco! Rocco! Open the door!"

It was the screams.

It was Amy.

The voice was clearly recognizable.

Rocco glanced at the bedside clock and softly swore. He was dead tired after the sleepless last few days. Eleven-thirty at night. Fuck. "I'll take care of this," he muttered, dredging up the necessary energy, easing Chloe's head off his shoulder. "Stay here," he said, rolling away.

"I'll take care of her. If she doesn't shut up, Mrs. Gregorich *will* call the cops." Shaking herself awake, Chloe rose from the bed. But nothing wanted to function after only

twenty minutes of sleep, and she stood, eyes shut, willing herself to move.

"Rocco, I know you're in there with that slut!"

That did it. Eyes wide open, Chloe snatched up her robe from the chair by the bed.

"You shouldn't go down there." Rocco was almost dressed, his pants on, his shirt half-buttoned. "I'll see that she goes home."

Chloe knotted the tie of her robe with a jerk. "You know what—I'm kinda in the mood to send her on her way myself."

Oh, fuck. "Just don't get too close to her. She's unpredictable." He'd seen Amy throw rocks or anything she could get her hands on at Steve so many times over the years, he knew she didn't aim for legs.

"I think I'm pretty well primed for her unpredictability," Chloe snapped, moving toward the door.

"All the same, stay behind me," Rocco said, beating her to the bedroom door.

He ran down the hallway and leaped down the stairs, three at a time, hoping to defuse the situation as much as he could before Chloe arrived. But she was fast and damned adept at leaping down stairs herself. When he jerked open the door at the bottom of the stairs, stepped outside and growled, "Would you stop your damned screaming," Chloe was only a second behind.

"How can you be sleeping with her, when I'm going to have your baby?" Amy cried, her screams having shifted dramatically to a pitiful wail.

Oh, God, oh, God, oh, God, the voice inside Chloe's head started shrieking before Amy had even finished speaking. *OH, GOD, NOOOOOOO!*

At a sharp gasp and a murmured, "Mother of God," Chloe swiveled around to see Mrs. Gregorich in her robe standing on the sidewalk between their houses.

"What the hell are you talking about?" Rocco snarled, advancing on Amy as though he were about to do her bodily harm.

"I just found out." She smiled and held up a pregnancy kit box.

He stopped dead in his tracks.

"Are you coming with me, Daddy Dearest?"

"You'd better go," Chloe muttered.

Rocco turned to Chloe. "It's not true."

"Of course it's true, darling," Amy replied silkily, lifting the box with a little wavy motion, looking smug and triumphant, looking way overdressed in a white silk pantsuit and aquamarine shell jewelry.

"In my day, people waited until they were married for these kinds of shenanigans," Mrs. Gregorich said with a couple of *tsk, tsks* and a lowering frown. "You could do much better, Chloe."

"Who are you?" Rocco grumbled, glaring at the elderly woman.

"Someone whose sleep was disturbed by your . . ." Mrs. Gregorich paused, momentarily at a loss for the proper word.

"Well, go back to sleep," Rocco muttered. "The party's over."

"Rocco," Chloe hissed, not sure he should talk to an old lady like that, although Mrs. Gregorich was a damned nuisance, monitoring everyone's activities in the neighborhood with the vigilance of a KGB operative.

"Don't start." Rocco glared at Chloe like she was the enemy.

"It will serve you right if they throw you in jail," Mrs. Gregorich said sharply, scowling at Rocco. "Men like you."

As if on cue, a police car turned the corner, sans siren at

that time of night or maybe sans siren because Mrs. Gregorich made a habit of calling the police and they weren't about to wake up the neighbors for her latest complaint.

Silence descended on the small group outside Chloe's door as the police car pulled up and two policemen got out.

Shit, Chloe thought. *This is going to be embarrassing.* Maybe Mrs. Gregorich should try sleeping pills at night. Not that she wasn't pissed as hell at Rocco, but the police really weren't required for this problem. A priest or minister maybe. Someone to let out the seams on Amy's wedding gown for sure.

"What's going on here, folks?" The tallest of the policemen spoke.

"It's a misunderstanding." Chloe smiled what she hoped was a bland, this-is-all-a-mistake smile.

"What kind of misunderstanding? We had a complaint."

"This woman woke me up in the middle of the night with her screaming," Mrs. Gregorich said, pointing at Amy. "A person has the right to a quiet night's sleep. It's not proper to wake up the whole neighborhood."

The officers glanced down the darkened street. No house lights were visible.

"She was just about to leave, officers," Rocco interposed. "Weren't you?" he added, giving Amy a threatening look.

"Yes—yes, I was." Amy slipped the pregnancy kit box farther behind her back. "I shouldn't have come over to visit so late."

"Visit, my foot," Mrs. Gregorich snorted. "This here man"—she nodded at Rocco—"has a lot to answer for."

The policemen scanned the group. "Anyone care to make a formal complaint about anything?" They knew Mrs. Gregorich never did.

Her father would be displeased if he had to come and get her from jail, Amy understood. Her mother would be shocked. "It was my fault, officers, and I apologize. I shouldn't have come over at this time of night."

"You okay with this, Mrs. Gregorich? Everything quiet enough for you to sleep now?"

Mrs. Gregorich curled up her nose and sniffed. "It was disgraceful—the noise and shouting, not to mention other even more disgraceful things. I don't know what the world's coming to when young people—"

"I think the shouting is over, Mrs. Gregorich," the tall policeman who seemed to be the spokesman interrupted. He surveyed the group. "Everyone agreed on that?"

A multitude of nods and affirmatives acknowledged his question, although Mrs. Gregorich was still muttering under her breath.

"All right then." The policeman nodded. "Everyone go home and let's not make a habit of this."

His last phrase was intended to be a warning to Mrs. Gregorich, but she looked him right in the eye and didn't blink. "I have my rights too," she said, the tight curls of her perm quivering with her indignation. "I'm a tax-paying, law-abiding citizen."

The policeman shrugged and turned away, his silent colleague, who'd looked the entire time as though he'd rather be somewhere else, following in his wake.

Giving Rocco the evil eye, Mrs. Gregorich said, "You should come to church, Chloe, and you'd meet the right kind of men—proper men who treat women with respect."

How did one respond? Chloe was in shock for a number of reasons, not the least of which was Mrs. Gregorich's last comment. *As if,* she thought. The last time she looked, the men in Greek Orthodox congregation Mrs. Gregorich was referring to were over sixty, probably more like over seventy. "I'm going to bed," she said, in lieu of discussing her dating philosophy apropos of men over seventy. Turning

away, she walked to her door. Mrs. Gregorich could stand
on the sidewalk all night as far as she was concerned. Nosy
old coot.

And Rocco had his hands full. Really. A baby. Wasn't
that just about the cutest thing one could hear in the middle of the night after a proposal of marriage from the proud
papa? She put the security chain in place. Let him try the
fucking code now.

As she walked up the stairs, she called herself every kind
of stupid for not having sense enough to send Rocco packing when she'd first see him walking toward her earlier that
evening. Lord, she was gullible—stupid and gullible and
ready to believe anything he said because she wanted him.
Even when she knew better. Even when she knew he could
talk any woman into bed. Even when she'd promised herself
to stay away from him.

So much for rational thought in close proximity to Rocco
Vinelli.

Had he ever been turned down in his life?

She pretty well knew the answer to that, she thought,
fuming with rage.

This perfume is for you, he said.

I named it for you, he said.

If her name happened to be Hot Pink, maybe he had,
damn his lying heart.

Walking into the bathroom, she turned on the shower
and stood under the steaming water, washing off every last
residue and scent of Rocco and his lying-ass perfume.

Then she turned on the television, wanting to know he'd
been lying about the ads too and found to her consternation
that they were being aired—teaser ads promoting the in-
troduction of Hot Pink next month. Not that it made anything any better or different or true. He could run that ad

for ten thousand women he'd pretended to name the perfume for.

Jesus God, she was witless.

She'd fallen into bed with him in all of fifteen minutes
after she'd seriously promised herself that she was turning
over a new leaf. That she was on a search for meaning in
her life and relationships. That hot sex was no longer
enough—or even necessary . . . well, maybe she'd not gone
that far. After all, sex was a normal healthy function, essential to well-being and contentment and mental feng shui.
But certainly, she'd promised herself to be a tad more discriminating.

And she'd believed all that crap about the nonengage-
ment and Amy's mental stability—although she couldn't
take issue with his assessment of Amy's mental health after
her few meetings with her.

Amy was either a very good actress or off her rocker, and
Chloe was betting on the second, supplemented with a good
dose of spoiled-child syndrome. Apparently she'd been used
to ordering the world to her golden-girl wishes since the
cradle. Damn psycho bitch.

THIRTY-THREE

ROCCO HAD HEARD THE SECURITY CHAIN slide into place—not that it mattered. He had to take care of business first anyway. "Give me your car keys," he ordered, putting out his hand.

Amy gave him a small considering look before deciding his growl meant business. But as she handed over the keys, she said, pettishly, "She's not your type."

"Shut the fuck up and get in your car." Without waiting for an answer he walked to the driver's door, opened it, slid inside and started the car.

No one spoke until they were through downtown and out on 394.

Rocco was trying to keep from choking her.

Amy was watching the tick in Rocco's cheek and sensibly waiting for his temper to cool.

"I'm taking you home and talking to both your parents,"

he said, as they moved toward the beltway. "You're not going to keep doing this to me."

"They won't like to hear that I'm pregnant and it's your child."

"They won't like to hear that you're lying."

"They'll believe me over you."

He shook his head. "I don't think so. I talked to your father. He knows I haven't dated you for a year."

"I'll tell him you have . . . although I don't suppose it has to be an actual date to get pregnant," she murmured coyly.

"Tell him anything you damned well please. I'm done with this crap from you." He punched the accelerator.

Amy had spent a lifetime manipulating her parents, but the talk she'd had with her father on Friday had made her squirm. He'd kept asking her questions she didn't like— about when Rocco had asked her to marry him, about the engagement, about their dating. He'd never been so blunt with her. He'd also never taken someone else's side against her. And now Rocco was going to confront her parents with what she'd said about a baby.

She quickly weighed her possible losses—Rocco against her parent's adoration—and found herself opting for the luxury of her life. On the bright side—she might have done enough damage to Rocco's relationship with *that* woman so it was beyond salvage anyway. Perhaps he'd be available after all. Time enough to pursue that path after she made sure to placate her parents. "I apologize for what I said. I'm not pregnant with your child."

He shot her a look. "No shit."

"I'll tell what's-her-name."

He slammed on the brakes, screeching to a stop on the shoulder of the freeway. "If you're fucking with me again, I'll wring your neck."

"Really, Rocco, there's no need for violence. It's no big deal."

Reaching out, he took her chin in his fingers and held it firmly so his gaze lasered her brain. "Tell me it's no big deal again."

His voice was harsh, his dark eyes piercing, and she understood chill sarcasm when she heard it. "My mistake."

"Thank you," he murmured, releasing his grip. He shoved the car into gear, pulled out into the busy Sunday night return-from-the-lake traffic and cut over three lanes to the ramp heading east, back into town. "You'll tell her we were never engaged. You'll tell her you're not pregnant by me." He slanted a glance her way. "I doubt you're pregnant by anyone. You don't like kids." He blew out a breath of relief and apprehension too, because no matter what Amy said, Chloe wasn't going to take it well. "And you're going to be so fucking polite you could be meeting the queen. If you're not, I *will* talk to your parents."

"I don't care if you talk to my parents."

He half smiled because he'd finally found a chink in her bitch-of-the-world armor. "Yeah, you do. So keep it in mind."

"You've turned out to be a real ass."

"You're the same bitch you've always been."

"I don't know what I ever saw in you." Sliding down in the seat, she stared out the window in a sulk.

This was one of those occasions when a heavenly choir of angels broke into song on high, Rocco thought—the music faint but verifiable. It was looking as though his troubles with Amy were finally over.

BUT CHLOE WASN'T at home when he drove back. Her car was gone. His jealousy meter immediately spiked into the danger zone and he said, curt and low, pulling out his cell phone, "Sit tight. I'll find her.

"Where are you?" he asked a moment later.

Chloe had debated answering when she'd seen Rocco's phone number and name on her cell phone screen, but she'd never not answered a phone in her life. A therapist probably would have a good reason for that. "I'm having a drink far away from your pregnant fiancée."

"She's changed her mind. Tell me where you are." He could hear noise, people talking in the background. He could picture some guy with his arm around her, motioning for her to hang up her phone.

"None of your business."

"She's going to tell you the truth and apologize."

Amy did one of those half-snort, half-sniff things as she stared out the window.

"Tell me where I can find you." Chloe couldn't have gone too far. He hadn't been away long. "Are you with Colin?"

"At least I'm not pregnant with his child."

Bitchy as her reply was, he was heartened. She wouldn't be talking that way if a guy was hanging on her. "I can straighten everything out. Amy's sitting right here. She's going to apologize. Word of honor."

"Somehow 'word of honor' rings a little hollow at the moment."

"Just tell me where you are. Don't you want Amy to apologize to you?" He was counting on Chloe's need for revenge. He was praying for it.

"I'm at Louie's."

That simple phrase was capable of parting the waters, soothing the savage beast, generating rainbows after a week of stormy weather. "Don't move."

"That's my line." Jeez, when would she stop being a wiseass? This wasn't the time. This was one of those times when you needed those folks from Florida who looked at chads with a magnifying glass to distinguish intent and genuineness.

"That's true, babe."

"I'm not your babe."

Ignoring her grumpy tone, he said, "Yeah, you are. Wait and see."

Firing up the car, he drove too fast down the residential street, swerved around the corner and pulled into the no-parking zone by Louie's front door. He gave Amy a don't-fuck-with-me look. "Talk to her politely or I'll tell your parents things you don't want them to hear."

She glared at him.

"You pushed me too far. I don't care anymore. And I know shit about you that goes back to junior high, so watch your mouth."

"This is out-and-out blackmail," she snapped.

He turned back to her, one hand on the door latch. It was fortunate she couldn't see his white-knuckled grip. "You're accusing *me* of blackmail?" Each word was uttered through clenched teeth.

Maybe it was just as well she wasn't going to marry him, she thought. He was getting hard to handle. The word "frightening" came to mind, but she was too arrogant to let it remain there long. After all, she was Amy Thiebaud. "For heaven's sake, Rocco, don't take everything so literally. This is all a little annoying, that's all."

Annoying? He thought of the cops, of Mrs. Gregorich, of Chloe's anger, of all the machinations prior to tonight. Amy had tried to ruin his life in a dozen different ways. He drew in a deep breath to keep from slapping that *annoying* pettish look from her face, slowly counted to ten, hoping like hell his temper held.

"Have you gone to sleep?"

She didn't have a clue, he thought. Everything was always about her. He jerked his head in her direction. "Get out. We're going in."

CHLOE WAS SEATED at a bar lined with elderly people; everyone had their eyes on the TV set. Judge Judy was looking peeved as two women screamed at each other.

"Ew . . ." Amy wrinkled her nose.

"They won't like you either. Just say what you have to say and you can go." He shoved her in front of him, nudging her back with his hand until they reached Chloe. "We're here," he said. "Amy has something to say to you."

Everyone at the bar turned around, Chloe included.

Rocco gazed down the curious faces and felt like *he* was in court. "Do you want to talk here or outside?"

"Here's fine." Chloe didn't feel like making it easy. She felt like making him pay. She felt like making Amy push a boulder uphill in the hot sun for about a month. And that was after she decided if she was even going to believe anything either one of them said.

"Start talking," Rocco ordered, nodding at Amy.

Amy's expression was sullen, her baby blues glittering with resentment. "Must we go through this charade?" she snapped.

"If you want to keep on living you do," he snapped back.

She gave Chloe one of those down-the-nose sneers. "Then I apologize, I suppose."

"Not good enough," Rocco growled.

No way good enough, Chloe thought, as sullen as her rival.

"I shouldn't have said what I said." Amy's voice was a modicum less snappish, but not in the least apologetic.

"About what?" Rocco prompted, his voice chill.

"Rocco, for God's sake"—her gaze narrowed as she took in the rapt audience—"we're in public here."

"Good. Then we'll have plenty of witnesses."

She tossed her hair with a little flick of her wrist. "This is really so ridiculous."

"We're standing here for as long as it takes."

"Very well," she said, huffily. "I'm not pregnant."

A collective gasp ran down the customers at the bar.

Amy's spine stiffened and she swiveled around to glare at Rocco.

"Keep going. You're not done yet."

"We're not engaged."

"And?" he prompted.

"We've never been engaged."

"Because?"

"Bastard," she hissed.

"You're done ruining my life. Because?" he repeated, coldly.

"Because I made it all up."

"Like you made up . . ."

"The pregnancy," she said, looking at him with fury.

He turned to Chloe. "Will that do? Do you have any questions?"

"When did you sleep with him last?"

Amy's mouth twitched, but Rocco said, "The truth or I'll be doing some talking of my own," and she said, each word virulent, "A year ago, last spring."

"Tell her how many times we did it." He was taking a chance, but he wanted Chloe to know.

It looked for a moment as though Amy was going to explode, her face turning red and blotchy, then white, then red again. "Four times," she muttered.

Rocco looked at Chloe. "Have you heard enough?"

Four times, she was thinking. *They'd* done it four times in—hell . . . twenty minutes once. And she'd lost count of the times they'd made love even in their very brief relationship. So if one-upmanship was a sign of victory, she'd definitely won. She held Rocco's gaze for a moment. "It clears up a few things."

"Are we done?" Amy spat.

Rocco swung around. "Here's your keys. Go." He shoved Amy toward the door, then turned back to Chloe. "I'm sorry," he murmured, "about her . . . the whole mess—everything. Do you think you can forgive me?"

"Hey, honey, I'd forgive him no matter what," an old lady shouted in a husky, cigarette voice. "I'll bet he looks great with his clothes off."

Laughter rippled down the bar, Rocco looked embarrassed and Chloe felt her first twinge of forgiveness. How much could she blame him for Amy's maliciousness? How much did she wish to harbor a grudge? He'd put himself on display here tonight to get her attention, to make her listen. That had to count for something.

"Could we go?" he murmured, touching her hand.

"I'm looking for dependable. Are we clear on that?" She didn't feel like rolling over yet.

His smiled was boyish and sweet. "Did I tell you I used to be a Boy Scout?"

"Liar."

"Well, I thought about it in the second grade."

She exhaled, the tension in her body ebbing. "Is she really gone?"

He glanced out the window. "Looks that way."

"I don't mean that."

"If you want to stay and talk about it, could we get a booth at least?"

"You don't like to be on stage?"

"Not usually—but whatever you want," he added quickly.

"Don't tempt me with whatever I want. I'm still pissed." She was having trouble shifting gears—saying, "Okay, you're off the hook. It's not a problem for me that you attract female attention wherever you go; I'm mature enough to deal with it."

"I could walk you home. Or we could take your car, but there's a nice moon out tonight."

She smiled for the first time since he'd walked in. "You're pretty damned accommodating, aren't you?"

"I'm on my best behavior . . . for obvious reasons. This has been one helluva ride. Could we go?" he whispered. "Please . . ."

"Go where?"

"Wherever you want."

"Not to my place." She wasn't quite ready to forgive and forget entirely; she could still see Amy standing on her sidewalk with the cops.

"You name it, we'll go there."

"I've never seen your place."

She'd said it like she was testing him. "It's not far," he said. "Let's go."

She grimaced. "I don't know."

"Let's walk back and you can decide on the way."

If she left the safety of Louie's, she was on her own. She'd never been able to muster the necessary restraint to deal with him; she wasn't sure she could do it now. "I might send you home," she said, sliding off the bar stool.

"Whatever you say."

They exited Louie's on a wave of cheers and whistles, but the walk to Chloe's was subdued, neither sure what to say.

A boatload of uncertainty and the enduring image of Amy at her door had Chloe's anxiety and indecision at peak levels—should she or shouldn't she, a running litany in her brain.

It was impossible not to notice her quietness. Rocco had already decided to leave this all for another day. He wasn't in the mood for battle, and at least Amy was gone—so he *had* another day.

"Why don't you call me tomorrow?" Chloe said when they reached her door. She felt like an actress in a clichéd movie, but she *did* need more time.

It was probably a good idea. He was exhausted anyway, not having slept much the past week. "How about dinner?"

"Like on a date?"

He smiled. "Yeah."

She nodded.

"Six-thirty?"

"How much did you mean—about getting married?" she asked, needing to know so she could maybe sleep tonight.

"I meant all of it."

Did other people hear violins tuning up at a time like this? She kinda thought hers might be playing all night. Reaching up on tiptoe, she gave him a little kiss on the cheek. "I'll see you tomorrow."

"Okay." He didn't make a move. Somehow he knew he shouldn't. He watched her open her door and go inside and then walked to his car.

If he was a betting man, he'd figure he had fifty-fifty odds.

THIRTY-FOUR

CHLOE CHECKED THE TIME AS SHE WALKED into her living room. Twelve forty-five. She needed to talk to somebody; she needed advice. But when she went to pick up her phone, she saw the screen flashing twenty-four messages and ran through them first. Six from her mother, starting Friday afternoon—something rambling about Rocco; five from Gracie, same start time—equally vague message; three from Colin, two drunk and one half-sober; five from Tess saying her mother was trying to get hold of her; another five from Rosie with the same message.

It was too late to call her mother. Gracie was a probable, but she didn't know if she wanted any family advice at the moment. What she needed was unbiased and sexually aware advice. Tess, the night owl, answered on the first ring.

"You must be waiting for a call," Chloe said.

"He said he'd call, damn him. And he's not at home."

With trouble in paradise, Chloe debated how explicit she should be about Rocco's marriage proposal or whether she even wanted to mention it considering his track record with women. "Rocco asked me to marry him," she heard herself saying as though her frontal lobes were asleep at their censuring switch. And when Tess shrieked, *"WHAT!"* in a completely nonsupportive tone of voice, Chloe found herself excusing and justifying and outright lying about what had happened.

"Well, that's more like it," Tess said. "I couldn't take any really good news in the mood I'm in. I wouldn't want to hear that there are nice, good, kind, loving men in the world."

"Bad weekend?" Chloe asked, thinking she could probably top anything Tess had lived through.

"Dave showed up drunk Friday night—late. He didn't come over at all on Saturday. And when he arrived here this morning, I could smell another woman's perfume on him—the bastard!"

"Oh, dear." There was no way to sugar coat that sorry picture.

"And your mother kept calling here looking for you," Tess said in her resentful tone that included everyone in the world at the moment.

"I'm sorry. I'll call her in the morning. Let me know how things go with Dave."

"They're not going to go anywhere. If he'd ever pick up his phone, I'd tell him to go to hell. Not that I haven't left a few messages to that effect already."

"It's really hard to know who to trust," Chloe replied, soothingly. Her current dilemma as well.

"You can't trust a single one of them," Tess muttered. "Not. One. Single. Rat. Bastard."

"You're probably right."

"Damn right I am. Rosie discovered the same sad fact. It seems Ian forgot to mention that he'd been divorced twice. She's not talking to him until she decides if she wants to date a man who's struck out on two marriages already."

"Rich people seem to get divorced more often. I suppose they can afford to."

"She doesn't know if she wants to consider being divorce number three. You know Rosie. She's always wanted the white picket fence and moonbeams and roses."

"Forever."

"Yeah. When you and I know better. There's no forever."

Tess wasn't exactly serving as the comforting, bolstering voice of friendship Chloe had been looking for tonight. Which meant she was on her own to struggle through her minefield of uncertainty and doubt. "Life sure can get complicated," she murmured. "It makes you wonder if there really are people out there who meet, fall in love, marry and live happily ever after."

Tess snorted. "Hel-lo. How old are you?"

"It must happen to some people. Otherwise, all the love poetry and prose through the ages wouldn't have been envisioned."

"Exactly. Envisioned. It's all a fantasy, darling. I'm thinking about going celibate in retaliation."

"You've tried that before. Have you ever lasted more than a week?"

"Well, even a week sounds good right now. Damn phony love and bastard men."

"Dave might have a good excuse. You never know."

"The mood I'm in, it would have to be the mother of all excuses—like he was captured by aliens or the CIA."

"You should give him a chance to explain anyway." How easy it was to be objective about other people's love lives. "I thought you said he goes paranoid whenever he sees his family. Maybe they came into town this weekend."

"If they did, he was too out of it to explain on Friday night."

"There's a possibility then."

"You're really stretching, sweetheart, but thanks for trying."

"Don't leave any more nasty messages until you hear from him—just in case."

"Okay, Mom, and I'll brush after every meal."

"You were saying how much you liked him a couple of days ago. Don't let your temper get in the way." Maybe she should take her own advice.

"Yeah, yeah, yeah. You know, screw it—*East Enders* is coming on. At least we *know* that's not for real."

"I'll talk to you tomorrow."

"If you don't get married," Tess said with a sardonic, slightly bitter laugh.

"Probably not," Chloe replied, tactfully.

"Smart girl."

Tess hung up. Chloe sat with the phone in her hand until the dial tone started making that frantic sound and then she set it down. Why was it so strange that she might think about getting married? Why did Tess have to sound so sarcastic about the possibility? Just because she'd never seriously considered the option before didn't mean it was completely out of the question. Just because Tess was angry with Dave didn't mean *she* couldn't have a sincere, impassioned love affair with Rocco. Oops, bad choice of words—"sincere"—what with Amy so recently standing at her door.

And then she thought about Lia and her three children, of what Lia had said about waiting, and her thoughts became even more muddled. Talk about emotional hell. Maybe she'd watch *East Enders* too. She was so tired she couldn't think straight. Switching on the TV, she half watched the cockney soap opera and decided, fantasy or not, her life seemed infinitely sane in comparison.

That moment of understanding helped.

It also made her recall, with almost a degree of comfort, her old saw about fish in the sea.

She wasn't going to make any swift decisions. For once, she was going to think before she jumped—in this case into marriage.

Rocco could wait.

Her mother would be proud of her self-control.

And as long as Rocco was miles away, she was even able to sustain her dégagé attitude. It was only that closeness thing that caused problems.

She fell asleep watching an Antonio Banderas movie, and her dreams were awash with confusing combinations of Antonio, Rocco and Visnjic—none of them less than lush, however, which made for a pleasant night.

Or half a night.

The phone rang at two thirty-four according to her lighted dial, and as she reached for the phone, she was thinking giddily maybe, maybe, maybe it was Rocco because all rationale aside, her wanting him was at peak pitch what with the sexy dreams and all.

"I just wanted you to know I lost you fair and square," Colin murmured or slurred—it was hard to tell. "But you're the best, Chloe, you're *awesome* . . . do you mind, Heather, I'm on the phone here—can you wait a minute, hey, cut it out—"

And the phone went dead.

It seemed she didn't have to worry about Colin falling into any deep depression over her.

But, as Tess would say, this was the real world—not a fairy tale.

THIRTY-FIVE

HER MOTHER'S CALL WOKE HER. AND HER
mother's long lecture on responsibility and reason
without once mentioning Rocco's name was an art
form of delicacy and finesse. "I just don't want you hurt,"
she said at the last in her only personal remark.

"Rocco asked me to marry him," Chloe said. Finesse had
never been her forte.

"Isn't he engaged to someone else?"

"Not anymore."

"I see."

It was a negative response regardless of the neutral tone.
"I told him I'd think about it."

"Good for you. Be cautious, darling. You haven't known
him very long, and he sounds as though he's not completely
stable when he jumps from engagement to engagement."

"He may not have been engaged before, but it's real complicated."

"Just use your head, darling. You remember how you wanted to go to school in Florence because Owen was going there, and then after you registered, you broke up with him. And the time when you were going to move to Alaska with Cole and had even packed when you met Kenneth. And then—"

"Okay, Mom, I get it."

"You're just impulsive by nature, darling, which is a wonderful quality and the reason you're so creative, but perhaps at times, er—well . . . you could be slightly more measured in your decisions."

"I'll try, Mom." It was always safer to agree than disagree with her mother. It made the conversations much shorter.

"But why don't you bring this new man in your life to dinner so we could get a chance to meet him? I don't suppose he fishes. Your father loves to talk about fishing."

"I don't know if he fishes, Mom. I'll ask him."

"Ask him if he likes chocolate cake. Most men do. I could make one for dessert. Or cherry cheesecake is another favorite for men, or strawberry shortcake. Do you remember how Uncle Ralph used to like strawberry shortcake?"

Uncle Ralph also used to like his brandy and any other kind of food. He weighed three hundred pounds. Which is why he died of a heart attack at sixty. "I remember, Mom," she said dutifully, not about to get on the subject of relatives.

"He and Uncle Ben used to fight over the last piece of shortcake."

"I gotta go, Mom. There's someone at the door." Once her mother started down memory lane, there was no telling how long she'd ramble.

"This early in the morning?"

"Maybe Mrs. Gregorich lost her cat again," Chloe lied. "I'll call you."

After having gotten off the hook, she wasn't quite up to making another duty call right then. She'd read the paper, eat something, have some caffeine and in general avoid calling Rosie until her brain was fed and she'd be more capable of all the little white lies that courtesy required.

She only read the funnies, because her life was in enough tumult already; the world would have to take care of itself today. Her espresso machine actually manufactured a good crema—something in the way of a miracle. Maybe it was a sign. And the burrito in the back of her refrigerator was still edible. Things were definitely looking up.

Now she knew how the Greeks and Romans felt—always looking for advice from signs and oracles.

Finally, she couldn't put it off any longer. She made her second duty call. She took care not to mention Rocco after having been warned by Tess of Rosie's problems. All she said to Rosie's sad lament about Ian's none-too-stellar track record with marriage was, "I know how tough it is to make up your mind about a guy who appeals to you."

"Isn't it, though?" Rosie said with another sigh. "He keeps calling and I keep telling him I need some time to think about us." She uttered a hiccupy little sob. "As if there's ever going to be an *us*."

"There's no rush to make up your mind." God, she was beginning to sound like her mother.

"I know . . ." Lapsing into a weeping fit, Rosie sobbed an unintelligible explanation of how she felt about Ian.

Fortunately, a word was decipherable from time to time, making it possible for Chloe to make appropriately consoling remarks of a general nature like, "Time heals . . . you know best . . . I know what you mean . . . and there might be a perfectly good explanation," although she got the impression he'd left wife number one stranded in Moscow, which made good explanations slightly more difficult in that case. But it was kind of weird that he'd tell Rosie about it. "How did you hear about that Moscow story?" she asked, suddenly curious.

"We went out to dinner Saturday night and ran into some of his friends. Melanie told me about it in the ladies' room."

Chloe didn't question the venue. Women always went to the ladies' room in packs. It must be some evolutionary relic. "How did she happen to talk about his marriages?"

"She pulled me aside and said there were some things I should know about Ian—for my own good."

"Oh, Rosie—not that old deceit. I'll bet Melanie had gone out with Ian herself."

"She didn't say she had."

"Ask around. Mark my words, she wasn't doing you any favors."

"Do you think so?"

"I'd bet money on it."

"You're not just trying to make me feel better?"

"Hell no. Don't you remember Stacy Lind? She was always doing shit like that. And most of it wasn't true. Ask Ian next time he calls whether he ever went out with Melanie. See what he says."

"Maybe I will. Do you think I could call him and ask?" A hint of excitement shimmered in her voice.

"What do you have to lose?" It's amazing how cool and objective one can be about others' problems.

"At the moment, not much." Rosie's giggled. "Actually nothing. Thanks, Chloe. You have a knack for getting right to the point. I *will* give him a call."

"Smart move."

"I forgot to ask," she said, all cheerful again. "How's everything going with you?"

"Good, fine, I'm hangin' in there." What could she say

when Rosie had her own soap opera going on? "Call me if
you need anything."

So FAR SHE was zero for three in terms of useful advice
that would unravel her current riddles of the universe. Since
she had no intention of returning Colin's calls, Gracie was
her last resort.

"Are we going to be having a wedding in the family?"
Gracie inquired brightly when she heard Chloe's voice.

"Not if I listen to Mom and some of my friends," Chloe
replied drily.

"Pooh on that. Listen to yourself. That's the only person
who matters. Tell me all about this romantic man who
drove up to the North Shore to find you."

"He never found me, for starters. I was at Gull Lake."

"But he found you eventually, I'll bet. I had the impression from your mother that he was quite intent on his
mission."

"I saw him last night. He asked me to marry him."

"I just knew it. I must have had a dream."

Chloe laughed. "If you have another dream, tell me if I
should accept."

"Do you want to?"

"In a way."

"But?"

"I just don't want to go too fast. I've only known him
for a couple of weeks and he's not exactly—"

"Reliable?"

"Something like that."

"Because of that Amy woman?"

"Among other things. He's too good-looking and he's
pretty smooth. You warned me about that."

"Sometimes you have to go with your heart, though.

There was a time in my life when I didn't, and I still regret that decision."

"The man in Japan?"

"Yes. I was young, too young probably, but sometimes age doesn't matter. On the other hand, your mother and I have never agreed on the merits of responsibility; it's never easy to weigh reason and love."

"At least you're not telling me no."

"I'd never do that. Does he make you happy?"

Chloe laughed. "Mostly. Although things are pretty volatile in one way or another."

"That sounds exciting."

"It is. And that's what I'm trying to understand—whether excitement equates with love or whether I'm mixing it up with sex and passion. I'm not sure I even know what love is. He tells me not to try to analyze it—just enjoy it."

"Maybe he's more sensible than you think. Bring him over for drinks sometime so I can meet this man who's making you think about love."

"He is, isn't he? Wow, that's a first. It must mean something at least."

Gracie laughed. "Since when did you start thinking this hard about having fun?"

"You're right. *You're right.* I'm making this all too cerebral. When did I become overly concerned with intellect rather than impulse—oh, oh . . . that might be him calling in."

THIRTY-SIX

 "HOW'D YOU SLEEP?" IT WAS A LOW, SOFT query.

"Hey. Could have been better."

"Same here."

"Things are looking up, though," Chloe purred. She only had to hear his voice and joy filled her heart.

"That's what I'm thinking."

She could hear the smile in his words. "It looks like it could be a great day." It does now, she thought, basking in the pleasure.

"A good enough day to skip work? I sold so much product last week, my sister gave me the day off. I'd like to take you up to my cabin."

"Why?"

"No reason. Do you need a reason?"

"Not really, but I have to pick up my car from Louie's."

"I'll do that while you're packing a swimsuit."

"It won't take me long to pack a swimsuit."

"I'm downstairs. It won't take me long to walk to Louie's. Throw your keys down the stairway."

"You're downstairs!"

"Sorta."

"You're so adorable." Reason didn't have a fighting chance against the tidal wave of happiness flooding her mind.

"I'm not sure I want to be adorable. How about rugged or strong or well-equipped?"

"Nope. Adorable. Although, I'll give you points for those others too."

"Good, because I'm thinking maybe we could take advantage of the well-equipped part now before we leave."

His voice sounded close, and looking up, she saw him lounging in her bedroom doorway, one shoulder against the jamb, his phone to his ear, his smile so beautiful it made her melt with longing. He was dressed for the lake in jeans and a T-shirt, the jeans riding low on his lean hips, the grey, athletic T-shirt taut over his hard muscled body, his virile maleness reminding her of a Calvin Klein ad where you're never quite sure if they're selling sex or T-shirts.

He snapped his phone shut and arched one brow. "Or then again, maybe you could help me drive and we'd get to the lake sooner."

God worked in mysterious ways. She'd taken off the chain lock when she'd picked up the paper, and look at her prize. Her own Calvin Klein ad in the flesh. "Help how?" she murmured, a ripple of heat radiating through her body, one particular possibility front and center in her mind.

"Sit on my lap while I drive," he said with a sexy grin.

"That's what I thought you meant." Her body was way ahead of her, every libidinous cell dancing the tango.

"So?"

"I'm hungry. You'll have to feed me if I go right now."

He laughed. "You're talking about food, right?"

"Very funny. That must be male humor." Throwing back the covers, she rose from her bed, wishing she'd worn something more sexy than her Mickey Mouse nightshirt. "I want something sweet and gooey, a caramel roll or creme puff to go with my latte."

He pushed away from the doorjamb, looking so gorgeous she was seriously thinking about attacking him, but not before she brushed her teeth and got rid of the taste of Louie's gin.

"You've got it, babe. Give me your keys. I'll be back in ten minutes with your car and something gooey. All you need is a swimsuit. At least for the daytime. If you want to stay and skinny dip tonight, I don't have to be back until morning."

"I should say no. I should stay home and work. I shouldn't always just do whatever you ask me to do."

"Do you like to water ski?"

She grinned. "Damn you. I suppose you have a sauna by the lake too."

He smiled. "And if you decide to stay tonight, I'll cook you s'mores over a camp fire."

"Ummm, s'mores, now there's temptation. On the other hand, my mother said I should be less impulsive and more considering in my decisions."

"So think about it for another few seconds."

She looked out the window, then gazed back at him. "Okay, I'll go."

He held out his hand.

She picked up her keys from her dresser and tossed them his way.

Catching them with a kind of lazy grace, he grinned and left.

Men always said, "Throw a swimsuit in your bag," like it was that easy, like women were like them and packed a duffel bag for two weeks in Europe. She ran for the bathroom wondering how she'd possibly have time to make herself presentable in only ten minutes. Lord, it could take her ten minutes trying to decide which swimsuit to take along. But then, maybe his seductive promise apropos of the car ride north gave wings to her feet, or maybe she'd lucked out and slept on her hair in just the right way, so it curled in provocative disarray instead of flat-as-a-pancake disarray. Ripping off her Mickey Mouse nightshirt, she quickly splashed water on her face and everywhere else she could think of that needed a splash, ran a comb through her hair, brushed her teeth, threw on a minimum of makeup (read: lipstick) and slipping her arms into a robe, dashed to her closet where she stood for probably seven of her ten minutes trying to decide what to wear.

North woods denim? Boaty stripes for the lake? Chinos and plaid? Was gingham too farmy—not woodsy enough? Something for the beach, maybe? He must have a beach. A cute little sun dress with colorful sandals?

"Jeez, women. Your car's back, the food's in my truck, and you're still not ready."

She swung around. "I don't want to hear, 'jeez, women,' like you've done this ten thousand times before. That would ruin my perfect day."

He held out his hands, palm out. "Let me rephrase that. I'm anxious to leave. Could I help you in any way?"

"You certainly could, Mr. Vinelli."

He grinned, readjusted his timetable and said with a dip of his handsome head, "How may I help, Miss Chisholm?"

She waved him toward her dresser. "Pick out a suit for me. Second drawer. And take back your money clip. It's in the kitchen in the drawer next to the fridge."

This might be the time to explain why he hadn't told her to mail him his money clip that day at Diversified Foods. On the other hand, this was more likely one of those occasions for which the phrase "let sleeping dogs lie," was coined. Considering her very good mood, he opted for the latter. As she turned back to her closet, he walked to the dresser, opened the second drawer, put in his hand and pulled out a suit.

"How about this?" he said, holding up a tiger print one-piece suit.

She spun around. "I don't like that one."

"Okaaay." As she went back to her perusal, he picked up a large canvas book bag hanging from a chair, emptied it of books, and stuffed it with the contents of the second drawer. Then he went to the kitchen, picked up his money clip, carried the bag downstairs and put it in his truck.

When he returned to the bedroom, she was dressed.

Some miracle must have occurred, he decided, but carefully refrained from expressing his opinion. It was one of those days.

What had actually happened was that Chloe had recalled the possible dynamics of their car ride north and understood that nothing but a dress would be functional. Which eliminated three quarters of her choices, maybe even seven eighths of her choices, seriously minimizing the theory of randomness, seriously simplifying her decision.

"Nice," he said, really meaning it. What he didn't say was that it looked easy to take off.

"Thank you. Did you pick out a suit?"

"I put a couple in the truck." Omission was diplomatic, not mendacious. "You can decide at the lake."

"And the food?"

"In the truck. We're all set."

She smiled. "You're very accommodating, aren't you?"

"We try, Ma'am."

"That was a sexual innuendo wasn't it?"

He shook his head and tried to keep from grinning.

Her gaze narrowed. "Everything's always about sex with you."

His brows arched. "Excuse me?"

"Let's go."

He waved her past and kept his thoughts to himself. There were times like this when it paid to have a poor memory.

SHE CHECKED TO see that her door was properly locked when she closed it, just in case. Amy wasn't going to stop being a wacko overnight.

He noticed, but wasn't going to touch that subject with the proverbial pole. He took her hand in his instead and said, "Thanks for coming along."

She supposed it wasn't sensible to say, "I'll go with you anywhere, anytime," in the event she sounded like a complete pushover. Especially when she'd only known him a couple weeks and her mother's lecture was still fresh in her mind. "It doesn't hurt to take a day off once and a while," she casually said.

He looked at her oddly.

She hated to think Mrs. Magnuson, the high school drama teacher, had been right when she'd said, "Stick with art, Chloe. I mean it," but maybe she'd overdone the casual tone. "I'm thrilled to go," she corrected. "I dreamt of you all night."

His expression lightened.

There was no point in mentioning Antonio Banderas and Visnjic. Men didn't understand comparison shopping.

As they moved toward his truck, she took note of the

lawn furniture piled in the back of the pickup and wondered if he *knew* she was a pushover or whether he would have gone up north with or without her. She wasn't sure she liked either choice. She waved her hand toward the furniture. "It looks as though you were planning on going anyway."

"If you didn't want to go, I would have taken the truck back home and gotten my car. We could have done something here in town."

"Oh." Men's simple directness could be charming.

He helped her into the cab of his truck and walked around the back, checking the ties on the furniture in a manly kind of fashion she found inexpressibly sexy, as though men were intrinsically take-charge kinds of people. Leaning against the passenger door, she lifted her legs up onto the bench seat and waited for him, her pulse beginning to race a little as she followed him with her gaze. He climbed up on the back fender to tighten a rope running over a wooden chaise. The play of muscles in his arms and shoulders as he worked was terribly arousing. She squirmed a little on the seat.

"You look really good," she said as he entered the cab a few moments later.

He knew that tone. His gaze swung around and held hers. "Not as good as you. Come here." Reaching out, he grabbed her shoulders and pulled her close enough to kiss. "Thanks for coming. Really, thanks."

And he kissed her so the tingles went clear down to her toes.

But he abruptly stopped kissing her and let her go. "I want to get there today." Blowing out a breath, he ran his fingers through his hair, inhaled, then turned on the ignition and, giving her a quick glance, took off.

She was sitting utterly still trying to decide whether

she'd break the spell if she moved—the spell that was causing her body to glow like a nuclear reactor.

He shot her another look. "I want to get out of town at
least."

She knew what he meant; they both did.

She turned her head toward him, but slowly so as not to
destroy the shimmering enchantment. "How far out of
town?"

His grip on the steering wheel tightened. "Lexington."
He was thinking, "I hope," because his erection was aching
something fierce.

It must have been mental telepathy.

Her gaze dropped to his lap and she smiled. "Or maybe
before."

"Give me some of that caramel roll," he said, thinking
distraction, pointing to the small box from the bakery on
the floor.

"After that, though, promise?"

He nodded and smiled. "Oh, yeah." They were both on
the same racing train.

The distraction served its purpose; she fed him small
pieces of the roll, ate some herself and by the time they'd
reached the beltway, they were semi in control of their li-
bidos. As they took the cloverleaf to get onto 35W, he said,
"Take a look up ahead. There's a billboard I want you to
see."

There it was. Her billboard. A bottle of Hot Pink perfume was set left of center on a pure white background, the
green base and pink flower top in dramatic contrast to the
immaculate white. To the right in magenta script were
the words PURE PLEASURE. Maybe this was love, she
thought, wanting to hug the world and more precisely, one
man. Which she did. "It's stunning," she whispered, kissing his cheek.

Curling his arm around her shoulders, he pulled her close and held her against the warmth of his body. "It's for you, babe, as they say in the song. And you're my pure pleasure, in case you were wondering." He didn't mention it cost him his season tickets for both the Vikings and the Gophers, along with his firstborn, for Sam to have his firm put together this one billboard and the TV ad in less than a week. Not to mention the triple overtime he'd promised to pay.

Chloe melted inside. "I'm speechless . . . and happy," she added. "And very, very horny. Do you suppose extravagant gestures like that are an aphrodisiac?"

"Anything's an aphrodisiac for you, sweetheart. And I mean it in the nicest way."

"We're almost to Lexington."

"I know."

"And no one can see us with these tinted windows."

"Yup."

"And there's no oncoming traffic."

"True."

"Does the seat push back a little more?"

He hit the switch and the seat slid back another six inches.

"Now try and relax," she teased, running her hand over the bulge in his jeans.

Brushing her hand aside, he unbuttoned and unzipped his jeans. "You can probably help me there," he said with a small smile, driving with one hand, sliding the other under the skirt of her dress, slipping a finger inside the crotch of her panties, stroking her slick labia in passing before pushing into her honeyed warmth. "If you have some time in the next four hours."

She almost came when he said four hours, the thought of having him inside her for four long, delectable, exquisite, explosive hours almost too much to resist. And she didn't come right then because he added another finger and then another to his soft stroking massage, and he talked softly of what he was going to do to her when they reached the lake, how he'd make love to her, and she wanted the pleasure to last. But she did come before he'd finished telling her about having sex with him on his boyhood bed.

Wiping his fingers on his jeans, he pulled her against his body while she came back to earth. In that quiet interval, he found himself questioning the really scary probability that he might never have run into her that night in the elevator. Everything about that evening had been unforeseen—his going to Amy's family party in the first place, the fact that it was downtown instead of at the country club, the rarest happenstance that he and Chloe had left their respective parties at the same time. The odds that Chloe had held the elevator door for him. Most people wouldn't.

So was he lucky or what?

"Do you know how lucky we are?" he said softly, stroking her arm.

"Cinderella and Prince Charming lucky," she said, her eyes still half shut. "And I don't mean the fairy-tale love stuff, I mean that we met at all."

It must be a sign, he thought. They were beginning to think alike. "No shit," he said, totally unromantic.

But she knew what he meant.

"We're past Lexington, right?" She sat up and stretched.

"Way past."

She looked at him. "So you're due."

"I have more patience than you."

"So you can wait until we get to the lake?"

"I didn't say that."

"Lucky for you, you didn't."

He grinned and glanced down at his erection, thrusting up through his opened jeans and boxers. "You think I couldn't get it if I wanted to?"

She took one look and tried to speak in a normal tone of voice. "Don't be smug."

He grinned again. "We're not smug. Just seasoned veterans."

"I don't want to hear about that, either."

"Retired veterans."

"That's better."

"Seriously, I don't know about you, but I'm in love. You can jack me around and I'll take it."

"Really?"

He laughed. "Don't look so hopeful."

He was so sweet in that masculine, nonsentimental way that was nevertheless as touching as the most saccharin tripe. "I'm feeling as though love might not be so scary after all."

"That's a start."

He winked, a wicked seductive wink that didn't have a hint of romance, but was assured as hell, sexy as hell and started up her engines again. "You shouldn't wink like that. It makes me hot."

"That's the idea. Here." He held out his hand. "Why don't you check out the traffic behind us."

It was amazing how he had only to look at her like that and give her those sexy orders in his husky tone and she was damned near reaching for her next orgasm. Her hand was shaking a little as she placed it in his, and he said, "Steady," in a deep, low voice, as though understanding. She hoped he didn't understand because this was the two thousand and tenth time he'd done this in his truck, but she quickly dismissed her caviling paranoia because he kissed her gently just then and said, "I'm really happy," in that perfect, sincere way he had so you knew he meant it.

He helped her straddle him, helped her slide down his hard, rigid penis. He groaned softly as she settled on his thighs, the full length of his erection buried inside her. She liked that small, vulnerable sound. She liked more that he was moving inside her from side to side as though keeping rhythm with the road. And when he pushed up, she liked that even more.

He drove with one hand. With the other he stroked her back or her breasts or slid his hand between her legs, lazily tracing the contours of her clitoris as he moved in her, as she moved on him. Soon their skin was slippery with sweat even though the air conditioning was on full blast. His eyes were slits against the sun and the violence of his lust. She'd come so many times, hers were half closed as she lay on his shoulder and felt him inside her, mile after mile.

She fell asleep in his arms by the time they reached Hinckley and he turned on the CD system and listened to all the variations of love songs that finally made sense.

When she woke up at the Cloquet turnoff, she moved off him and leaned against the door, resting her feet in his lap. And they drank their iced lattes that had melted and ate the rest of the caramel roll and cream puff and talked as though they'd known each other forever.

She even invited him for dinner at her parents' in a moment of weakness, but when she tried to renege, stammering and stumbling over a really lame excuse, he said, "Hey, it's okay. I have to meet them eventually."

"But things don't always work out, and then what?" She meant for herself. She had a long history of relationships not working out.

He took his eyes off the road and smiled at her. "A day at a time, babe. We're not building the pyramids. We don't need any long-range plans."

She felt such a sense of relief she wondered if she wasn't really a completely mature adult. "Perfect."

"See how easy it is?"

"Are you sure you're not a therapist?" He seemed to understand her in a mildly troubling way.

"How about I'm *your* therapist." He flashed her a smile. "Let me know when you need more love and affection and chocolate-chip cookies."

THIRTY-SEVEN

VERMILLION WAS QUIET, ALTHOUGH SOME of the cabins had families there for the summer. But the racing boats and water skiers and droves of fishermen from the weekend were gone.

Rocco's cabin had been built in the forties, the logs painted and repainted scores of times, the two-story structure perched on a cliff over the lake, surrounded by towering Norway pines and beautifully secluded—which wasn't always the case on Vermillion. He showed her around the main cabin and then took her down to the shore on a switchback staircase that wound through the pines clinging to the granite. The beach was lovely white sand. A boathouse and sauna were set on the shore along with another small guest cabin. At the end of the dock a small sunfish sailboat was anchored.

He was different at the lake, a little less smart-ass, quieter, she would have almost said boyish, although with their ride up such a recent memory, the word didn't quite fit. He made them lunch from a well-stocked refrigerator and pantry, ham sandwiches, an antipasto salad from one of the local resorts, potato chips that some woman in Ely made by hand and sold for about a hundred dollars an ounce. But they were definitely worth it. They drank a beer from the brewery in Duluth with their lunch and then went to sit on the screened porch overlooking the lake.

Chloe sat while Rocco carried in the new outdoor furniture he'd brought up. She'd offered to help, but he'd said, "Take it easy," leaving the rest unsaid, the part about her needing her strength for later. But he'd smiled when he'd said it, so she knew.

They made love in his boyhood bed, and if her day wasn't perfect enough, he said, afterward, while he was holding her in his twin bed next to the one his brother had slept in, "I've never done this before—in this bed, I mean."

She got a little misty-eyed for a moment thinking of him being young and at his grandparents' lake place, of saving his bed for her, but then he spoiled it all by adding, "I think I broke my toe on the bed post."

But that was the smallest of little blips in her happiness radar that day because there was no question he was happy and she was happy and the world in general—the warm sunshine and singing birds and clear blue sky—was a backdrop to their bliss. He couldn't get enough of her, which worked out just fine because that not getting enough worked in reverse, too.

Late that night, bundled up against the cool night air, they shared a chaise he'd carried down the steep steps, and watched the fire he'd built on the beach. The northern lights shimmered green and red overhead, outshining the moon and stars.

He'd brought down what they needed for s'mores, and

they'd been waiting for the fire to burn down. Roasting marshmallows required coals, he'd said, and she was so mellow and content, she didn't tell him she always made torches out of her marshmallows because she couldn't wait.

But waiting wasn't a problem tonight as she lay between his legs, her back to his chest, his arms around her. This kind of waiting was right up there with Christmas presents and learning to ride a bike. Unalloyed joy.

When the coals were ready, he squatted before the fire and made them both s'mores with a simple ease and naturalness that reminded her how little she knew about him.

But learning more would be fun, she thought, clutching the wool plaid blanket around her, gazing at the stark beauty of his face in profile against the firelight, the strength of his body beneath his jeans and flannel shirt hers to share.

She watched him roast the marshmallows and assemble the s'mores, thinking, how did he know she liked the Hershey bars all the way to the edge of the graham crackers, and how did he know she liked her marshmallows roasted until they had a little touch of black—like that—so the faint taste of charcoal melted into the chocolate?

She'd never had the occasion to think, let alone use the phrase, "soul mates," but at that moment she was sorely tempted.

But he turned just then with the gooey cracker in his hand, arresting her imminent gaucherie. "Here," he said in that lush husky tone she adored. "I'll feed you."

This must be love, she thought—marshmallows, chocolate, firelight, the moon in the sky and Rocco smiling at her like that.

There was a real good chance this might work out after all. . . .

SUSAN JOHNSON, award-winning author of nationally bestselling novels, lives in the country near North Branch, Minnesota. A former art historian, she considers the life of a writer the best of all possible worlds. Researching her novels takes her to past and distant places, and bringing characters to life allows her imagination full rein. But perhaps most important . . . writing stories is fun. Please visit her webpage at www.susanjohnsonauthor.net.